The Shape of the Atmosphere

By
Jessica Dainty

pandamoon
publishing

© 2016 by Jessica Dainty

This book is a work of creative fiction that uses actual publicly known events, situations, and locations as background for the storyline with fictional embellishments as creative license allows. Although the publisher has made every effort to ensure the grammatical integrity of this book was correct at press time, the publisher does not assume and hereby disclaims any liability to any party for any loss, damage, or disruption caused by errors or omissions, whether such errors or omissions result from negligence, accident, or any other cause. At Pandamoon, we take great pride in producing quality works that accurately reflect the voice of the author. All the words are the author's alone.

All rights reserved. Published in the United States by Pandamoon Publishing. No part of this publication may be reproduced, stored in a retrieval system, or transmitted in any form or by any means—for example, electronic, photocopy, recording—without the prior written permission of the publisher. The only exception is brief quotations in printed reviews.

www.pandamoonpublishing.com

Jacket design and illustrations © Pandamoon Publishing

Art Direction by Matthew Kramer: Pandamoon Publishing
Editing by Zara Kramer, Rachel Schoenbauer, and Saren Richardson: Pandamoon Publishing

Pandamoon Publishing and the portrayal of a panda and a moon are registered trademarks of Pandamoon Publishing.

Library of Congress Cataloging-in-Publication Data is on file at the Library of Congress, Washington, DC

Edition: 1

ISBN-10: 1-945502-10-X
ISBN-13: 978-1-945502-10-1

"Listen now, for the sound that forever more separates the old from the new."
NBC Radio Broadcast
October 4, 1957

Dedication

For my parents
who not only showed me the stars
but made me believe I could reach them

Four walls to hear me
Four walls to see
Four walls too near me
Closing in on me

—from the song "Four Walls," performed by Jim Reeves, 1957
—written by Marvin Moore and George Campbell

The Shape of the Atmosphere

I

The day before my dad and sister died, my father woke me in the middle of the night to watch the stars explode.

It was October 4, 1957, my sixteenth birthday.

For months he'd been talking about some big global competition. "Pretty soon it won't just be stars up there, Gertie. The world is racing. It's going to be us or them. We're going to win, aren't we?" he'd said.

Tonight, the sky looked like a mess of glitter from too far away. "So did we lose?" I asked, scanning the smear of gold, my eyes blurry with sleep. The satellite was a dot of light traversing the sky, like a star that couldn't stay still.

"Appears that way," he said. And I panicked, imagining this marked the end of our time together studying the sky. "But we don't know yet. It might be a marathon we're watching. Not a sprint. I bet we'll catch up soon." He nudged me in the ribs and smiled, and I didn't care that my mother hid downstairs in the pantry, finding comfort in small glass bottles rather than in us.

"Goodnight, Gertie," my father whispered, his chin warm on the side of my head. My lids were heavy. I fought to keep them open, to keep this moment going, sensing the importance of it, though I knew I didn't fully understand.

I only liked hearing my name when it came from my father. My name, Gertie MacLarsen, sounded like someone had taken a bag of smooth sounds and smashed it against the wall until nothing but edges remained. I detested Gertrude even more, though, and so I kept the jagged version of my name. I was ugly as I rolled off the tongue, long before you ever saw me. My father took my name and rolled it around in his mouth to soften it before spitting it out into the air. If I closed my eyes, I was almost beautiful to listen to, those nights in my room when it was just us.

"Look!" he said, pointing, my head jerking up. Sputnik had faded, disappeared, but the stars shone brighter than I remembered seeing them in a

The Shape of the Atmosphere

while. He knew more about the sky than anyone, my father. He could find combinations of stars and connect shapes that did not exist in my eyes until he drew them for me. He bought the telescope for my twelfth birthday, and the nights he didn't come sit with me by the window I would look through the lens and try to locate the shapes—the bear and crab, the goat that looked more like a crooked square with horns. But I could never find them on my own. He had always promised a night like this, though, when we'd see something that would change the world.

I fell asleep on my father's chest, the rise and fall like the ebb of water.

In the morning we listened to the news of Russian success, a ship that sounded like a potato being launched into space and circling the world. My mother made pancakes, something she rarely did, and my sister braided my hair, also something rarely done. It was a Saturday, my birthday celebration, and my mother had not woken us as she usually did for our weekend chores.

Instead, we listened to the radio all morning, as the news turned to music and back to talk again. My sister and I played Chinese Checkers, and at lunch my father served us on trays in the TV room where we got to watch TV in the daytime, a luxury typically allowed only to my mother.

By the afternoon, we had spread out like air, pushing to fit all limits of the space around us. I made a sandwich in the kitchen, my mother's elusiveness hovering like a ghost from behind the pantry door. I could hear my father rummage through his office, looking for something. My sister got dressed upstairs for her field hockey game.

My sister and I grew up a hallway and a world apart. The two-year difference between us stretched out further and further with each grade, each life milestone. My father tried to stretch himself with us, but no one can reach quite that far, and before long, he spent more time at her field hockey games, more hours at the kitchen table helping her with homework. The time at my bedroom window was the only part of the day I could claim him from her.

Yet we were both equally distant from my mother, though my mother would often stroke Allison's hair, or kiss her forehead at night and then carry on, as though late for something and without enough time to do the same for me.

Jessica Dainty

My sister told me that when I was born, my mother refused to hold me. My sister was only two at the time, so how could she remember? My father didn't deny the story, though.

"Your mother was in a lot of pain, dear. She needed time."

My father had stood ready, prepared to call me Annabelle, a name I yearned for with an intensity unknown to most five, six, then seven-year-olds. At sixteen it remained one of the few things I still prayed for.

In my mother's arms, when she held me for the first time, I became Gertrude, branded ugly by a woman who probably never again held me quite as tightly as she did in that initial meeting, when she decided for me who I would be. I protested in cries. She put her hand over my mouth until my father took me away.

I didn't remember when my mother started retreating inside the recesses of our kitchen pantry. She used to sit in the green chair in the den, knitting or reading her Bible. We went to church every Sunday, but somewhere along the way her position as president of the Daughters of Isabella went to Rosa Winnow, and she no longer directed the church fundraisers.

As my mother became more elusive, she retreated because of smaller and smaller things: my pants torn at the knee, my sister wanting to go to a night movie instead of a matinee, our growing independence in the light of her overwhelming departure.

When I was thirteen, my mother cried when I won a watermelon-spitting contest at the church fair.

"A girl should not know how to spit like that," she'd said, her face buried in my father's shoulder.

My father, on the other hand, crafted me a trophy out of aluminum foil, a crude rendering of a pedestaled star that I kept on my dresser until my mother threatened to send me to confession if I did not throw it away.

"It looks cheap, Gertrude, and we will not have any false idols in this house."

Instead, I hid it in my closet behind my old shoes. I took it out the nights I watched the sky alone and set it on my desk. I turned to it and smiled, as though it commanded the seat next to mine, large and father-shaped.

The Shape of the Atmosphere

Somewhere in our childhood, instances speckled along the way like a glistening trail of stars, my sister and I almost knew each other—finding each other in the midst of our dimmed hallway and holding on with a fierceness I imagined could overwhelm when under the title of a different kind of love. We stayed up late giggling, her telling me stories of high school, what it meant to have boys actually see you and push your hair behind your ear before smiling and walking away, leaving you weak for more.

We would fall asleep curled up in each other, like when we were seven and five, before we separated like planets traversing the sky. It was as though we floated in orbit, starting together and then traveling apart, pulled by something as natural as gravity. I waited, alone now, for when our paths would cross again.

My mother's orbit did not circle. The trajectory of her path shot out slowly, but in a constant direction. She floated away, and we had not tethered her to anything because we either did not see it coming or did not know what could hold her.

My mother's rustling from behind the door brought me back into orbit. I washed lettuce and put it across one of my slices of bread.

"Have you seen my watch?" my father called from across the house. My sister's feet padded down the hallway above my head.

I could hear the watch on her skinny wrist, from inside the pantry, like chains clattering. She'd worn it this morning, seemingly unaware of the oversized weight on her arm, as though she noticed no difference between her thin gold band and my father's thick metal watch. It had appeared there sometime after breakfast.

"Have you seen my watch, Gertie? Allison's going to be late." He came into the kitchen buttoning the cuff of his shirt.

"How do you know you're going to be late if you don't know the time? Seems to me like you don't really need one." I smiled, spreading mayonnaise on my bread. I could imagine my father's delight in this exchange if his other daughter's commitment was not more important.

"Where's your mother?"

My sister came down the stairs, and I intuitively moved my body in front of the pantry, not knowing why I thought to protect her.

Jessica Dainty

I shrugged my shoulders.

My father sighed. "Goodbye, Alice," he called to the closed door behind me. And then to me, "Allison's got a game. Want to tag along?" My father was the only person who ever invited me anywhere. I often transposed his words to the mouths of Roger Danielson or Mark Deluge, allowing myself the normalcy of a girlhood fantasy every now and then, up to the point our lips touched in my mind and I felt a wave of embarrassment.

"No thanks. I have homework to do." I did not like sharing my father with my sister's achievements. But last night had left me bubbling over with excitement, and I debated whether I did want to go to talk about what we had seen shooting over us in the sky.

I could hear my mother's rustling through the shelves of the pantry and quiet, shallow sobs like gasps of air between sips. Someone should stay here with her.

I almost missed my father's kiss to the top of my head, my sister's dismissive hand wave to my unwanted and unneeded "good luck."

I watched them go. I heard my mother's voice and imagined my mother's breath wafting out in flutters, that devout Catholic woman who whispered her prayers in waves of whiskey and rum, the occasional peppermint schnapps. I could not picture her in there, a woman who scoffed at my father's nightly centimeter of scotch, barely enough to swirl a quarter of the way up his glass.

"Gertrude, if you're out there, please walk away. Please. Walk away and leave me alone."

I did not think she thought I stayed. She probably assumed I had left the space when my dad and Allison did. I heard my mother cough, sniff, and swallow a sound I can only describe as part of her dying right there, just out of my reach. I'd stayed for a woman who wanted nothing to do with me.

I touched the outside of the closed pantry door. I walked away. This was my gift to my mother.

* * *

The Shape of the Atmosphere

In 1957, in our salt-boxed neighborhood, it was not uncommon for the local police to stop by our front door. The neighborhoods were small where we lived, and the adults had grown up together. The few who left were still talked about with fondness and pride. But the ones who stayed shared something deeper—this ordinary acceptance of stagnation, of trading dreams and ambition for the genuine everyday smiles of those who had known you before you knew yourself. That's how I liked to imagine it anyway. Perhaps because it dripped of something romantic, sweet, but more likely because I yearned for something like the earlier part of my day with my family, a coming together as rare as a meteor shower. I longed for any companionship, stemming from something as basic as simply being alive, together, in the same place.

When my mother answered the door, the clock read after six. My dad and sister weren't home yet, but they often stopped after her practices and games for ice cream or a root beer float, a routine habit I was fiercely jealous of. I heard my mother greet Bobby, someone she had gone to high school with, and whom, if I had to guess, my mother loved at some point in her life. By the lilt in her voice, the slight golden edge to her tone, I imagined some part of her still did, and the thought made me smile for the brief second I separated my mother from the woman hidden behind the pantry door each day.

Bobby's voice always surprised me, less so when I couldn't see him and compare the heavy, always-red cheeks and the incredible broadness of his body with the incredible softness of his words—his tone that shared its goldness with my mother's when she spoke to him.

Tonight, I could not hear his words, or the raspy way he breathed in between sentences. Just the lowness of his voice, a tone that could bring nothing good with it. Everything hung quiet until she screamed and then the house crashed down around me, and before I knew it, I was running down the stairs.

My mother knelt on the floor in broken, ugly prayer, her butt lowered to the ground between her splayed out knees. I could see her house slippers poking out from under the starched hem of dress, her legs at sloppy angles, her hands grasping for each other, missing, and then giving up in a tangle of fingers. I couldn't help that my first thought stuck to the absurdity of my

Jessica Dainty

mother's formality, her dress of clean lines and hair of pinned curls, that somehow kept its form even when her body's reaction escaped her control.

I knew without asking, even before I saw my mother on the ground, and Bobby, in his dark uniform standing baffled, looking completely unsure of what to do with his own body in our brightly lit foyer, that it was my father, my sister, possibly both. I vomited onto the black and white tile of our front hallway, and while I couldn't remember eating anything, the substance hung thick and orange, brackish in my mouth, and it splashed onto my mother's perfect hemline, onto the filthy bottoms of her slippers.

My mother opened her arms to me for the first time since my early childhood. I fell to her because her eyes showed a need more important than my own, and she cradled my head against her chest, her chin resting above me where my father had last kissed me goodbye. I wanted to wipe her away, to save the spot only for him, but they now shared their goodbyes there. My mother let me go after only a moment, pulled herself up, smoothed her dress, avoiding the dark splatter, and prepared to present herself to the world both a widow and non-mother, despite my standing there beside her.

* * *

Bobby helped her to her green chair in the den and she sat there for two days. I did not see her leave once. But on Tuesday morning, I came downstairs to find an empty den and a closed pantry door. Notes clung to the counter with phone numbers and times. Before she had locked herself away, she had arranged to have my father and sister memorialized and buried.

I hadn't gone to school Monday, and I did not know when I would go back. Both schools, my old Catholic school and the new public school, sent baskets of sympathy, rose and yellow colored, smelling like spring, a season that seemed further away than even the other side of my telescope.

Food and flowers overwhelmed our front stoop, but no one ever stayed after ringing the bell. No one visited. No one offered to help. I started the week preparing meals for two, but after a few days, I had realized the food went to waste, and I only made for myself. By midweek, I ceased even

The Shape of the Atmosphere

that. I ate cereal out of the box, the occasional apple, but mostly survived on hidden stashes of red licorice and lukewarm bottles of Coca-Cola.

The house felt different now, although in reality, not much had changed. I did not see Allison much before, but she no longer avoided me from across the table, from down the hallway. One of my earliest memories was being overwhelmed by my sister's acceptance by everyone. She was older than I, and I no doubt watched her with that attentiveness anyone pays to someone better than they in some way. Throughout our school years, I watched her on the playground, in the cafeteria, those brief windows of sightings when we filed past one another in the hallway. She laughed, twirled and sucked on the ends of her hair, pointed to scribblings in blue-lined notebooks, sat at a table with actual other living bodies.

And she ignored me with such incredible ease in those public settings that I found myself staring at her for extended periods of time at home, watching television, from across the dinner table, as though she were a stranger who had somehow implanted herself into our house.

Yet without her here, the air felt heavier, and I had been sleeping on the floor of her room, away from my telescope and the reality that my father would not be coming in to point out Sirius and Polaris, clusters of light in the shape of some mythical figure or creature.

My sister's room lingered, suspended and too empty for me, her perfume bottles and makeup unfamiliar and unimportant, even in light of the fact that they belonged to her and she was gone. I soon instead spent my nights in my father's office.

My mother had rarely gone in there, even before she started locking herself in the pantry. Here, she deposited report cards, bills, to-do lists, but she never stayed. It had served solely as a depository for her, a sanctuary for him. He loved the darkness of the wood trim, which my mother had tried to brighten by adding yellow curtains he never seemed to open. One day she left a crucifix on his desk, his office being the only room in the house without one. Even the pantry where my mother committed what were possibly her only sins hung heavily with one. He met her halfway and put up a bare cross of the same dark wood as the rest of the room.

Jessica Dainty

"Catholics use a crucifix because they're obsessed with death, the sacrifice. Everyone else uses the cross because for them it's about the resurrection. Why do we have to stare at a dead guy all the time to be reminded to be good?" I was certain my father had never said this to my mother, and my insides bubbled with pride to think he chose me as the one person he revealed this to. "What ever happened to hope?"

The cross still hung there, vacant and sharp at the edges. I liked its barrenness.

Next to the cross, a frame held a picture of me from when I was eight. My sister was not in this room, only me and my father. I missed him. I had tired, even over this past handful of days, of leaning on the outside of that closed pantry door for support, for companionship.

I walked the room, fingering the books, his green lamp, his cup of pens. He kept a small blanket in his bottom left drawer, his toothbrush and shaving blades in the top left, so he could use the downstairs guest bathroom instead of the one accessible only through my parents' room. I easily deduced my father had often slept in here, that perhaps he had been gone longer than just this one week. That both he and my mother had orbited around each other for who knows how long.

The realization surprised me. And yet, I didn't feel like crying or screaming. I didn't feel anything. I nosed around and found matches in a drawer filled with paperclips and tape, a pair of scissors that felt too heavy to cut with any sort of deftness. But everything felt heavy just then, sitting in my father's office surrounded by his things, the smell of the tobacco he kept hidden like my mother hid her peppermint schnapps, of the awful starch my mother pressed his shirts with, of the mustiness that came from his large pores. I remembered sitting on his lap as a small child and imagining those black dots on his nose as craters on the moon or some secret planet that belonged only to us.

I lit the candle he often worked by at night, when the house darkened and he wanted something softer than the harsh overhead light or the green tinge of his desk lamp. The flame flickered and shook as though it too no longer belonged here and couldn't stay. I lit a second match and watched it burn, the flame licking toward my fingertips, the heat soothing but

The Shape of the Atmosphere

dangerous, and when I realized I felt nothing as I sat there in my father's space, I turned the match upside down, the heat stinging my fingers briefly before I snuffed it out on my arm.

    I dug out my father's hidden ashtray, clear and square, bulky in its unnecessary thickness, this thing made to hold ash. By the time I heard my mother's slippered feet down the hall, the near-silent latching of her door, the unnecessary lock as though I or anyone else would dare to intrude, the bottom of the tray lay hidden below a line of thirteen matches, each belonging to a seared welt on my forearm, like blooming hills of red flowers.

    After twenty-seven matches, I stopped, my arm red and glowing. I wrapped them in toilet paper in the guest bathroom before flushing them down the toilet. I still felt nothing, but wet a cloth and went back to sit in the cavern of my father's office, waiting as the pain slowly worked its way to the surface as though buried and coming back to life. Before long, my arm seared as though it had not simply been burned but engulfed, alive with flame. I vomited in my father's wastebasket, and draped the coolness of my mother's embroidered hand towel over my arm. I closed my eyes against the pain, but smiled to know that, yes, I could in fact feel something.

    Over the course of the next few nights, the hills filled in with rivers of thin red, flowing behind the shine of my father's razor blades. Never deep enough to really bleed, only to sting and to watch the life inside of me rise to the surface, as though until I saw it, I did not believe it was there.

* * *

    I had never attended a funeral before, but in the church everything held form; opening prayer, readings, Gospel, Homily, Eucharist. The homily I usually tuned out, listening only on the days Father Duncan donned the white and purple frock of holiness and stood in front and slightly above us. He wasn't as definitive in his rulings of life as the others seemed. He often talked of the years before he took his vows as a priest. The first time he did this I sat shocked, my mouth dropping open, an audible gasp at the realization that such a possibility existed—a life before priesthood and, more baffling, the choice for the change.

Jessica Dainty

I thought vaguely of becoming a nun after I first learned this. I knew I couldn't do it because I could not bear giving my mother that much joy, as awful as it sounds. But still, I imagined all the things I would do first, so that I could share my stories and shock and amaze the next generation of children who looked at me and did not see humanity, but rules, fear, an all-knowing entity.

My list of things to do depressed me. I couldn't even imagine greatness for myself without thinking it ridiculous, a girl given ugliness at birth. Especially because at the top of my list, I put make love. Eleven when I started my list, I only had a blurred abstraction in mind of what that meant, one that involved tenderness and sweat and the soft whispers of *oh God oh God* I sometimes heard from my father when my parents no doubt thought I slept but instead stood listening, bleary eyed behind my closed bedroom door.

Now as Father Duncan spoke abstractly about death and rebirth, Heaven and love, I looked over at my mother, followed her small hands as she scratched at the tip of her nose. Her profile struck me, caught me off guard. Her beauty did not shock me as much as the suddenness with which it overwhelmed me. I had never noticed this woman, whom I saw every day and who could not, even through searching my memory, look so different now than in any other moment of my life.

And yet, just then she did, what with the slight slope of her nose, the tinge of olive to her skin that came from nowhere obvious in her Hungarian/Irish background. The deep well of her large blue eyes crested like an actual ocean, or a sinkhole, so deep but seen from the side so that the surface of the water shone almost iridescent, a trick to the eyes as to whether they were even there at all. My mother never wore makeup for the simple reason that her lids disappeared when she opened her eyes anyway, as though her facial structure changed position every time she blinked to allow more room.

In this moment, I couldn't help but see my mother and father as lovers, as young and burgeoning, a word I'd read in my sister's diary when talking about Oliver Saranson, the new boy in town who wore black jeans and t-shirts and dark sunglasses even in the winter. And my knowledge of the world opened, for a split second, and I did not know how I'd ever come up from a grief so deep.

The Shape of the Atmosphere

I spent the rest of mass reciting Hail Marys in my head and locking my eyes onto the missal so my thoughts wouldn't stray. I promised God I would be better. That if I was, I would no longer be the reason my mother locked herself away now that I was all she had left.

The funeral mass lasted even longer than the High Masses, which stretched out endlessly, the smell of incense in those interminable ceremonies making my head and throat scratchy. I found myself floating slowly away on Father Duncan's prayers, his simple offerings based on this man he barely knew, who despite my mother's pleas, rarely found his way to church. He tread lightly on the topic of Allison, eyeing me occasionally as though for approval to speak of my sister, who seemed no more mine than his, this girl who lived down the hall from me and who, I liked to think, I almost knew.

When he began singing in Latin, I drifted fully away, imagining myself swimming in his words, not as in water, but as in light and air swirled together in a thickness similar to ice cream. My mother nudged me awake, and I could see the petulance in her tempered breaths, how even they stayed, how still her eyes remained, how to anyone else, she looked almost peaceful in her grief. The beauty I'd seen before hovered, wispy at the edges, and I held my breath, afraid it would blow away.

At the cemetery, it wasn't as cold of a day as I would have expected for a funeral. Or rainy. No clouds punctuated the sky. The trees filtered the sun. I tried counting the leaves, but my fingers twitched when I lost count. Father John presided now, my least favorite of all the priests. He used to walk the halls with egg salad on his shirt, and I hated his fingernails, how they seemed too long and always yellowed. His words filtered in over the numbers in my head, and I started counting those instead.

He-Was-A-Good-Father. I bounced the words inside my mind, as though they trampolined off the inner walls of my head. *He.* Left. *Was.* Right. *A.* Left. *Good.* Right. *Father.* Left.

My mother held my hand in both of hers. The day was too warm for October. I wore long dark sleeves to cover my arms, but the sun's heat and the overwhelming pressure of my mother's hands became too much. I rolled up my sleeves and saw my mother eyeing my welted arm with a look more empty than any I'd seen yet, as though I were not there, and she stared at the ground instead, at my father and sister far beneath us. I pulled my sleeve back down.

In the car, after the service, she pushed my sleeve back up and ran her fingers along the bumpy surface. The pressure was light, but my arm throbbed. She raised my arm to her face and pressed it to her cheek. We stayed like this all the way home, my mother sobbing into my skin, her tears burning me all over again. By the time we got home, she leaned into me with her whole body, her head buried in my collar. I stroked her hair and helped her inside. I tucked her into her bed and closed the curtains. I kissed her forehead and wondered what it was a mother felt for a child in moments like this, when the roles were as they should be. I left her—angry and bitter that I was not the one being tucked in. How could she have gotten this all so wrong?

I went and sat in the pantry, holding her bottles up to the light inside. Thirteen bottles in all, each no bigger than my palm. There was a rainbow of muted earth tones, from clear to a muddy brown. I opened one of the clear bottles and dabbed some onto my fingertips, crossing myself with the liquid—unholy holy water, a blessing for the unblessed. The smell tickled my nostrils and made me want to sneeze. I considered dumping the bottles out, feeding the contents to the kitchen sink, letting the drain gulp them down and be done with it. My arm stayed gritty with tears and stung. I left things as they were, hoping tomorrow would do its job and move only forward.

II

The next morning, when I answered the door and felt the coolness of the air, I did not immediately notice my father's black, soft suitcase sitting just off to the side.

I expected the four neatly squared bottles of milk on our doorstep, my father's newspaper that my mother never read but did not know how to cancel, or even a covered dish, an onion quiche or homemade lasagna, which we received less and less frequently but still sometimes got from caring or simply nosy neighbors. I did not expect a man in a suit, a black town car, and a gentle but seemingly far away voice saying, "Gertrude MacLarsen, I'm Dr. Rosslins from the Willow Estate Sanatorium. We are here to pick you up for treatment, on your mother's insistence and by order of her as your legal guardian."

Before I could process what was going on, I heard the voice again.
"Is this your bag? Please, follow me."

I'd heard my mother's shower this morning; I knew she had gotten herself up and had the initiative to get herself ready for the world. I'd made coffee and oatmeal, had even put a flower in a vase for her and waited to eat together. She did not come out, and the oatmeal grew lumpier and cooled. The coffee, my father's beverage of choice, not mine, smelled burnt.

"Mom," I called. "Mom, there's a man here." I fingered the rosary through my shirt. I'd put on the rosary my mother gave me for my First Communion when I woke up. I planned to wear it every day.

"Your mother knows we are here." He handed me a form, signed by my mother. Her loopy, beautiful script tarnished the page, and it shouted at me ugly things I could not fully hear.

Dr. Rosslins picked up my father's bag. This man in a black suit, a day late for the funeral, took me by the elbow and led me away.

The Shape of the Atmosphere

I turned back. My eyes searched the windows. Thirteen in all and my mother's face—a regretful smile, a weak wave—in none of them.

* * *

I was amazed to discover I had fallen asleep and had to be woken up as we turned on to the long drive leading up to the sanatorium, or what I assumed to be the sanatorium—a large pale building not so unlike the White House in my mind, though without the rounded, south-facing side of columns. Still, it was massive in its own right with rolling lawns and purposeful-looking trees scattered about. The building didn't strike me as unpleasant in and of itself, though my mouth stung with bitterness, as though the bile I'd spewed on my mother's pressed dress and our front hallway had somehow made its way back to me.

I rested my head against the cool of the car window and tapped a rhythm out as I waited to see what would happen next. Dr. Rosslins cut my tune short, however, with the curt clearing of his throat.

"Gertrude."

"Gertie," I said.

"Gertie"—he paused—"your mother wants you to be here. To get well, to be able to return to her and live in good health." He stared at me as though he could see inside of me. "Can you tell me why you're here?"

I knew why my mother had sent me here. I was not the daughter, had she been forced to do such an unjust thing as choose, that she wanted to be left with.

But I'd heard stories of people being sent to sanatoriums, to the institutions—women who had tried to pull babies out with clothes hangers, ones who ran naked with clumps of their hair in their fists, men who thought little girls were prettier than women or who saw Jesus in clouds. I did not think I was one of these people.

Dr. Rosslins broke into my train of thought. "Can you?"

My catechism lessons had taught me well. Tell them what they want to hear. "Because I'm…unwell," I said.

Jessica Dainty

"And how are you unwell?" He pivoted forward as though intensity of interest alone could cure me.

"Because."

He nodded, and though I felt I had nothing else to say, I went on, "Because I don't feel anything anymore, nothing inside. And I embarrass her." My arm tingled under my long sleeves and I tucked my hands under my legs, grateful for the cool morning. I noticed one of my sleeves was rolled up, and I had a small, bluish bruise forming on my inner elbow around a tiny dot, like I'd been pricked. I couldn't remember what had happened after getting in the car though, so I pulled down my sleeve, grateful they hadn't looked under the other one and seen my signs of mourning or whatever they had been. I dreaded to think what my mother had packed for me in the suitcase, and I reveled to be wearing a pair of slacks, knowing I'd have at least one article of clothing that was not a flowered, starched dress for as long as she kept me in this place.

"You'll have a few days to settle in and you'll meet with me the next few mornings. We will do a full physical and mental assessment over the course of the week, but just enjoy settling in and meeting everyone. You'll be on Ward 2 for now, and I'm fairly confident that's where you'll stay. Jessica will escort you in." He ducked out of the car as though that were his true profession, this ability to slip away without means of stopping him.

The woman outside the car, Jessica I assumed, stood no taller than I, and seemed no more than ten years older either. She looked young and plain, and though I had yet to see anyone else who belonged to the estate as a patient, had she not worn a pressed, white orderly uniform, I couldn't say I would know whether she worked here or lived here.

"You'll have to check your bag at the front so they can look through it. While they do that, I'll show you around the commons area and to your temporary room while you're in the initial assessment stage." She walked, always slightly behind me, so that her words floated up in waves and I had to slow and look back every few steps to catch them. She prompted me to open the door and I hustled through. I stuck my arm out to keep the door from slamming on her, knowing she was there to block my way should I have anything in me to run.

The Shape of the Atmosphere

Where would I go?

"My mom packed it."

"What?" She stopped and looked at me as though realizing I spoke some unnatural language when she'd already spent so much time instructing me.

"My bag. My mom packed it. I don't even know what's in there."

"Well, I guess you won't miss anything then, if they toss it. Here's your temporary room. I'll give you a couple minutes. You look like a wreck. When you're ready, meet me in the front hall. Once they've checked your bag, they'll send you to the lavatory to shower while we set up your room." She refused eye contact with me, as though I were contagious just by looking. "We're sort of short staffed so it may be awhile. Take your time, but don't be more than an hour. I'm behind the desk. Just ask for me if I'm not there." Jessica darted away before she finished speaking. She closed the door behind her.

I couldn't tell anyone how I'd gotten there; Jessica had moved so fast, I'd absorbed nothing of my surroundings. The room I was in was small, and though not overly impersonal, too bare and white to feel homey. The cot had a thick blanket folded at the foot and a generous-size pillow. A small round table sat in one corner, covered by a lace doily on top and a brass lamp with a cheerful, crinkled shade—a bright cherry, the only pop of color in the room.

A small washstand stood in the corner, but the basin and pitcher sat empty, the bottoms thick with dust, and I assumed it was only decoration. We'd had one in my own home, one that we never used, and I often hid my licorice laces in it when my father brought them home. My sister and I loved them equally and I would hide them from her so she couldn't steal them. The non-use of the porcelain dishes was evident when I had to pick the dust off the sticky, red strands. Still, it was worth it to have them all to myself. They'd served as my meals for the past week or so.

I still hid them even though no one remained around to steal them.

Other than in relation to my father's bag, I had not thought of my mother once since entering this place. I felt a deep shame, not at that my mother thought I needed to be here, but at the notion that the house was more bearable without me in it.

Jessica Dainty

I waited for what had to be at least forty-five minutes before making my way to the commons area where I had entered and where Jessica had told me to meet her. Luckily for me, it was immediately outside of my room, or else I was not sure I'd have found my way. She was nowhere to be seen, and had I not known the walls and halls were filled with people, that the facility was almost at its maximum occupancy (something I'd heard someone in a white coat say on the telephone as we walked in), I could have easily believed I was here alone. Even that I was dreaming, walking these too-clean halls searching for my father or sister or even, should my subconscious be so daring, my mother.

I found my way to the desk and Jessica sat behind it filing her nails with a small, pointed metal strip.

The commons area was actually nice, somewhat homey, with circular tables covered by nice linens. There were large bay windows and activities scattered about from playing cards to jigsaw puzzles.

I stood before the desk, Jessica still filing and not looking up.

"I'm ready. Is my bag done?"

Still not looking up, "Just about. We will drop it off in your room once you're cleaned up. You can go down the hall to the left and Sarah should be there. She'll get you directed to the bathroom."

When nothing else was said, I turned to find my own way.

The hallway I turned down struck me as clinical and for the first time I was fully aware that I was in a sort of hospital. The walls and tiles were completely white and the lights above, instead of softening the lack of color, made the hallway more garish, and I fought the urge to squint.

A woman I assumed was Sarah stood at the far end, tapping her foot and picking at her nails. She didn't even look up as she ushered me into a dimly lit room with high rectangular windows of bumpy glass that distorted the light coming in. If I hadn't known it was midday I may have been at a sudden loss for my orientation, for grounding myself in time in the filtered daylight of what I realized, as my eyes adjusted to the change in brightness, was a sort of group bathroom. I counted five showerheads separated by tiled juts of wall. Toilet stalls with no doors glared at me from the back of the

The Shape of the Atmosphere

room, and my stomach sickened at the lack of privacy. Today, I was the only one in the room besides Sarah. I doubted this would always be the case.

"Take your clothes off. Here's your soap. You have five minutes. You get one towel and your clothes will be hanging here." She motioned to a row of wooden pegs on the far wall and I could see two splotches of white. I could only process the ten-yard walk I would have to make in the nude to get to them.

I still couldn't tell you the color of her eyes; she kept them cast away from me. Her hair was a muddy brown, like the darkest of my mother's liquor bottles, but without the sheen, as though this place had drained her of gloss and lent it instead to the sharp edges of the room, the metal shower knobs and faucet handles, the dulled but shiny drains. Her voice fell in blunt echoes in the empty concrete and glass room, making me feel hollow and desperate for her attention.

"I'm required to stay in the room. But I'll face away. I know it's sort of a rush initiation. The first day's the worst."

"So it's not like this always?" I asked.

"No. You just get used to it." She was already turned away from me, an action that raised in me mixed emotions of both shame and gratitude. I wondered if the aides were naturally this impersonal or if it was a job requirement.

Here I was, sixteen years old, standing naked in front of a stranger. My sister had not even seen me unclothed, not since we were young children and would run through our fenced backyard in our underwear or share the bathtub at night, splashing and laughing as though we knew and loved each other and foresaw nothing in our futures able to change that.

The soap she handed me was down to its last uses and had hairs stuck to its surface. I didn't waste my time trying to get them off. She didn't give me shampoo so I rubbed the soap there too, trying to lather my hair and rinse it as well as my body. I hadn't showered since the previous morning, and not knowing when my next chance would be, I tried to clean everything thoroughly enough to last me awhile.

"Five minutes. Water off."

Still sudsy on my legs and hair, I tried to rinse the last bit clean, but Sarah came over and turned the water off. At least she had been kind enough

Jessica Dainty

to bring me my towel, and I covered myself quickly. She didn't return to her chair and I left my hair and legs dripping, unwilling to drop my towel to dry them under such close attention.

"Get dressed and we'll see if your room is ready. Someone will take you on a quick tour of this building, though you'll mostly learn as you go."

Once back in the main hallway, I was swept away quickly by someone I had not seen before, ushered into a small room, my bag at the foot of a bed, the door closed and latched behind me, left with nothing but whatever my mother had thought to give.

* * *

Again, I was grateful for the pair of slacks I'd put on that morning. That morning.

It seemed like weeks ago, months even, as though home were already the abnormality and this new, frightening place the norm. My mother had packed only, as I thought, starched and ironed dresses, cardigans, clean underwear and stockings, a toothbrush, and a single picture of my sister. There was nothing of my father in there, and I was saddened at my mother's ignorance of me, or at her pettiness to keep him all to herself or to forget him entirely. The photograph of my sister was somewhat recent, from Christmastime it seemed, by the suggestion of strung lights in the background, glowing orbs of white, like tiny apparitions. She smiled, and I wanted to throw her into the trashcan, but instead propped her up against the wall on my bedside table.

Though I had no idea proximity-wise their location to one another, this room was similar to the first, but it had a four-drawer bureau, a mirror, and the bed, slightly nicer than a cot, was covered in a patterned quilt. There was no washbasin, but a lamp still punctuated the bedside table, the shade green here, instead of red. On the table sat a typed page, a schedule I noted, when I looked more closely.

6am—8am Showers, breakfast, free time
8am—10am Treatment

The Shape of the Atmosphere

10am—12pm Guided activity time/therapy
12pm—1pm Lunch
1pm—3pm Individual/group therapy or occupational therapy varies by day
3pm—4pm Free time
4pm—5pm Varied daily activities, Sunday visitation, 3rd Saturday of each month estate social 4pm-7pm with late dinner
5pm—6pm Dinner
6pm—8pm Room check, medicinal administration, free time
8pm Lights out

    Although I did not know what some of the time slots would hold, for the first time, I felt somewhat grounded and safe, knowing, at least in theory, what my days would entail. Nowhere did it outline for me what my treatment time would hold, but it was nice knowing I'd have some consistency and therefore would learn what to expect.

    There was no clock in my room, and I did not remember seeing one in any room I'd been in since I'd arrived. There may have been one behind Jessica's indifference in the aide station, but I couldn't remember. Regardless, my door soon unlatched, and Jessica told me it was dinnertime, that she would show me where the cafeteria was, and I figured it was about five o'clock.

    "You won't always be locked away in there. Just today, since we don't want you getting lost. I'll be taking you on a short introductory tour."

    "Fine," I said.

    "Well, you are on Ward 2, a good place to be, above others. That's where I am most days. So, welcome. We'll be seeing a lot of each other."

    On my brief tour, Jessica pointed out the main lobby area as where we could spend free time. She explained the books were open to use, as were the pre-set-up activities. I could ask for a key to the lobby bathroom as long as I did not lose bathroom privileges. The nurse's station and the medicine counter both abutted the common area room, and she reminded me about the whitewashed hallway that led to the group bathroom.

    "You have one visit there in the morning and one at night. Only one shower a day though, and Ward 2 showers in the morning. You share this bathroom with Ward 1. They shower at night so we don't run out of hot water."

Jessica Dainty

"How many wards are there?"

"Hmmm, oh, four, but you don't have to worry about the other two. They are on separate levels and other than the dining hall, which some Ward 3 patients attend, all facilities and activities are kept separate. Someone will show you the recreational room, the Occupational Therapy options, the craft room, and the grounds over the course of the next few days."

She still spoke fast but stayed beside me this time, not behind. And I found her presence comforting. I did not think, seeing her now, that she could be much older than I, not by more than five years.

I pulled my cardigan around me as we exited the main building and walked out under a breezeway toward a separate set of doors. The air was not cold. I just wanted to shrink into myself, to melt away. The sky was cloudy and I could not see any stars. I had no real concept of Heaven, but I squinted at the sky, wondering where my father would be, if he were up there. I longed for my telescope, as though I could look through it and see not only Venus and Orion, but his form orbiting about in a shock of light.

"Here we are." Jessica ushered me in through a door I would have rammed into had her voice not broken my scan of the sky.

The cafeteria was more like a dining hall from the one year of summer camp I'd attended, a Catholic camp where we couldn't rent canoes without reciting the Nicene Creed mistake-free.

Long tables filled the room, with benches on either side, a chair on each narrow end. I was shocked at the number of people, and though the room seemed to be segregated into four sections, there had to be at least one hundred people in the space. Jessica led me to the farthest corner on the left side of the dining room, and explained it was Quadrant 2, the only section I was to eat, sit, and socialize in.

"Each quadrant is sectionalized based on classification. Ward, illness, et cetera. In fact, some of the patients do not even eat in this room; they are too disruptive and uncontrollable. Those able to conduct themselves in a group environment are allowed to dine here. Quadrants 3 and 4 are patients from Ward 3 and are judged on a day-to-day basis, so don't get too used to faces you see over there." She spoke almost as though I were on tour at a boarding school or fancy summer camp. "You are on Ward 2, which means

The Shape of the Atmosphere

you can eat here in Quadrant 2, make your own meal choices, and get yourself to and from the dining hall. You have to stay either here or in the common area until lights out though. Rooms are off limits."

"What if I need to go to the bathroom?" I asked.

"Wards 1 and 2 have access to the common area bathroom I showed you, as long as they get the key from the desk, whenever they need it. Otherwise, you'll be able to use the restroom during the morning showering time and at night when you brush your teeth. Enjoy your dinner." And she was gone, zigzagging back across the room to the door.

I looked for an empty chair. A number of them were scattered around, next to women swaying slightly, some talking to themselves. Others laughing and socializing as though at a Sunday brunch after Mass. Some women sat quiet, with little or no food in front of them and I wondered if they had already eaten. I had been so overcome with the events of the day that I'd neglected to notice how hungry I was. The food looked sloppy and unappetizing, but my mouth watered at the runny potatoes, the thin gravy and flat biscuits, the pieces of meat I saw women sawing at throughout the room.

The food did not taste any better than it looked. It reminded me of my mother's cooking when I was younger, before my father had sent her to classes and she had come back quieter, an apron forever hanging over the handle of the oven door. She was always so solemn when she first sat down to eat, her mouth thin and, I think now, afraid, until my father took his first bite and sighed appreciatively, which he always did. Then we, my mother, sister, and I, would raise our own forks and eat, as though his verdict decided for all of us whether the meal was safe.

Even with this memory flooding back to me, I thought of my father as a kind man. And not just because he was there when my mother was not, because he had wanted to name me Annabelle or because he showed me the sky. But because he read to me when my mother went to bed early with a headache, because he put silly little notes in my Jesus lunchbox, because he invited me to sit by him while my sister played her sports. Because he called me Gertie when even my mother more often than not reverted to Gertrude.

I laughed out loud envisioning my dad taking his first bite of this dinner and gagging or better yet, spitting it across the table, but I swallowed my lapse in judgment quickly. Others at the table shot me looks, and I remembered where I was and that, no doubt, I was always being observed.

For the most part, the people around me looked, dare I say, normal. All appeared older than I, but some still held youth in their faces, young women or wives no more than eighteen or twenty. To my left, an elderly woman squinted at her plate, stabbing her fork always just to the side of her cut meat. I placed my hand on hers, and guided it down, the beef tough even as we pushed through it together.

She turned and grinned, mostly toothless, one eye fogged over, like a glass bottle filled with smoke. "Thank you, dear. And don't worry, it's not so bad here. I'm Gladys."

"How do you know I'm new?" Even though she was looking right at me, there was no way a woman unable to see her plate would know every face, considering the number of them in the room.

"Because you're still kind. Not to say there aren't some nice ladies here, but for the most part, meals are pretty solitary experiences. Everyone is afraid there's no guarantee they'll be back for another meal so they just eat, is my guessing."

I smiled, and then realizing she couldn't see my reaction said, "You are probably right."

"First day?"

"Yes. Though it seems like weeks could have passed already, for all I know."

Gladys laughed but her lips stayed pressed together when she smiled. "I've been here three years now. Ever since the eyesight went. My daughter is young. Four boys and a working husband."

I felt apprehensive, as though my next question would split open this new world with information I wasn't supposed to have. "So you're not, you're not…" I searched for the word and then settled on, regrettably, "Crazy?"

"Only if still being optimistic that when the oldest of my grandsons marries and moves off that I'll be asked back makes me crazy!" She coughed.

"I thought this sort of place was for people who were…unwell."

"Are you"—she turned to me as though she could see me—"unwell?"

The Shape of the Atmosphere

I thought of my mother asking me to leave, of vomiting on her neatly pressed dress, of the nights with my father's matchbook and razor blades. Of my silent rage at a closed pantry door.

"I don't know. Maybe."

"Well good luck to you then." She looked around as though she could tell if someone was nearby, watching, who may overhear her. "Because this sure as hell ain't the place to get better."

* * *

After dinner, the women filed out, quadrant by quadrant. Once out, I recognized faces from Quadrants 1 and 2 in the commons area.

In the commons area, some of the women played bridge, a group of four or five worked, backs bent, on a large, scattered jigsaw puzzle. One woman sat reading in the corner, while many others stood here and there in small clusters talking. A few congregated by an open, though barred, window smoking, tiny red blots of light floating near a blur of hands. Everyone was not present, as the commons area would be filled had all fifty or sixty-plus patients of the left half of the dining hall been congregated in the space. About twenty women stood in a single file line before a doorway whose placard read NURSING STATION and, in smaller print, MEDICINE DISPENSING. Another line stretched down the hallway to the bathroom, and I deduced from what Jessica had told me that they must be patients from Ward 1 going in for their showers.

I walked the perimeter of the large room, counting the outermost ring of floor tiles. Seventy-three and a half by fifty-seven. The bay window cut into my clean, straight line on the next wall, and, instead of continuing around it, I sat on the sill and looked out into the sky, which shined light only in the middle, the horizon already dipped into dim.

The view here was lovely, and I was struck to find beauty in a place I had no reason to hope to find it. Even the windows, the fine mesh metal sheet that covered each one, seemed warm in the soft light. The black iron of the girding panes was painted white, for a more idyllic effect I assumed. I could tell they were originally black, as the white looked bubbled and bits of

Jessica Dainty

it stuck out as though at any moment it would flake to the ground, like snow. The window was so large, I could climb up on the sill and sit if I wanted to, a narrow, dormant radiator spanning the length of the bottom. As the weather dipped cooler, I knew braving the hurdle over the hissing thing would be riskier, but tonight I stretched over and pressed myself to the cool glass.

The grounds, from this view, were open and regal nonetheless. Large pines, oaks, even a birch here and there seemed to come together in a colorful display of foliage. The sky still boasted a hint of blue and the leaves clung to handfuls of green though Autumn was taking over. Not yet six o'clock and already dark around the edges.

A large weeping willow, the facility's namesake, no doubt, stood solitarily in the middle of an expansive field, and I wondered if we were allowed outside. I longed to walk the grass, to look inside the hanging protection of the willow.

I loved walking barefoot in the morning and letting the cool dew numb my feet and toes. When I opened the door to Dr. Rosslins that morning, before I understood what was happening, how my life was about to change, when all I felt and knew was the coolness of the early Fall air, I had been thinking about taking such a walk. My feet now ached at the thought of it, and I looked around for kindness in someone's face, so that I could ask them questions, find out what the future days held for me in my indefinite span of time in this place.

Gladys sat in a chair on her own, but I doubted the shortness of staff Jessica had alluded to allowed a personal escort on the grounds. She probably did not get out much without someone to accompany her. I made a note to offer to take her, should such a thing be allowable for me, but for now, sought someone else to speak to—extend myself to—and hope for reciprocation.

A small woman perched on an ottoman, reading in the corner. Perched really was the proper word for her. She was skinny and bird-like. Her frame reminded me of what I remembered of geometry: angles and lines, connected and measurable. She appeared young, though not a teenager like myself. Probably a young wife or mother, and I was struck by the seeming normalcy all around me, the fierce curiosity I felt to know these women's stories.

The Shape of the Atmosphere

"Mind if I sit here?" I lowered myself into a smart, wooden chair. The woman was staring at her book, but not reading, I noticed, as I watched her eyes, which were wide and still.

"Hello? Is it all right if I sit here?" She still did not respond to me, so I took a book from the shelf nearby and tried to pass the time. After several minutes, the woman slumped down in her chair and blinked rapidly as though someone were blowing directly into her eyes.

I made a start toward her.

"Oh, no. Please don't get an aide. I'm fine." Her voice was quiet but resolute and did nothing to contradict the bird-like image I'd already established of her.

"I wasn't. I was just making sure you were, are you alright?"

"Oh, I'm fine." She sat up taller, smoothing the front of her dress. "I just go still sometimes. Always have, ever since I was a child. Sorry if it seemed I was ignoring you. Have you been waiting on me long?" She was so attentive that I found myself speechless at her alertness, at the awareness in her eyes, in the deliberate movements of her body, when moments ago she had been absent of herself.

"Oh! How rude of me. I'm Elizabeth." She extended her hand, her arm like a wing reaching out for flight. I imagined her body as hollow, the way we learned birds' bones were, and that she, this woman who seemed so heavy in herself five minutes ago, was about to take flight right before me. If she did, I hoped she would lift me with her.

"Gertie," I said, shaking her hand. "First day." I hoped that was all I needed to say to open the gates of communication.

"Oh, you poor thing! And you're so young. I've been here since I was nineteen, almost five years now. I barely remember my first day though, it was so long ago and I was so traumatized coming in after the accident and all. But the day-to-day isn't so bad, on the good days anyway."

Her words were so fast and light I almost lost track of them. I smiled and nodded as my mother had always taught me to do, even though my father told me, if I wasn't really listening, nodding was simply just rude and embarrassing if the other party ever actually caught on to your ruse.

Elizabeth, however, seemed unconcerned if not unaware.

Jessica Dainty

"Five years. Wow. I met a woman earlier who has been here for three years. Is that normal, to be here so long? She didn't even seem unwell to me, just blind."

"'The families pay, and so we stay.' That's the running joke with the patients. Not to say there aren't some real crazies here. Arlene over there in the blue." She pointed a bony finger. "She eats her hair. Even bends down after shower time to pick it out of the drain. Can you imagine such a thing!?"

I couldn't help but gag, the runny potatoes seeming thicker as I had to swallow them back down, but Elizabeth passed it off with a wave of her hand and a chirping laugh. "Francis, the one sitting alone in the corner, is convinced she is Saint Francis of Assisi brought back as a woman. Thinks she's here serving God's will. She's so calm and peaceful. No doubt she'd be on Ward 3 or 4 if she thought she was someone less desirable!" Elizabeth stroked the cover of the book on her lap. I could tell from the gilded lettering that it was a Bible. "I tried to get close enough once to tell her God doesn't exist in a place like this. But she wouldn't listen to me."

"You don't believe in God?" I had never really been around anyone, other than the children in public school with me, who were not overwhelmingly Catholic.

"I believe. I believe he's out there. Mostly anyway. Just not in here." She smiled weakly as though the corners of her mouth were fighting against a heavier weight, and she gave up quickly. "I'm tired now, if you don't mind. I'd like some time to myself. I wish we could go to our rooms, but they have to check them each night. Nice to meet you."

She sat so upright on the ottoman, that I could not imagine she was relaxed, but she closed her eyes and exhaled, as though the air between us was a formidable distance now. I too closed my eyes and leaned against the stiff back of the chair. I was too tired to seek out someone else for information, to be further unbalanced by these other women's problems or, more disturbing, lack thereof. Elizabeth had mentioned an accident, but, upon observation, her face twitched slightly, and I did not dare disturb her with my nosy curiosity. She seemed no more ill than Gladys or, as I sat here amidst women who ate their hair and imagined themselves to be saints, than

The Shape of the Atmosphere

myself. Nothing struck me here as overwhelmingly awful, but I was not encouraged. I feared what the next day would bring.

Once the nursing station line disappeared, Jessica came out and announced bedtime. The women filed out methodically, in all directions to different hallways. No one lingered. There were no annoyed sighs at an unfinished hand of bridge or at the needed time to secure a final puzzle piece in its proper slot. Everyone looked like organized chaos, no formal lines and yet everyone moving in an invisible order, in and out of one another's paths, solitary but as though choreographed in a grand chorus of movement.

I had no idea which direction my room was from here. I had not been processing my surroundings in relation to my other surroundings. I knew the color of my table lamp, remembered the garish glow of the white hallway, the commons area bathroom, but I could not point myself toward any of them.

I had not seen anyone on my hallway earlier. It was as though I had been in here alone. Soon I was the only one left in the commons room. Neither Jessica nor Sarah, not even the unfamiliar girl who had ushered me to my room after showering, was anywhere around.

I went to the aide station, could hear rustling from behind the closed door. I hesitated but knocked lightly, as though it would open to my mother and her liquid comforts.

"I'm sorry, but I don't remember where my room is." There was no answer, and I knocked again. "Hello? I need some help please."

No one came to the door, and I decided to go by the process of elimination. I remembered turning left to get to the dining hall from the hall that abutted the commons area. There were three hallways immediately to the left, all similarly lit and colored. I entered the first, closest to the right of the nurse's station. All room doors were to be open when empty. I remembered that. The only time we were allowed to close them was during the night. They did not lock from the inside. All the doors on this hallway were closed.

As I turned down the second hallway, an orderly rushed at me. "What are you doing out of your room, young lady?"

Jessica Dainty

    I tried to explain in a stammer of speech that it was my first day, that I did not recall how to get back to my room, that I had only been led away from it, not to it since I'd had any element of my bearings. As she got closer, I saw that it was Sarah. She hurried me back down the hall by my arm.

    "What is your name?"

    "Gertie. You were with me earlier. It's my first day. I'm sorry. I just don't remember."

    While she flipped through papers on a clipboard, I burst into tears. I had not even cried over my father's and sister's deaths, over their bodies being lowered at an unbearably slow measure into the ground, and here I was crying over room assignments. I felt her hand tighten on my arm, and thought, as a woman, perhaps she would be more sensitive, more understanding.

    "You better get it together, for your sake as much as anyone else's. Anything can be written down for any reason in this place. You don't want to be found wandering the halls when you should be somewhere else." We stopped in front of a door with the number 17 on it. I liked the oddness of the number, and ridiculously, this seemed like a small gift at the moment. "Don't get lost again. Got it?"

    She was rushing back down the hallway before I could cross the threshold. I closed the door behind me. I lay down. I took my sister from the side table and wrapped myself around her, imagining our planets had finally come together, lazy and limping, hovering and heavy, but still.

III

The next morning, after wake up—which consisted of a loud opening of my door, the pulling back of my covers, the sharp snap of my window shade, and a curt order from the receding back of an unseen aide—I took cautious care to note my hallway's relation to the commons room and dining hall. On the left side of the aide station, it was the right-most corridor.

Ward 1 patients went to the dining hall first, whereas it appeared my ward got corralled into the group bathroom. The line extended down the whitewashed hallway, and I recognized no one as I waited toward the back of the line. As I got closer, I saw Sarah handing out soap, towels, and placing toothpaste on everyone's toothbrush. I had neglected to bring mine, unaware of the morning routine. I found this immersion tactic annoying, as I would love to give my teeth a thorough cleaning after last night's dinner and subsequent gagging.

I realized, too, that I somehow missed the opportunity to freshen up before bedtime. In my whirl of confusion and obvious exhaustion, I had not even thought of it last night. I was too concerned with finding my room, with fitting into this strange new world, now my home whether I wanted it or not.

When I got up to Sarah, I held out my finger for some paste. "I forgot my toothbrush." I forced out a short laugh, a shrug of my shoulders to lighten the exchange, which felt heavy and awkward.

"No toothbrush, no toothpaste. You can brush them tonight." She moved her attention to the next in line.

"Please. It's only my second day. I—I—I didn't know. And I'm sorry about last night, about getting lost, and not being able to find my room, if that's what this is about. I didn't mean to put you in any sort of bind, if that's what I did." I tried a smile this time.

The Shape of the Atmosphere

Sarah looked at me as though she had no idea what I was talking about. She looked again at my finger. "No toothbrush, no toothpaste. You can brush them tonight. There's your towel and soap." She motioned toward a cart.

I took a white towel and pulled off a square of soap from the mound of stuck-together pieces.

"Go to the bathroom first if you have to. Order goes toilet, shower, out. No going backward."

It wasn't much, but I was grateful for the information. Inside, the women worked like an assembly line. They unclothed in measured motions, as though programmed. Women brushed their teeth as they sat on the toilets, the stalls open for all to see. Their towels hung over their shoulders, their squares of soap balanced on a knee or held in one hand. Once done, they moved swiftly to the showers. I had seen five showerheads the first time in here and assumed five showered at once. But the women clustered together, sometimes three or four naked together under one of the heads. They were efficient and, though some talked and laughed, most conducted themselves impersonally.

Some who had not brushed their teeth on the toilet, lathered with one hand and brushed with the other. Others rinsed and spit first and then simply held the toothbrush in their mouths while they scrubbed with both hands. Once done, they rustled their hair and wrapped the towels around themselves, deposited their soap on a slippery, increasingly leaning tower, and exited out the door, I assumed, to go back to their rooms to dress.

I absorbed this all quickly, for everyone's process seemed to take less than a few minutes. I took my cue from the women who brushed their teeth in the toilet stalls, deciding this would be my way, once I remembered my toothbrush. In a way, I was relieved to have forgotten it. I felt like I hadn't had a proper shower in days, despite my trip yesterday, and I wanted as much time to cleanse myself as possible.

The showers had cleared out a bit by the time I made my way to them, since I had been at the end of the line, though none was empty. I saw Elizabeth in one stall, but thought this was an odd time to reintroduce myself, so I entered one a couple to her left, next to a hunched woman who looked older than Gladys and who, God forgive me, I hoped was blind as well.

Jessica Dainty

She wasn't but she was kind enough to face away while we both shared the weak water pressure. The stalls, now that I really looked, were surprisingly low. I could see over the top of them, could look into other women's faces if I wanted. I recognized Arlene, and I yearned again for my toothbrush.

I had just started shaving my legs a few months ago, and I could feel the stubble growing on them. At first I had been embarrassed, ashamed at this obvious sign of womanhood. Now I hated the tickling friction my legs caused one another when they touched, and I wondered if we were ever allowed to shave.

"Two-minute warning. Ward 1 is exiting the dining hall. Two minutes."

I thought of my nights in my father's study, watching the thin red line marble my pale skin. I turned to see Arlene's body crouch to the drain. I had my doubts about the availability of razor blades.

The older woman had finished and left, and I had the shower to myself. I re-lathered my hair and rinsed, rubbing again under my arms and between my legs, the two places my mother always stressed as the most important.

I was just wrapping my towel around my body, ringing out my hair, when Sarah called for water off. I walked back toward my room, the first hallway to the left of the aide's station, leaving moist footprints all the way behind me, like disappearing breadcrumbs not meant to help anyone.

* * *

The dining hall was less crowded this morning, as the wards rotated in shifts. I saw both Gladys and Elizabeth at separate tables, already eating. Elizabeth had only a cup of, I assumed, coffee, and a scone with red smears in it. I said good morning to Gladys as I passed, eyeing her oatmeal, which looked thick and gruel-like.

"You obviously survived your first day, my dear. Cheers to you then." She raised her glass. I squeezed her shoulder in acknowledgment before walking on.

I was actually amazed at the range of selection for breakfast—pancakes, scones, biscuits, oatmeal, coffee, tea, even orange juice. This was more than I had ever been offered at home. My mother cooked dinner every

The Shape of the Atmosphere

night and might make us a sandwich now and then, but breakfast was not her strong point. She put on the coffee for my father and bought boxed cereal. The pancakes we ate the morning of the accident were a rarity.

And there was maple syrup. And cream. Real cream. My mother for all domesticity never bought cream. Milk was just as good.

"Plus you'll keep your figure better." She always said, as though at eleven, twelve, even thirteen I had one to try to keep.

When I was twelve, when I noticed the new tenderness in my chest, the early signs of development, I spent hours each night willing those annoying new growths away. I was oddly ashamed of them, the signs of this natural transition into womanhood, but also of fulfilling these wisdom-shrouded threats of my mother. Terrified that I, a child whose mother rarely claimed her, guided her, taught her, would be truly responsible for 'keeping' anything. How do the unkept learn to become keepers?

"Um, waffles please?" I disbelieved they were actually, in any way, for me. The pancakes looked better and I'd always liked them more, but, despite what the memory held for me, I wanted that awful day to keep them for itself. Until the night of Bobby and my mother on the floor, it had been one of the better days I could remember for awhile.

The lady placed two on my plate and shuffled me by with a roll of her eyes. I didn't want to press my luck. I took them, poured on some syrup, and sat at the nearest table. I'd already shoveled three bites into my mouth before I realized I was not even tasting them, just devouring them, practically swallowing them whole. Without the syrup they would have been chalky at best, but the thick syrup sunk into the divots and permeated the crispy squares, and each bite was like an explosion of liquid sweetness. My father would have smiled at this meal, given an approving nod, had he been able to witness my enjoyment of this moment.

I'd had coffee only once, at a debutante party for a girl named Rhonda when she turned fifteen the summer before. I'd known her from Catholic school, though she was far from holy. I heard her mother had caught her in the coatroom of the golf club with one of the thirteen-year-old altar boys, but these rumors only made it to me after the fact—secondhand whispers in Sunday school, in the hallways from a few of the kids at public school who went to my church. I only attended the party because Allison was invited, and I assumed the mother thought it rude to invite one without the other, me always being the other.

I'd noticed that the wards had placards at the start of each hallway. Ours was called The Debutante Suites. I'd seen debutantes, Rhonda no exception, throw fits grander than any I'd seen in here yet, ripping at their hair, screaming over ice sculptures or the wrong flavor of cake. I couldn't help but find amusement in the name's unintentional parallels. We were misfit debutantes, stripped of our freedom to act spoiled, rash, and impulsive, because in here we were seen through different lenses.

At Rhonda's, after she stomped off in the middle of a song because she had wanted the big band version, I heard whispers of "Well, it is her party" and "That's a shame" far outnumber "What a brat" and "Why I never…"

The women surrounding me appeared well-mannered, quiet, even distinguished in their poise given their situations. I scratched at my stockings, my peach fuzz stubble prickling through. The aides had taken my clothes from yesterday, to wash I hoped, though I had not yet had the courage to demand answers.

The coffee urn was near empty, and I'd heard my father say that the bottom of a coffee pot was like licking an ashtray. I wandered back into the commons area, and decided to test my privilege level.

"May I use the bathroom, please?"

A nurse, distinguishable from the aides by a small red cross on the left chest of her uniform, looked me up and down. "Ward?"

"Two," I said. And then for effect, "Debutante Suite," I added with a smile.

She placed a key attached to a strip of wood nearly a foot long. "You have three minutes. Through that door, to the left."

The key was heavy, as though to remind me of the weight of this privilege, of the tangible difference of losing such a freedom as using the bathroom any time I wanted.

A young woman I'd never seen before sat in a chair outside the door marked POWDER ROOM.

"Are you in line?" I asked.

The Shape of the Atmosphere

"No, I'm on watch." She looked at her watch. "Your three minutes start now. Hang the key on the hook before you go inside."

I didn't actually have to go. Inside, the room was small but nice, and I had an inkling that this was where visitors went to use the bathroom. The counter held fragrant soaps, thick paper towels. The toilet was clean. Best of all, it was behind a door—that locked. I didn't care that the key hung outside on a hook, available for anyone to barge in on me. I stood in the corner and counted to 180. I'd lost track of time since being in Willow Estate, and the numbers felt unnatural, the normalcy of counting seconds, passing time.

When my three minutes were over, I flushed the toilet and ran the water. I fingered the soaps, shaped like shells and flowers, and thought of putting one in my pocket but didn't know how little I had to do to have such privileges as this stripped away from me.

"Thank you. Do I just bring the key back to the desk?"

She rushed me along with a wave of her hand, but I almost didn't care. I could have been at school, at home even, making choices for myself. I handed the slab of a key back to the nurse.

"That was closer to four minutes. Next time I'm marking you down. Three strikes and you lose bathroom privileges for a week."

I nodded, but said nothing. I saw that the hallway leading to the bathroom was empty and figured Ward 1 was finished with its morning rounds as well. Not many people appeared to be left wandering in from the dining hall, and the commons area was becoming more crowded.

On my way in I had noticed that the building stretched higher than one story tall. In fact, the size suggested at least three or four stories, and I wondered about the setup of the other levels. Did each have a common room? A dining hall? A group bathroom? As far as I could tell, Wards 1 and 2 were the only wards on this level. And from what I could see and from what I'd heard, Wards 1 and 2 were apparently the most 'normal.' But Jessica did say that Ward 3 patients ate in the dining hall, their presence determined each day.

I stood in front of the windowsill, as though enjoying the view, but really wondering what my mother would think of this place she had thought better for me than home.

Jessica Dainty

"Gertrude?"

I turned reluctantly toward my awful name.

"You are meeting with Dr. Rosslins and Nurse Peters this morning. They'll start evaluations to slot you for therapy. You can go down that hallway there and someone will come to meet you. Afterward, someone will show you around a bit more."

I seemed to follow a lot of fingers lately. Hand motions, dismissive waves, hurried points, all telling me where to go but not where I was going, or what was waiting for me when I got there.

I'd gotten used to having strangers around, not just the other patients but the nurses and aides too. It was amazing what I could get used to in one day's time. But the constant presence of people other than myself was eerily easy to deal with, even for me, someone who had spent most of her time alone.

They did what they called "check-ins" here. Every twenty minutes or so, I was aware that someone was looking for me, had found me, and made a note of it. Sometimes they called my name, and I raised my hand in a sort of odd roll call. Other times, you just saw searching eyes, a settled recognition, a flick of a pencil-holding hand on a chart, and a moving on. I could almost convince myself it was a game, like hide and seek, and I longed to, if I were braver or more rebellious, cower behind a curtain or in the bathroom past my three minutes to witness what would happen if they could not place me.

I did not recognize the aide who led me outside, though she must have been aware of who I was, as she started describing the grounds and the setup of the buildings.

The grounds had a garden, a pond, and sectioned areas available for sports and recreational activities. Once my assessment was complete, my occupational therapy options could potentially include these areas in the spring, summer, and early fall months.

"Many women love to do gardening for their OT. The men opt often for mowing the lawns and taking care of the landscaping, though women can help with that in some capacity should they be interested."

"Men?" I said. The idea of men being here had not crossed my mind.

"Oh yes, see those buildings over there?" Again, the outstretched finger, my eyes following. "Those are the men's wards. Did you get a

The Shape of the Atmosphere

schedule yet? The Saturdays when you have estate socials, the men from Wards 1 and 2 will come over. There's usually food and music and just an opportunity for people to practice the societal norms of etiquette and interactions. All chaperoned of course."

I could not see the pond from where we were walking though the aide promised me I'd get a full grounds tour should I earn grounds privileges.

"Well, here we are. After your session with Dr. Rosslins, someone will take you over to the recreation hall and show you your other OT options."

The building she left me in front of was much smaller than any others I'd seen or been in since I'd gotten here. The front door had Dr. Rosslins' name in large, angular print on the door as well as the names of a Dr. Isaac and a Dr. Robertson, with a Nurse Peters and a Nurse Irene listed below in smaller font. I went in and sat on a hard metal chair in a small holding room.

Dr. Rosslins came out to greet me himself. I followed him into a small office, fully furnished with a rich wood desk, files, a lamp too similar to my father's for me to look at for more than a couple of seconds, and a plump red-faced nurse sitting perfectly erect in a chair next to an empty chair. Mine, I assumed.

"How are you finding it here, Gertrude?" Dr. Rosslins had not even finished lowering himself into his chair and he was asking questions, his expensive looking pen already poised above an open folder with scribbling on the tab that resembled my name.

"How am I finding it?" This seemed like an odd question to me. Odd enough to repeat. *Finding it.* "Fine, I guess. Just settling in."

"Yes. You seem to have made a smooth transition and we appreciate you embracing your new surroundings. I'm just going to ask you a few questions, and Nurse Peters here is going to a make a few notes as well. We have a number of visiting therapists and we want to place you with the most appropriate one, as well as give the nursing staff an idea of your status and potential needs."

All I had seen the nurses do so far was hand out tiny cups full of pills. I assumed my "needs" referred to that area specifically.

Jessica Dainty

"You mentioned a lack of feeling on the car ride here. Can you elaborate on that? Do you mean a lack of emotional feeling or a lack of physical sensation? Or both?"

The stillness of his pen worried me, as though when it began to move it would take off with such force I would be unable to stop it. Did they want me to be normal? To be crazy? Which would fare me better here, I couldn't tell. Arlene was by far the strangest character I'd met, but she always had an aide with her, always had attention, care, company.

"I'm not sure."

The pen still hovered, though the tip was lowered and touched the paper, in deceptive rest.

"All right. Why don't you tell me a bit about what's happened in your life recently? We know you've suffered a tragedy. Care to talk about it." The last was not a question, nor was it as kind as an invitation.

About what? A sister I rarely knew, being gone. A father who literally gave me the stars leaving me with a mother who gave me nothing but ugliness in a name.

"My father and sister died. My mother did not."

The pen had come alive. "Hmmm, and is there something about that that bothers you?" Dr. Rosslins asked without halting his writing.

"Yes."

"What?" The pen stilled, and his eyes lowered onto me in false patronage, like a suffocating hug.

"What do you mean?" I was confused. I was fully clothed and yet I felt naked.

"Your statement implies you found this circumstance unfair. That it was your father and sister and not your mother. Are you angry with your mother?"

"I do not have a mother. I mean, I do not know her. How can you be angry at someone you don't even really know?" Their stares, both of them now, made me feel queasy.

They glanced at each other and nodded, and both penciled something down in unison, as though they heard each other's voice without speaking. And I was the crazy one.

The Shape of the Atmosphere

"How did you deal with your family's tragedy? With the death of your father and sister?"

I saw their pens at work and I could not formulate my thoughts.

"As anyone would I guess. By mourning." I was sick of this and didn't want to give them anything else to write down about me. I felt something inside of me I'd never known before, this sort of burning bubbling bitterness that not even my mother had been able to elicit from me. I had screamed, cried, and wished, but only because I cared that I did not love her and that, from what I could tell, she did not love me. These people, I felt had no decent intentions for me and were enjoying this.

"Were the burns and cuts on your arms part of your mourning?"

I lightly fingered the receding bumps on my forearm. They were now a purple color, and could have looked like raised, lumpy veins had they been blue instead.

"No. Maybe. The first one maybe. They just seemed to fit."

"Fit?" He raised his eyebrows as he raised his question.

"What I was feeling."

"And what were you feeling?"

This time, if I'd had a pen, it would have been mine that halted, wavered in its forward path.

"I'm sorry?"

"You say it fit what you were feeling. What were you feeling?"

I swallowed my next breath and held it. I did not want to feel alive in this space. "I don't know."

The pen, the non-verbal conversation passed between their eyes.

"And did this make things easier or more difficult?"

"What?" I felt very far away now, as though they'd already given me whatever medicine they were marking down in my chart for me to have.

"The burning and cutting. Did this make things easier or harder for you?"

I wondered if my mother had not seen my arm that day, cried her crocodile tears into it on the way home from the funeral, if she would have even thought to send me away. Or was she just looking for a reason?

"Not easier."

Jessica Dainty

They didn't ask me any more questions then, because I started crying, and they handed me tissues and told me it would be okay, but never touched me, and eventually led me back out where another stranger came to collect me and lead me, with the point of a finger, onward.

* * *

I do not remember much about the rest of the day other than that after dinner, when the line had dwindled in front of the nurse's station, my name was called by an impatient, too-thin nurse with a clipboard. I walked up to her from the window, where I had been watching the shadows of the willow tree dance on the ground. I wanted to know what I had to do to get out there, even just for a few minutes. My tour of the recreational building, craft building, and OT rooms that I got after leaving Dr. Rosslins' office were hazy. I think I signed on for laundry three days a week, the chemical steam stinging my eyes into a nod. I remembered a tennis net, some balls and racquets, and some version of a pool at the rec center but did not remember if I was allowed to use any of them.

"I'm Gertrude," I said, walking up to the window. I may as well embrace it since no one seemed to remember or care about my name preference.

"Here." She handed me two cups, one in each hand. One I could tell held water. The other, more than one pill by the tiny clicks they made when she pushed them at me.

"What is it?" I did not extend my hand.

"What the doctor ordered." Her hands did not move. "Chlorpromazine, 25mg. Just take them alright? My arms are getting tired."

I took the cups from her, and turned to walk away.

"No, sorry. Have to take them here." She penciled something on her clipboard, probably charting my slight reluctance. She didn't even look up as I popped them into my mouth and swallowed them down.

"Lift the tongue." She lowered her glasses and glanced into my mouth. "Good. Let us know how you feel tomorrow. The doctor can make adjustments."

The Shape of the Atmosphere

We were dismissed to our rooms shortly after, and I curled onto my bed, wanting nothing but something of my father with me. Instead, Allison stared at me from an awful photograph. I barely heard the door open and the aide announce "Check-in!" over the tearing of my sister's face.

* * *

I felt tired in the morning, as though I hadn't fallen to sleep rather quickly after my self-pity tantrum the night before. My sister lay in pieces on the floor. I had no trashcan in my room. If I did, I had a feeling it would be nailed inconspicuously to the floor. The dining hall benches were, as were the chairs on either end. And the smaller end tables in the common room. What would they do if they ever wanted to redecorate?

I remembered my toothbrush this morning, but I was not quite able to get it together and was ushered out of the showers still sudsy, my mouth dry with residue.

I was not overly hungry at breakfast either and I opted for the gruelish oatmeal with honey on top. The way my father used to eat it. I didn't like honey though, and after the second bite I thought I might gag and poured it into the garbage before wandering back to the window in the commons area.

"Gertie," I turned, shocked to hear my name in that form. Jessica stood waiting for my response, as though asking permission to continue. No one seemed to ask anything here, silently or not. They just took and did.

"Yes?"

"You'll be seeing Dr. Rosslins again this morning. Would you come with me?"

I followed Jessica out the front doors and down the gray slate steps. The walk was the same as it had been yesterday, but seemed easier today. I liked Jessica more than Sarah and the others I'd met, despite her ambivalence on the day of my arrival. I wondered if such a thing as friends was possible in this place, especially between a patient and an aide.

"We're a little early," she said as we came to the smaller building that housed Dr. Rosslins' office. "I can sit with you while you wait for a minute or so, but then I have to run back to help with treatment in the hydro room."

Jessica Dainty

I had been wrong to estimate Jessica as ten years older than I. She couldn't be more than nineteen or twenty. "How long have you worked here?"

"Two years. I'm still an aide but take nursing classes at night. I'll be working as a student nurse soon."

I liked the idea of Jessica as a nurse. She seemed kind and not detached. I wondered if she had a sister.

I was about to ask her when she looked at her watch. "Sorry, but I have to go. Have a good appointment."

I'd glanced at Jessica's watch before she ran off. It was still fifteen until eight. I could see the willow tree in the distance. It sat almost directly between the lines of the buildings but further off. I wondered if I had time to get there and back before I was called in. I leaned back instead and closed my eyes. I began to swim laps in my mind, back and forth, left and right. I concentrated so hard that fatigue spread through my arms like a tangible weight and I found myself breathing in deeper, more rhythmic breaths.

The water had been my summer sanctuary. In the summers, I walked to the club pool, as young as six, on my own with my towel and goggles. I'd dive down and watch the light show, the sun fractured across the bottom of the pool. I was winning the race my father spoke of, the light, bits of star floating around me. The pool was my ocean, my universe, and the possibilities were endless. Sometimes I'd sit on the floor with the bottom of the ladder on my shoulder to hold me in place, and I'd pretend I lived down there. I'd count the seconds, seeing how long I could make it before I had to return, to emerge from this place where there was no sound, no thoughts but silence, no avoidance because I was purposefully alone.

I would run my fingers along the bumpy surface floor, measuring time against my expiring breath. When I turned eight, I started swimming in the lane with the red sides. As far as I could tell, I was the only child who dared to enter. I swam back and forth, my arms taking on a rhythm of their own. I often could not stop though, feeling I needed one more lap, anything to not go home, and then one more, until the lifeguard finally told me I had to leave before the sun, and I'd walk home exhausted and fall into bed, happy with my excuse to not sit at the table and chew quietly under my mother's eyes.

The Shape of the Atmosphere

"Gertrude." I was on lap thirty-two when Dr. Rosslins' voice broke through. I completed one more for thirty-three, my chest pulsing. But I still brimmed with anxiety as though it could boil up and out of me. "Please come in."

I opened my eyes. I could distinguish the outdoor tennis courts in the distance, a badminton net. I'd seen croquet sets being carried in and out by aides. I wished I'd paid more attention to the size of the pool. I stood to walk inside.

This meeting with Dr. Rosslins did not focus on my father or sister or mother. It did not focus on my welted, blooming arms, or the tiny marbled scars that were the result of my father's razor blades the last nights I spent in his office.

Instead, he let me choose what to talk about. I sat, holding his stapler in my hand, clacking it in a sporadic rhythm until I caught his eyes pleading with me to stop.

I put it down and sighed.

"Did you see the Russian satellite when it crossed the sky?" I knew nothing else.

"I heard about it. Is that something you're interested in? Space?"

"I don't know. I liked looking at the stars. It was my birthday, the night Sputnik flew. Like my own private birthday candle the size of the sky."

Dr. Rosslins smiled. Perhaps he was not as bad as I had thought.

"Past tense?"

"Hmmm?" I had let myself fall back into the shape of my bedroom, into the memory of my father's rising and falling chest as I fell asleep.

"You said you 'liked' looking at the stars. And that wasn't that long ago." He turned a small desk calendar toward himself. "Not two weeks ago even."

"It was something my father and I did together."

"What did you like about it, aside from your father?" He kept his eyes down, like someone approaching an animal they were not quite sure would not bite.

"Do you think what's out there is like what's down here?" I said, embarrassed by the ambiguity of my question.

He rested his pen and looked up. "What do you mean, like people and animals and cars?"

Jessica Dainty

"No. I mean. I mean." I shook my head. I meant a word that meant emptier than any word I knew. Hollow. Shapeless. "Nothing."

"Hmmm. Well if you think of it, you can tell me. How's that?"

I smiled—the taut, pulled-back face of a stranger with no choice but to look up and acknowledge the person passing by.

"You have your physical assessment tomorrow. You'll also be meeting with Dr. Isaac, our newest and most progressive psychiatrist. He'll run you through a few more therapy methods and then we will finalize your schedule. I foresee no change in your ward placement, though, and we'll probably cycle you through a few group therapy sessions to find the best fit, but we'll work it out. Won't we, Gertrude?"

His windows were so low, I couldn't see the blue of the sky.

IV

"Shower quickly and put your dressing gown on and we'll exit through that door and go to the Treatment Wing to meet with Dr. Isaac. He's our newest psychiatrist."

Sarah had met me in the hallway, the same white hallway that led to the bathroom. Inside, she ran the water briefly, not being so kind as to face away this time. She turned the water off before I'd even gotten warm under the showerhead.

I put on the dressing gown and the material surprised me, a sort of mix between cotton and paper. My wet hair seeped into it and the back of the cloth clung to my body. I dried my front as best I could so that nothing would be see-through. I was used to having a male doctor, and though I dreaded the few minutes when I had to drop my underwear and hold my breath while he examined me, I had the comfort of knowing it was coming, knowing it would be fast, and knowing I would be clothed and covered the rest of the exam. I hugged the flimsy gown to my body as I made my way out the door, not knowing what to expect.

We went out a door and down a set of clanking stairs. Sarah abandoned me in front of a blank metal door. There were no chairs so I leaned against the wall, waiting. Eventually a young man came out, confirmed my name, told me his, and led me in. He seemed vaguely handsome though I was not fully able to absorb this sort of information given the circumstances. His hair was brown and his face angular. His eyes were an odd green color, like baby food, peas or green beans, cooked and strained. I locked onto them and did not let go, hoping they could hold me should I start to drift away.

This area of the center was completely different, even from the sterile white hallway that led me to the bathrooms. The light was weak and flickering and the walls were bare concrete, almost as though it was a cellar,

The Shape of the Atmosphere

gutted out and allotted into rooms. The room itself was concrete, though white curtains covered the gray slate of the walls and the presence of a standard-looking exam table almost convinced me I was in a regular doctor's office. A tub sat in one corner as well as a table stocked with cotton balls, syringes, tongue depressors, and other typical medical tools.

This, the first time I was completely naked with a man, was at sixteen, in a concrete room, and no formal introduction. Dr. Isaacs did not even shake my hand. His fingers felt like slimy grapes as they tapped their way around my abdomen, my knees, my throat, under my arms. When he finished touching me, I sat there, still exposed and embarrassed while he asked me questions like "How old are you?" "Who is the president?" "Do you think that you're going to Heaven or Hell?" as though my answers of *sixteen, Eisenhower, blank stare,* were more transparent, honest somehow, when I sat completely bare.

This young, attractive man—that in another situation I may have gone home and envisioned holding hands with, smiling at, this man who somehow had a file on me, who would have known about my inflamed arms even if I had not stood naked in front of him—made notes without speaking. He scribbled, cleared his throat, squinted at my body so that I felt like shrinking into myself, into the cold concrete wall behind me, all without a comforting word.

He then showed me pictures of black splotches, a crucified Jesus, a dead body, and asked me to react in one word. He told me I was dirty and asked me to respond. Then that I was clean. He confused me with his methods. Both Sarah and Dr. Rosslins had called him progressive. The only other time I'd heard that word was when my father talked about John F. Kennedy. And all I knew about him is that people believed he might be our next president and that he was Catholic. The man in front of me was not a politician, but the adjectives my father used for politicians—untrustworthy, smarmy, charming—popped into the space between us, and I thought I began to understand how the wrong men win things sometimes.

I felt the pressure build in my stomach, the musty air of the cellar room reaching my consciousness. I fought to keep my anxiety inside of me, to not let this man looking for sickness see anything he could scribble down

Jessica Dainty

in my file and pass along to someone else, someone who would decide what I ate, where I slept, how many people I showered in front of, this girl who, in the past two days, had been naked in front of more people than she had in the entirety of her adult-ish life. Were these even the progressive methods Dr. Rosslins mentioned? If I failed these would I have to move somewhere new and alien all over again?

When I thought I was done, I put my gown back on. Dr. Isaacs made a move for the door. I followed him, but he instead led me to another room, a room with Dr. Rosslins. I stood for an unbearable length of time, though it was probably only a couple minutes, backed into a wall, turning a quarter turn, touching my toes, doing jumping jacks, holding my breath at their command while they whispered at a level I could barely hear.

I eyed Dr. Rosslins, the man who had disrupted my life at my doorstep, had dropped me off in this place, and yet whom I had begun to like. I did not want him here, in this room, connected to this moment. I had left him yesterday morning feeling calm, feeling safe in my belief that I could trust him. Now I stood in front of him, his finger going in a circle telling me to turn, his eyes and mouth neither asking nor answering questions.

"Oh, are we still on for golf next weekend?" Dr. Rosslins' face was angled in profile, his words directed at Dr. Isaac next to him. I could see his eyes on me each time I finished my circle or changed activities. I was happy when I got to turn away, and I slowed my revolutions so I was facing away more than I was facing forward.

"Morning right? 8 a.m.? Susie is making pot roast. You and Jan should come over."

"Splendid."

The normalcy of their conversation gutted me, and when I finished my current circle they were both facing me, mouths in flatlines across their annoying jaws. They stared at me. Dr. Rosslins lifted his finger to motion for another circle, and I could not help it. I began to cry. Not just to cry, but to weep hysterically and I had an epiphany of overwhelming dread that this is what they had wanted from me, this sign of instability, so that they could do with me what they wanted, scribble in their pads with no hesitation that I was unwell, emotionally distraught, in need of whatever treatment they had to give.

The Shape of the Atmosphere

Dr. Rosslins stood and brought me his handkerchief, offered an abrupt attempt at soothing with a whispered "there, there." I felt a pat on my back, which felt more like he had tried to brush away a fly and touched me by accident. Then they left me weeping, crouched over, snot dripping from my nose, trying not to gag, unsuccessfully, and vomiting into the drain in the floor that looked like a judging eye staring up at me. I sat on the dirty floor until someone came to get me, someone I had not seen before and I was led through the hallway and back to the bathroom, to my clothes. I would have given anything to be allowed back into the shower, even in its openness, to let the water fall over me, to camouflage what the doctors had no doubt seen in me as some kind of sickness.

Instead, I found that my clothes had fallen and were wet from the water on the floor. I dressed, sucking my stomach in and tiptoeing as though I could pull my skin away from the cold material. I took a roll of tape from a craft table set up in the commons area.

Once in my room, I pulled my wet clothes off and sat naked on my bed. I taped my sister back together, piece by piece and watched her take form like a constellation. I imagined my father's finger guiding my way. *The corner piece first. The ones with the white edging. And then the middle fills itself in. There you go.* Still, the picture wasn't quite right. The lines were off somehow, and my eyes, my memory, were not strong enough to fill in the shape alone.

I put on a dress and a cardigan, still chilled from the wet clothes. I went to the commons area and looked for Gladys or Elizabeth, but both sat solitary, occupied with tea and books, and so I orbited the room, pulled at the fray, wondering if I pulled hard enough, if I could float off and be forgotten.

"OT time ladies. Those of you going to the kitchen, line up with Sarah. Laundry room, with Patrice. Gardening with Jessica. Reminder that this is the last week for gardening. You'll have to sign up for a new OT with the desk or in your therapy sessions by Tuesday."

I lined up in front of the aide I did not recognize, assuming she had to be Patrice since she was neither Jessica nor Sarah.

Although hazy, I had remembered the laundry room accurately from my tour with Jessica. At first the smell hit me soft and sweet, like powdered freshness, as though they had somehow bottled flowers and sprayed them

Jessica Dainty

out in an intense concentration. Before five minutes passed though, my eyes burned and my nose reddened at the edges, raw.

Today I steamed. I stood holding a giant hose that exploded shots of air so hot, my mostly healed arm began to tingle from the heat. I passed the hours watching wrinkles fall away, like the chocolate ganache my mother poured over heavy cakes. The richness rippled down in waves and then magically, hardened flawlessly, like a candy skating rink, shiny and smooth.

I returned to my room sweaty and red, my face puffy and sore from the detergents and oppressive room. Still, it had felt good to be down there, to be doing something predictable and constant, and my morning fell away like the wrinkles. I wondered what my mother was doing. If the piles of dishrags and clothes still hid the mudroom floor, if the pantry door was closed or open.

I fell asleep and slept through dinner.

"You can't be in here. Rooms are off limits until lights' out."

A small blonde aide herded me into the commons room. I found Elizabeth and sat across from her but her eyes stared blankly and did not find me. I leaned my head back and slept again, wondering what it would be like to fall away from myself as Elizabeth seemed to. And would I even care if I couldn't find my way back.

* * *

The next morning, I woke unsurprised by where I was. This depressed me.

During the time I had been meeting with Dr. Rosslins, the schedule in my bedroom read TREATMENT. He did say something about visiting therapists and I knew we had group therapy Monday, Wednesday, and Friday afternoons, which I heard was sometimes run by Dr. Isaac, for the calmer wards anyway. But if treatment were one of those, wouldn't they call it THERAPY, as the later time slot did? I ran my fingers down the mesh frame in front of the commons area window. If I got close enough, I could look out with no distortion from the metalwork or white bars, like looking

The Shape of the Atmosphere

through a peephole or having tunnel vision that took me directly to the willow tree, to anywhere outside of here.

The bathroom hallway cleared and the commons area became more full. Jessica told me that during the morning and afternoon around breakfast and lunch we were able to use our rooms. We were still subject to check-ins but they were not off limits as they were in the evening hours, when they were given, I guess, a full search. I went to my room, hoping when eight o'clock came around that they would miraculously forget about me. It was cool this morning, and I already had goosebumps on my arms. I could not imagine standing anywhere unclothed, especially in the dampness of wherever those initial exam rooms were.

A head poked in. "Check-in, Gertrude!" Head poked out.

She was way too cheerful. I'd been checked on five times since I'd been up. If they were in fact on a twenty-minute schedule, I had twenty minutes left until I had to face whatever was coming to me. I lay down on my bed, hoping to rest for a bit, to make the time shorter or to stretch it out. Just to pass it without thinking. I closed my eyes.

My father sat next to me in my bedroom, the telescope pointed up at the night sky, though my room, where we sat, lit up with the sun.

"Show me Pegasus again?"

And he turned a dial, rotated the base, and let me have the lens. There she was, boxy and un-horse-like.

"Does she fly?" I asked.

And my father laughed at me and motioned for me to look again but this time he pushed me through the lens into the sky, and I reached for the white wing because up here she was not shapeless and hard at the edges but beautiful and made of stars, alive like flame. I touched her dancing, burning fur, and my skin caught fire. I stared at it, feeling nothing, my hand melting away in front of me.

The voice of a nurse awoke me.

"Check-in Gertrude. How are we feeling today?" I sat up, groggy, wondering why she wasn't leaving. Didn't she have other people to check?

Jessica Dainty

"A little tired. Can you tell me what the doctor gave me again?" I wiped a dribble of drool from the side of my mouth with the back of my hand and wiped the wetness on the quilt.

I recognized her as Nurse Irene, as I woke up more and more. She and Nurse Peters appeared to be the two in charge. She glanced at the chart in her hands and then back at me. "It's called chlorpromazine. Nothing serious. Helps calm you down. And you're on a very low dose. He's just trying to help quiet your mind, make you more comfortable."

"Well, knowing what's going on is what would make me more comfortable." I felt a tinge of guilt at my possible rudeness, and looked down, tracing the stitching on the quilt. "I just feel like I've been sleeping a lot."

"I'll make a note of it and they'll review and make any needed changes. For now though, you start treatment today. You'll be joining Nurse Peters for your first hydro session. This therapy aims to slow down your body, to calm you. Now, doesn't that sound nice?" This wasn't Nurse Peters. Nurse Peters didn't sugarcoat, and for all her forwardness, she didn't come across borderline condescending or patronizing as this Nurse Irene did.

"Sarah will meet you in the commons area and take you down."

Down. Goosebumps popped up on my arms and legs. I didn't yet fully know my way around, but I knew where the "down" I'd been was, and I was not hoping to return. Perhaps treatment differed from assessment though. Perhaps it would not be as bad, as humiliating.

Five other women stood in a group with Sarah just to the side of them. I'd spent enough time in water to know what hydro implied. Nurse Irene said it would calm the body. After rushed and often cool showers, I supposed the potential for some sort of warm immersion wasn't something to fear.

The women filed into line and followed Sarah down the hall. No one spoke. No one exchanged glances. I knew without asking that no one was new to this but me. They did not present fear of the unknown. They knew exactly what was waiting for them. I envied them but the anticipation, anxiety, hyper-awareness, unquiet—the final even despite everyone's off-putting silence—almost made me glad I did not know where we were going or what we were going to do.

The Shape of the Atmosphere

We entered a stairwell I had not been in before, and though where we came out looked the same as the dank basement walls I remembered, I had no idea if we were in the same place or not. We entered through a door labeled HYDROTHERAPY ROOM. The interior looked like a group bathroom but with bathtubs instead of showers, and no toilets. Eight tubs, all oversized and big enough to fit multiple Elizabeths in each, occupied the room. The edges of the tubs had a border of raised studs and a tarp-like material rolled up at what seemed to me the foot end of each tub.

"Welcome, ladies." Nurse Peters' voice was both comforting and frightening. I stand by her not sugarcoating, but she spoke as though she knew no pleasant inflection could hide the truth that what she was saying, that what she was about to do, was awful. "The aides will help you in."

Aides, three total for the group of us, stood by the tubs. I watched as everyone disrobed. These women were seasoned. There was no shame. Instead I saw something worse, a sort of confidence in their brokenness. An acceptance of humiliation, of inhumanity, of whatever sickness they had inside them, if they had one at all.

I did not know any of the women in this group though some of the faces had passed through my line of vision over the past few days. They were all from Ward 2 like me, and I think one of the women occupied the room next to mine. I followed them in suit, unclothed and climbed into the tub. The sides were deeper than I thought they would be from the outside, and the aide put a block of wood at my feet to push me back so that my head rested more naturally against the back rim of the tub.

The aides rotated around the room, securing the tarps into place, as though we were being covered for baking. To hold the heat in, I imagined.

"Everyone settled? Alright ladies, the aides are here if you need them." And then as an aside to the aides, not intended for us, "At least a half hour today. Definitely not less."

The foot of each tub had a black rubber hose that came up from a spigot from the floor. The aides began turning on the water, four rotations I counted on each handle. Finally, one came to me. She turned the handle and walked to the back wall where I noticed water tanks lined up. She flipped a switch on the back wall and checked something with red lines on it, a temperature gauge perhaps.

"Alright, ladies, just try to relax."

The tub was cool against my skin and I felt a slight shiver. I was eager for the water to fill up. I pushed against the block of wood, trying to raise my head up so my neck rested a bit higher on the ridge of the tub.

"Try not to move. We don't want to have to reseal you." I could not tell which aide spoke. I'd noticed Sarah but had not seen Jessica. All three of the women stood in the corner now where the lighting didn't quite reach. They were smoking, passing a glowing circle of red from one to the other.

My hose lurched, the water reaching it and spurting through. At first it was just a trickle, and I could not tell whether what I felt was the tub or the water. As it traveled from my calves to my buttocks though, I made the awful realization that it was not the tub's coolness I was feeling. The water was cold. Ice cold.

"Mine is cold," I called.

"Supposed to be, dear." I knew Sarah didn't speak because she never used "dear," or hadn't in any situation with me, but no one came over to me. The sentencing was done from across the room.

I bit down on my lip. As the water filled in over my shins, I kept my hands in my lap and made myself think of the willow tree, of the sun outside. Even in the cold of winter, if my upper body was warm, I was warm. The coldness didn't bother me much on my legs. When it worked its way between my thighs though and started licking up my back, a tightness throughout my body took hold. I had the urge to urinate as well as the thought that I already had and that I didn't have to go all at once.

The water hit my elbows and I could feel the goosebumps not only on my arms but on my breasts, my nipples protesting. My back ached and I realized that I was holding my body off the bottom of the tub, pushing my feet against the wood block with such force that I had raised myself up a bit. I took a deep breath and on the second attempt, let my body lower down. I gasped, the water so cold it took my breath away. My shoulders shook, convulsed really, and my teeth chattered. Two women to my left were speaking to each

The Shape of the Atmosphere

other, as though at a spa. I began to cry and thought I might throw up. Would they let me out if I did? Perhaps I could make myself.

And then I couldn't take it. I thrashed. "I have to get out." I tried to push against the rubber covering but it was hooked like buttons and I couldn't push it off from the inside. My head throbbed, and the lights went from dim to flashes and back to dim. The glowing red orb floated in front of me and smoke danced up like a charmed snake. The water filled up so fast I thought it would overtake me, fill the room, drown us all.

"Just try to relax," I heard the red orb say, and then there were two orbs, like glowing red eyes, and I began to cry again, or maybe to scream, the voice was so far away.

"I have to, I have, I have to go to the bathroom," I said, my teeth chattering like my words. And I did. I had an overwhelming urge to defecate. "Are we almost done?"

A whirring suddenly ceased and my hose jumped again. The water bobbed against the rubber casing. It was up to my neck now.

"Done? Honey, time starts now."

I watched her unhook and lift the bottom of the tarp and dump in a bucket of ice.

Then something in my stomach released. Even from above the tarp and from within the diffusion of water, I could smell the foulness.

"I'm sorry. Excuse me. I think I had—I had an accident." I nodded my head in indication.

"Thirty minutes. Sorry. Nurse's orders. You'll get to clean up afterward."

And they left me there with their laughing, and another red orb, and my black hose, which had somehow become a snake and I saw it slithering into my tub. I kicked and screamed at it, afraid it was going to bite me, and I remembered my dream from the morning and thought maybe it was fire beneath me. That I was melting away. I reached for myself, my fingers clumsy, numb and cold. I could not find myself. I was not there.

* * *

Jessica Dainty

I woke up coughing water. Nurse Peters pressed a warm towel to my head and poured hot water into my mouth. I gagged on it and spat it out. It felt like pure flame. I still sat in the tub, but Sarah was unbuttoning the tarp and about to pull it back. I remembered the accident, and I tried to stop her. I couldn't bear the embarrassment.

"No, please. Can you just let me? You said I'd be able to, to clean up?"

She eyed the underside of the tarp and rolled her eyes. She tossed a clean towel on the floor.

"Use the spigot in the corner. You have two minutes."

"The first treatment can be a little shocking, but we've seen very promising results." Nurse Peters removed the towel from my forehead and stood to walk away.

"Do you even know what you're trying to get rid of?" I still felt a little out of it, but I noted her pause and hurried scuffle away.

* * *

I scrubbed myself, scratched with my fingernails, but with no soap and only cold water, I still felt dirty walking into the dining hall. My lips quivered, and I returned to my room to grab a cardigan.

"Why your lips are perfectly blue!" Elizabeth sat with a cup of tea and book in the commons room. "I swear I'm chilled for a week after hydro. I always joke that I warm up just in time for the next session." She sipped the steaming liquid. "Isn't it awful though? My first session is the only time I saw God in this place, but I'm pretty sure it was one of the aides. I don't do well in the cold. Miserable time, but the rest of the week you do feel more calm. At least I did. Maybe just because I was relieved to be out of there."

The speed of her words amazed me. And in listening to her, I also realized how young she really was, even for twenty-four.

"Are they actually trying to treat anything here?" I asked. She cocked her head at me like a chicken. "I mean, are they treating us all the same? Because we're obviously not."

"No. Therapy is different. It's more personal. And not everyone goes to hydro, if that's what you mean."

The Shape of the Atmosphere

I'm not sure if that's what I meant, but I was too exhausted to harass her for answers.

"A little sunshine would do you well. Do you have grounds' privileges? We could go for a walk? It looks beautiful outside."

"I don't know. No one's told me anything."

Elizabeth leaned forward. She looked like she could teeter right off her chair if she went too far. "And no one will if you don't ask. It's been worse lately because they're so short staffed. You know, we had doors in the bathroom up until about six months ago, but then they didn't have enough people to supervise and the morning routine got to be too much. Wards 3 and 4 never had them. But we did. What's the point of moving up if you get treated the same?" She huffed back into her chair.

"You used to be on another ward?" I hadn't thought about this before, about who had been where, about the potential for improvement, or deterioration. I hadn't given the place enough credit to think they were actually trying to make anyone better, if any of us even needed such a thing.

"That's not entirely fair though I suppose because you don't get grounds privileges on those wards, and you don't get to go to the dining hall from 4. Food comes to you and if you choose one thing in the morning and then change your mind, well then you're just out of luck, aren't you?" I wasn't sure whether she didn't hear me or was just very good at ignoring questions and situations she did not want to be a part of. She had made her way out of the "crazier" wards after all. She was either actually getting better or was very good at playing her role.

"What day is it?" The question surprised me, not just because Elizabeth felt the need to ask it, but because I did not know the answer.

"Umm, Wednesday. Maybe, I don't know."

"It's Thursday, dears," one of the older aides chimed in. And with a tap on each of our heads and a too-cheery smile, "Check! And check!"

Elizabeth and I looked at each other and smiled. And then giggled, and then we were both laughing, and she grasped my hand in a way that brought me back to myself, stirred some warmth beneath my skin.

V

The next day I attended my first group therapy session, which on this Friday consisted of sitting at a typewriter and copying a page of print.

"Sit up tall, ladies. Elbows light, wrists up."

"How is this therapy?" I asked leaning over to the person closest to me, a woman I'd seen and heard at nights in the commons area. Her name was Susan.

"Preparing us for the real world, should it ever decide to claim us. Job training."

"What if you don't want to be a secretary?" I asked.

"Oh, don't worry. Every other week we get etiquette classes. You have the option of just being really polite and constrained for a living." And she smirked at me and rolled her eyes.

"So is there even any actual therapy?"

"There are talking days. Fridays, however, training and social branding. Sounds better if they call it therapy though. You can get away with almost anything under that title, don't you think?"

Her sardonic tone surprised me. How did the place deal with someone so openly judgmental of what they were doing to her? And then I almost choked on my thought. Why weren't we all more judgmental of what they were doing to us?

I wondered why she was here.

When typing ended though, she bolted from the room, and I did not see her again until nighttime when we stood in line waiting for pills, lifting our tongues to prove we'd swallowed them down. Susan kept hers out a little longer than necessary before going to sit by the bookshelves. She scared me a little, in her obvious confidence, something I did not have or pretend to have, and I instead sought out Elizabeth. She put her book down, and we

The Shape of the Atmosphere

played Canasta at a side table before being called to bed, my body already feeling the pull of my medication toward sleep.

* * *

The following morning, I was just as groggy if not more so from my two-pill dose the evening nurse shoved at my nose the night before. My mouth was dry and water seemed like the most important thing I'd ever wanted or needed.

The sun shone through my windows. I was surprised to think I'd woken up before the nurse came in. I staggered out into the hallway and saw women already dressed, playing bridge, turning the radio dials and listening to some sort of slow instrumental music.

A jumble of:

"No, too slow, too slow. Where are the records, Sarah? Don't we get the records?"

"Juniper scratched them all last time. There's only Elvis and you know Nurse Irene will never allow it. You're stuck with the radio."

"Who gets makeup?"

"Is there an aide to supervise shaving? I'm like an Amazon!"

"Does anyone know a good station?"

Those were the parts I caught. Women set out empty bowls and platters, taking steps back, moving them to another table, observing, moving them again. Sometime during the night, someone must have unscrewed the sofa and chairs from the floor in the middle of the room and moved them out along the edges. The space was open and frantic.

Elizabeth sat in the midst of it, still and quiet.

"What's going on?" I asked when I finally worked my way through the hustle.

After a second, her eyes fluttered and she looked at me as though trying to figure out who I was. "Oh good morning, Gertie. It's estate social day. Third Saturday of every month, the men's wards, the well ones anyway, come over for a little party. There's dancing and punch and sometimes cookies. It's actually quite lovely, though I know many of these women have husbands and little ones at home. I don't know what they get so worked up over. You'd think they'd never been courted before."

If I closed my eyes, I could imagine Elizabeth came from a different era altogether. She was so funny in her bird-like smallness, her oddly proper language.

"No one woke me up this morning. Is that normal for every Saturday?"

"No. There's so much commotion on these days they usually just let people sleep in. The less awake, the less to worry about. They still run checks. I saw Jessica run into your room at least four times. But there's no treatment other than medication for Wards 1 or 2 on these Saturdays unless specially mandated. I seem to be in the minority, but I sort of loathe the break of routine. I feel restless."

"If they're this busy, think we could get out for that walk?"

"I only get supervised walks. If you haven't been cleared yet, they may say no, but we can give it a try." Elizabeth actually looked excited. "It gets so stuffy in here when they add all the other people, I'd love to get out a little before they fill up the room."

She walked over to the nursing station, her book clutched to her chest. She was so thin, the book almost covered her waist from the side. I thought I remembered her mentioning a family, a child. I couldn't imagine anyone so small having carried a child. My mother was by no means a large woman, but she had curves she both thanked and cursed us for.

Elizabeth turned back to me with two thumbs up, the book held to her side by her upper arm. "One of the student nurses is going to take us. She'll be out in a minute. Oh, the garden is so beautiful this time of year, right before everything starts to die. Almost as though it knows it's about to go and thinks, might as well give it my all." Her silence swallowed her voice abruptly. She tucked her chin down and ran her fingers across her lips, humming.

The nurse came over. She introduced herself as Josephine. Josephine was unmistakably a student by her bumbling words, her awkward leadership, trying to take us out an obviously locked and bolted door before being directed by a patient to use the front door. If I wanted to escape, now was my time. The thought hadn't even occurred to me until then. I assumed I was trapped here, but the walks to Dr. Rosslins', the open grounds…how hard would it really be? Then I thought of my looming empty house and

The Shape of the Atmosphere

realized that the unpredictable horrors of my days here were not enough to send me willingly back to the known ones there.

Outside, we took a side path between the two buildings. The gravel path we were on wove its way through the estate lawn, over the hills, split off for the gardens and the tranquility pond, which I'd heard was not much of a pond at all, for fear of drownings. There was a cluster of men playing horseshoes, and though I knew they also lived here, were coming later today, the physicality of them unbalanced me. As though they had instantly appeared like ghosts because someone had told me they existed and I now believed.

"I'd like to go to the willow tree," I said. I could see it off in the distance, the closest I'd been, but no visible path seemed to lead there.

"No, the gardens, please, oh, please the gardens." At first Elizabeth's voice was soft and then it built in speed and volume and soon she was shaking and shrieking. "The gardens! I have to see the gardens!"

"Yes, yes, the gardens. The gardens will be lovely." I nodded affirmatively at the student nurse, who looked terrified. Elizabeth wrung her hands and I took them in mine to calm them. They were rubbed raw and some of her knuckles were cracked and bleeding. But she did not pull away and we walked hand in hand behind Josephine.

"It's just that the gardens are just so lovely this time of year. Did you know that?" She rested her head on my shoulder now as we walked. She was just enough shorter than I that we could manage this without awkwardness. For such a frail thing, I was surprised by the weight it added. "My boy, Alexander, loves the garden. Used to sit there in the daisies while I weeded."

The walk was short and we reached the gate within minutes. The garden was quite nice. There were a few more men here, sowing some rows and planting seeds. It seemed a bit late in the fall for such a thing but they looked content. One woman bent over a patch of wild green pulling anything weed-like. She'd come up with giant handfuls, look at them as though they would bite her and then shake them off to the ground like a snake. An aide sat to the side, observing.

Elizabeth led me to a wooden bench on the far end. We faced back toward the hospital but the building sat just far enough below the hill that you could only see the roof, the top floor's row of barred windows.

Jessica Dainty

"I love sitting here."

I loved just being outside. There was a garden like this near our town pool and sometimes on my way home, if I wasn't too tired, I would walk along the edges counting the flowers. I only counted the yellow tulips though because they were bright enough in the fading light and because yellow was my favorite color. I realized this only now, sitting in a place that told me each day there was something wrong with me, but where, for the first time surrounded by so many bigger and worse things, I was actually at an odd impasse of peacefulness. I had favorite colors. I had a friend in Elizabeth, though an unpredictable one at that. A potential second friend in Jessica. I was more normal than I'd ever been.

"Please don't tell anyone about my little outburst earlier." Elizabeth had taken her hand back and was wringing them again. "I've been a little jumpy lately but it always passes. It's the time of year, I know it is."

"I won't tell anyone. And I don't think we have to worry about that one either." I motioned toward Josephine who stood as though staked into the ground and unsure how to get back out. "Can you imagine her overseeing a hydro session when she can't handle a walk in the park?"

We laughed and Elizabeth got up to smell the flowers. She picked a yellow and pink flower I'd never seen before and broke it off a little below the bud.

"For the party," she said as she slipped it behind my ear into my hair. "A girl's got to look her best when she's asked to dance." She smiled at me but she was gone again, remembering some past I had no connection to. I let her go, not trying to pull her back. But when Josephine timidly asked us if it was okay if we headed inside, we eyed a silent agreement not to torture the poor thing.

* * *

After lunch, I helped hang streamers and a faded green welcome sign. Sarah assigned me to put out the cookies which I could smell baking since before lunch. I stuffed two into my pocket and shoveled a full one into my mouth while arranging them on the platters. Women giggled from all areas of

The Shape of the Atmosphere

the room. Nurse Peters set up shop at a table in the corner and women lined up to have their makeup done. Some women wore lipstick, a touch of rouge each day, but cosmetics were part of the privilege roster. My mother packed me none, so whether I could have it or not was of no importance to me. Most, I'd guess, just did not care to put forth the effort for what our days normally entailed. Hydro, tears from therapy, God knows what else was out there that I hadn't even been put through yet. It all got washed away one way or another.

The Catholic school did not host school dances, at least not until senior year when they would offer a version of a prom. I'd only attended one dance, last year in my public school. Our school dance in ninth grade was themed *Out of this World*, and the whole gymnasium hung with glittering silver stars that made the floor seem like a sort of funhouse version of the universe, as though one wrong step and we really could fall right through, gravity free and floating.

I'd spent the night fingering the crinkled paper from a cupcake I got from the refreshment table. I was almost asked to dance by a boy in a black blazer and greased hair, but even though my heart fluttered at his approach, he was shorter than I and I didn't like his crooked, nervous smile, so I turned away and shoved a second cupcake into my mouth in one giant, unattractive bite.

Here I couldn't exactly act crazy to get out of the same situation. Perhaps it was a desirable quality here, a sort of mark for compatibility. *Is she too crazy for me? Oh, she seems to possess the exact right amount of insanity. I'll ask her.*

"It's almost four o'clock ladies. The gentlemen will be here any minute. Music will start at five. Though we left the cards and puzzles out, please try to use this time to be social. Interactivity is pro-activity!" Nurse Irene's pep annoyed me. I wondered if rooms were off limits.

Susan, who as far as I could tell was in here simply by virtue of the fact that she was in her thirties and still unmarried (my mother either would have called her a tart or taken pity on her "poor misfortune" depending on her mood), asked if she could smoke, and following her lead, the room lit up like a bonfire.

Jessica Dainty

Everyone had a one cigarette per day allowance, but Wards 1 and 2 could get up to three for good behavior. I imagined by the amount of smoke that the women had pooled theirs for weeks and ignited them all at once.

Jessica turned on a couple of fans by the corridor hallways and the smoke dissipated quickly enough. I didn't know why the sight of Elizabeth smoking surprised me. She just seemed so pure of, well, everything. I'd heard my mother reference that my father used to smoke, that he quit because she didn't like it, and the more time they spent together, the less he smoked. Eventually it was just easy to stop. I've only seen one photograph of my father before he was my father, and he stands, leaning back against a white car, a cigarette in his hand, a second behind his ear, dark sunglasses on the top of his head. He was the most handsome man I'd ever seen, and though it sounds strange, I was deeply jealous of my mother, looking at that picture. That this woman who had nothing to give me, had had enough of something to give him that he took it, dropped everything else, and ran.

"Ooh, here they come, here they come." The women swarmed like birds to prey.

An older man in a white coat led the line, a doctor I had not yet met. I wondered if the men had separate everything. Doctors, therapists, maybe even treatments. Had they known the pain of a half-hour-long ice bath? The men in line looked as nice as possible for anybody with limited means to dress up. I doubted many had thought to pack the tuxedo when being sent off to this place. Most wore khaki or black pants, a button-down shirt. Only a few wore ties, and I saw one adjusting it and could tell it clipped on. It made sense they wouldn't allow something long and tie-able to go around the patients' necks. In fact, I was surprised they allowed panty hose. Perhaps they weren't strong enough to pose a threat. I hated them but wore them tonight regardless. I'd originally come out in my trousers, which had been folded and left at the foot of my bed after breakfast, but Elizabeth's disbelief sent me back to my room to change into one of the ugly dresses my mother had seen more fit for me. The line for shaving had stretched too lengthy and I'd sacrificed my chance to the doe-eyed women around me, most likely dreaming of being asked to dance.

"Oh, I'd rather die than have him notice my legs," one had said.

The Shape of the Atmosphere

The line of men came with a set of three male aides. Two of them were older, like the doctor, but one was young, probably in the earlier part of his twenties. The patients appeared to follow the same set-up. Many of the men were middle-aged or older, with the slight creasing around the eyes my father's had begun to keep even after he stopped smiling. A few patients were younger though, the last in line the youngest looking of all. I liked his face even from across the room. His hair was like a wave of powdered chocolate, if such a thing were possible. Almost all the other men had gelled their hair, slicked it one way or another. His was clean and looked touchable, inviting.

I'd never been particularly successful with boys, partly due to my fear of what liking them meant for me. The inevitable womanhood, the marriage, the babies. I knew I was getting ahead of myself, but the thought terrified me, and my mother was not open with details. Even at sixteen, I still was not overly clear about what exactly needed to take place for another human being to come along. And I'd heard my mother talk about the one or two high school girls who got themselves "in trouble" each year. Her words handed them such a heavy mark of shame that I could not imagine the humiliation, the embarrassment. I imagined myself as Hester Prynne, outcast and blamed. And not just blamed, but blame-worthy.

I admired instead, the younger aide. After all, he was an aide. I was a patient. I'm sure the interaction would be limited and I could watch him and enjoy his presence.

The hour until the music started would be a long one. People stood around as though some odd spell had fallen over everyone. No one spoke. No one moved. Finally, one of the older aides walked a gentleman whose head never quite stayed still over to the refreshment table and introduced him to Helen, a woman on my hallway who as far as I knew only said the world *apples*.

It was a game for some of the more bored on our ward. "Helen, what would you like to eat today?" *Apples*. "What would you like to play on the piano?" *Apples*. "Would you like something to wipe your nose?" *Apples*. She was self-reliant in every other way though; otherwise, I'm sure she would be on Ward 3 or 4.

Jessica Dainty

I watched, pitying the aide's choice for jump-starting the party with conversation. The silence hung, almost tangible, as though I could reach my hand out and get it stuck in the thickness of unspoken words. A few men and women who were obviously friends had settled into the outskirts of the room, a scattering lingered near the refreshments, but everyone else remained stagnant. Nobody knew me here, knew whether I was quiet or loud, popular or strange (other than by mere virtue of being a patient here), and I felt brazen.

"Has anyone tried the chocolate chip cookies?" I announced, my voice shaking in immediate regret. "They—they really are lovely." I walked up to the elderly gentleman with the one-worded Helen. His shoulders curved over and down as though his whole body could be rolled up from head to toe. "Would you like a cookie, sir? Come with me." I walked arm in arm with him to the table. He shuffled his feet on the floor like my sister and I used to do on the carpet when we were kids, trying to make a spark, our fingers outstretched, slightly bent in anticipation like veins strangled of life, waiting to explode.

I poured him some punch and handed him a cookie and others followed. Shufflings and murmurs trickled in and soon there was a low hum to the room as people *Mmm*ed at the cookies, said how do you do, and started settling into conversation.

I sat the old man down with Gladys. He had mentioned he had grandchildren too, and I hoped they would find enough to connect on to free me up. I wanted to get away to my room. My chest pulsed from my bout of public speaking and I wanted to calm down a bit.

"That was a nice thing you did in there." I had almost made it to my corridor, an oscillating fan the only object between me and some release. "You're linking everyone else up and now you're running off to be alone. Why don't you come socialize?" The young male aide placed his hand on the small of my back and guided me back into the room.

No man, outside of my family and now Dr. Isaac with his unwelcome explorations, had ever really touched me. The boys at my school stayed away for the most part. In their defense, I kept my head down or shoved cupcakes into my mouth to avoid them.

The Shape of the Atmosphere

With this man's hand there, my body hummed and sensation radiated outward from that spot. I felt like I might explode and I couldn't help it. I exhaled audibly, pushing the air out. I was overwhelmed. I smiled, nervous.

"What's your name?"

"Gertie." In this moment, above all other things, above having my father and sister back, above having a mother who did not hide herself away, I wished for a beautiful name so that he could hear it and it would roll off my tongue and spiral into his mind softly and find a place to stay. Instead, it came out abrupt and hit the air ugly. My legacy.

"I'm Jonathan. Gertie?" I nodded. "That's a nice name. I've never heard it before."

"It's short for Gertrude. But I like that even less." He smiled so I smiled too, and I imagined my name wasn't so bad after all.

"So what are you in for?" We had come to the window and he leaned forward, more in my space than his. I wondered if this was flirting.

Nobody had asked me that yet. The question startled me. What was I here for? Because my mother did not want me? Because I had hurt myself? Because whatever was behind that closed pantry door with my mom had pulled her too far away to get back to me?

"I, um, I don't know really. Part of my family died. I think my mother and I both found it hard to deal with."

"I see. Well, consolation can be my specialty. Maybe we could take a walk later and you can tell me more?"

My heart leapt and cringed at the thought, but before I could answer, a drumroll of speech broke in.

"J—J—J—Jonath—th—th—an?"

Jonathan stood up straight, assuming once again the formal stance of an aide toward a patient.

"This is Clement. Clement, this is Gertie, short for Gertrude." I had watched Jonathan as intently as possible without staring, and I now found it hard to pull my eyes toward this new person. It was the young male patient, the nice looking one with soft hair.

Jessica Dainty

"H—h—h—h—h—h—ow d—d—d—d—do you d—d—d—do?" Clement extended his hand. Based on his speech, I expected it to quiver but his handshake was strong and controlled.

"Nice to meet you. Clement?" I asked to be sure I had it right. He nodded. "Like the Pope," I said. "I think there have been fourteen of you." He laughed without hesitation or stutter and I was overcome by who he would be without difficulty speaking. Certainly not somebody in here. He seemed normal otherwise. I suppose that went for all of us though. Who would Arlene be if she didn't eat hair? Me, if my family had not died and I had not mourned them by self-inflicting pain. Probably, just a girl, at a social talking to two cute boys. Then why was it simpler in here than it had ever been out there? Maybe because I had nothing to hide. At least nothing to lose.

"Do you need something, Clement?" The patient opened his mouth, but then closed it and instead pointed with a finger toward a man in the corner who would not let go of the ladle for the punch bowl, despite several people reaching for it. "Ahh. Okay. Excuse me," Jonathan said. He bowed his head and touched me again on the small of my back before walking toward the opposite end of the room.

I clasped my hands in front of me and rocked back and forth on my heels. Clement shoved his hands in his pockets and kept his eyes on the ground.

"Want to see if we can go for a walk?" I finally said. The idea of walking with Jonathan had reminded me of my outing with Elizabeth, and I longed to breathe the fresh air again, especially since the smoking had not stopped but only increased since the men had come. Clement looked at me, as though startled I was still there. "I can see if an aide will take us."

"S—s—sure."

After some bargaining, Nurse Irene sent us out with one of the student nurses. I said I needed some fresh air and that I'd been feeling better after my walk with Elizabeth this morning. The smoke was giving me a headache and I was going to have to either go outside or go to my room. I knew she'd want to keep rooms off limits to cut down on the need for spread out check-ins. I was getting better at their games.

"I'd like to go to the willow tree," I said once outside. Clement walked on the path next to me, but with as much space between us as

The Shape of the Atmosphere

possible. The student nurse cut off the gravel walkway at the top of the hill. I felt rebellious at first, but then the grass became more flattened and brown beneath our feet and I knew we were on a well-tread footpath, one that had bore other travelers before.

The tree loomed, simply put. I turned to find the window I often looked out from, but the building stood further away than the tree ever seemed to from the other side, which struck me as strange, considering how much larger it was than the willow. The hanging branches made a claim though, staked the ground as their own, waving their drooping leaves like a flag.

Inside, the light was brighter than I expected as though the leaves were aflame just on the other side. The trunk looked almost like two separate trees had fallen into each other and danced for decades, twisting themselves up in some romantic affair. They'd grown old together. The bark was wrinkled, the exposed roots like stepping-stones to join them.

I sat down in a groove formed by part of the trunk as it fought its way in to the ground. I wanted to stay here forever, running my fingers along its old skin, its body that almost seemed to sway with the wind, as though breathing and alive. Not just alive as a plant is known to be, but alive as a soul is, aware of me and sheltering me, sharing with me this moment of peace.

"It's beautiful, isn't it?" I said. Clement had stayed near the opening in the drooping branches. He stood, unsettled as though lost, turning one way and then the other.

"Would you like to sit? Relax?" He came and sat next to me. I pretended he was Jonathan for a minute, but then noticed his hands, raw and red like Elizabeth's, and I felt bad for wishing he were someone else as though he didn't exist. If I had been braver, I would have taken his hands in mine as I had Elizabeth's, but I'd never been with a boy this way before. The nurse stood inside the tree with us, which made the moment both easier and more awkward.

The silence was nice though, and my inner peacefulness did not break open with the additions of these other people around me.

"Can I call you Pope?" I asked. I liked the sound of it. If I couldn't have a great name for myself, I liked the idea of creating one for someone else.

Jessica Dainty

     Pope smiled and leaned back against the tree and closed his eyes. His hair was more blond than I'd thought inside the commons area. Not like chocolate but like a mixture of sunlight and dirt, dark and light all at once. And before he closed them, I'd noticed his eyes were a grayish blue like a slab of slate that longed to be a gem of aquamarine but was stuck somewhere in between. I leaned back too and we stayed like this until the nurse, now on the outside, said she could hear the music starting, that we should go back now if we wanted to dance. I kept my eyes closed and smiled, because in my head, I already was.

* * *

     I liked that Pope didn't talk much. We didn't dance together but sat and played Go Fish. He used fingers and a flash of a card to tell me what he wanted, a wave of his hand in invitation to choose if he did not have what I wanted. Then we moved onto Gin Rummy while people blurred by us. Gladys danced on the outskirts with the man I'd sat her down with. They both smiled and I could hear her laugh, that touch of gold that made me think of my mother.

     The music volume was turned down a bit song by song until it stopped all together and the men were called back into line. Pope stuffed his hands in his pockets and said goodbye silently with a smile and a shoulder shrug, his cheeks just pink enough to make me blush too. Once they were gone, we cleaned up and helped move back the furniture which someone would no doubt screw into place sometime over the course of the night. Then we went about our nightly routine. After brushing my teeth, using the bathroom, and taking my medicine, I went to my room and whispered about a boy, to my sister's black and white presence, before falling to sleep.

VI

    I woke up fully aware that today was Sunday and that Sunday was visitation day. I dressed in my mother's favorite dress and when people started showing up, I sat by the window where the light would come in and hopefully flatter my complexion. But the sun began to burn the side of my face, my left arm, and I watched Elizabeth smile and giggle with a man I assumed to be her husband. They left for a walk and I went to sit with Gladys who was also alone. She was sniffling so I said nothing. I just sat in the empty chair next to her and let her cry for me too.

* * *

    My next week in Willow Estate started with no Elizabeth. She was not at breakfast. Or lunch. Or dinner. After her walk with her husband the day before she had come in cheerily enough, but at dinner she started shaking and crying and two aides had escorted her out. By the time she reached the breezeway she was screaming, and I saw Nurse Peters bustling toward them with a syringe in her hand. And then they were gone. I asked about her at breakfast, at treatment, which today was occupational therapy, but no one would tell me anything.

    "Worry about your lines right now honey. That crease is going to go off at an angle." Women around me in the laundry room shuffled clothes from washers to dryers and clotheslines to steam presses and then to folding. The pressing I was apparently not up to par on.

    When the aide had walked away though, Arlene leaned over. "Just because you don't see her, doesn't mean she's not here." She said this with a wink and a smile. "She'll come back. She always does."

The Shape of the Atmosphere

I re-steamed the pair of slacks I was folding and set up to iron the crease again. I wondered if they might belong to Pope, but then I thought of Elizabeth and pressed the iron on them until they burned.

* * *

Gladys and I enjoyed dinner next to one another each night. She told me about Samuel, the elderly man I had introduced her to at the social, about how his family had sent him here after he'd fallen asleep while watching the grandchildren and one had tried to climb up on the stove.

"Did anything happen to the child?" I asked.

"No, he was fine. But that doesn't matter when they're looking for a reason. He told me they'd been suggesting he visit one of the new homes that opened for the elderly. He wouldn't go. And why should he? There's nothing wrong with that man. Nothing at all!" Gladys was a quiet but forward woman. When her voice rose, the passion with which she spat out the final words made me smile. How her family could imagine she wasn't capable of taking care of herself, I could not fathom.

"Do you like it here?" I asked.

"When I first got here, I hated it. I was angry and annoyed. But now, I don't know. Would I really want to return somewhere where I'm unwelcome? They only want me here because my family is paying for me." She reached her hand out for the salt shaker. I slid it toward her. "But that's something, right? I mean, isn't it? To be wanted, whatever the reason?"

I knew she could not see my nod, but I could not answer her. I wanted to punch through the table, to kick and scream, before I would give in to the fact that I might agree with her. To actually acknowledge, despite the nakedness, the embarrassment of hydro, the humiliation of being made to feel I am unwell when I am not, that being here, where people called me Gertie and asked me how I was and held my hand on walks outside, that perhaps I was not altogether unhappy.

I helped Gladys to the chair she liked in the commons area by the fireplace they never lit, at least from what I had seen, and then sat by the bay window. It was almost November now. I could feel it even through the closed window, the coolness that held no guarantee of regressing back to warmth, even for an afternoon or two. The willow bared even more of itself than when Pope and I had sat under it, and the barrenness of it made me feel like crying. I loved the fall, despite the closing of the town pool, the end of my endless laps, but here I felt it would be too cold and dark, especially if there was no Elizabeth.

I looked over where she normally sat at night, a book in one hand, a cup of tea in the other. Susan sat there instead, her dark curls making her sharp nose soften in shadow. She held the Bible that Elizabeth read each night. She did not read it, and it was an odd sight to see her quiet, as she normally always had something to say about womanhood, feminism, anything in general. Whatever she said, she said it with purpose. I wished I had anything to say that I believed in as much as she seemed to believe in every word that came out of her mouth.

"Excuse me," I said to the aide sitting behind the half door of the nursing station. I did not recognize her, but she looked at me with eyes that told me she was not new. They were too tired. "I heard there was a chapel here? Is it still open? May I go?"

Another aide I did not recognize walked me down a hallway I had not been in before. At the end, on one side sat the small kitchen women could bake in for recreation. This was where the cookies for the last social must have been made, why I could smell them baking. Across from it there was a room, narrow but long. A handful of chairs sat in rows, enough for about ten women to sit at once. Up front, there were two places to kneel before a hanging crucifix. To the side there was a grotto to light candles and a small fount of holy water. An aide sat in a chair near the candles. Where there was fire, there was supervision, I thought.

I sat in the back row of chairs, my chest tight. I had not come for me, and I knew I had not come for my mother either. Something inside of me had wanted this though. To be here, where God, perhaps my father, maybe Allison, was just a little bit closer. They'd taken my rosary the day I'd come, finally returning it after my final assessment had been done. I had not put it back on, though, and I felt as though maybe I should have brought it.

The Shape of the Atmosphere

Perhaps I would belong more, in this space, with it on. It rested instead on my side table, near my sister.

I went up to the front but did not kneel. I simply stood there, looking at the bleeding Jesus before me. He looked back at me, his eyes so pained and sad that I wanted to climb over the small railing and touch his hands, wipe his forehead, whisper to him as I wished someone would whisper to me, *It's all right. It will all be over soon. One way or another. You just have to have hope.*

I nodded to the aide on my way out, thinking of my father whispering to me in the quiet of his office. "What ever happened to hope?" I pushed my hands into my pockets as though I could find it there, but of course there was nothing, and I sat back by the bay window watching for something, anything, in the sky.

* * *

Hydro marred my Tuesdays. I woke up as I did on the first day of school: full of dread. I hated the start of school, the awful stiff uniforms, my lunchbox with a glowing Jesus on the front, the Mother Mary's veiled head bowing down from one corner, my sister next to me, and my mother's words *God is watching you* pounding in my brain, to the point where the tickled spot my father had kissed me on the side of my forehead had faded. When my mother pulled us out of Catholic school and put us in public school, the Jesus lunchbox and dread went with me.

My sister didn't sit next to me on the bus, that first day of public school. When we arrived and exited the ugly yellow box, I did feel a slight tug on my backpack and then saw the shrinking figure of Allison as she ran ahead, already making friends. Once in my classroom, I saw the white slip of paper poking out from my front zipper. All it said was "try to have fun lonely girl" in my sister's unmistakable bubble lettering. And I went to the bathroom and cried because it was the nicest thing my sister had ever done for me.

Still, walking into that new classroom was worse than the day I found my mother's handwriting on a student withdrawal form on my father's office desk. My mother had filled in the reason for my withdrawal: *child's instability and signs of wavering devoutness.* I found this an odd choice. Wouldn't she want me there? The fact that my sister was going with me did little to uplift me.

I took the act as a definitive resignation of her mothering of me. A metaphorical towel, thrown in, her hands wiped clean. She hadn't even used my name. The only place it appeared was at the top, in a script that was not my mother's but that many of the nuns seemed to share, and I spent the day envisioning who it could have been, hoping it was Sister Magdalene, the only nun who smiled at me, and who in that moment as I sat unclaimed in my father's office, I replaced my mother with.

I had sat, pulling the metal beaded chain on my father's green glass lamp. I walked away with tiny imprints in my fingertips. When my mother saw them and asked, I told her I'd been praying the rosary.

"Whatever you were praying for, you must have wanted very badly," she joked, her head already turned away from me.

I knew, with everything, that she was right. I just had no idea what it was that I wanted.

All I knew now was that I did not want to sit through another hour of hydro. The inevitable check-in came, though, the roll call to line up, the march down the too-white hallway to the too-dank stairs.

Women around me were talking and laughing. I entered almost able to forget the terror of the last session, not quite sure if it was as bad as I remembered. This time I did not soil myself, but later in the common area sipping tea, I felt a warmth between my legs. After negotiating a few extra minutes, I took the bathroom key to find my thighs smeared with red.

The times a girl needs her mother. Take one. Though I doubted mine would have been much help. She'd see this as both a celebratory start to womanhood and as the start to the chance of me getting myself "in trouble" all in one.

Nurse Peters sent Susan with me to show me how to use the thick white pad she'd given me, the tiny tube of cotton that looked like a white bullet.

"Welcome to womanhood. It's a bitch," was all she said, before crouching in front of me and coaching me on insertion techniques. I did not attempt in front of her. There was no knock at four minutes, or even five. Susan called in only once to ask how I was doing. The tampon had hurt to

The Shape of the Atmosphere

put in, and I sat looking at my fingers, stained with red, wondering what Eve had thought after the Fall, the first time it had happened to her, with no one around to talk to, no mother anywhere in existence, as she was to be the first.

"I'm fine," I said, washing my hands. The first sign of my inescapable plunge into womanhood swirled down the drain, a diluted red. When my sister had gotten her period, when she was fourteen and I twelve, she and my mother had spent hours in the bathroom. They made it seem like a magical, secretive thing, whatever was happening behind that door, and I almost yearned for it, to know my mother in the way that Allison did in that time together.

Allison had always taken immense pride in becoming older. She wore her first bra at ten, the cups dented and hollow under her shirt. After her period, she began taping her tampons to the outside of her purse, until our mother threatened to not let her leave the house. Her brazenness only fueled my embarrassment, my obvious lagging behind. I was not womanly and I did not want to be. My mother sent Allison to etiquette lessons twice as often as I. She had to go to a doctor and put her feet in stirrups and let a man actually stick his fingers inside of her, instead of just the quick look I dreaded on my visits.

Being a woman seemed like too much work, too much pressure, that resulted in hiding in pantries, getting yourself "in trouble" or, in my case, being sent here.

I left the bathroom, and Susan still waited for me on the other side.

"You okay?" she asked. "No cramps or pain?" I shook my head. "You're lucky then. I want to rip my uterus out when I get mine."

I smiled weakly. Susan came across too strong for me. Her presence made me uncomfortable.

"Well thanks, you know, for your help and all."

She didn't leave and I had no choice but to walk back to the common area with her and sit in the green chair across from her. This green chair was nothing like my mother's. The cushions were too forgiving, and I sank into it. I wished it would swallow me up. Susan didn't try to talk to me. She just sat there, holding the same book again, Elizabeth's book, and closed her eyes. I watched her fingers trace the gilded lettering until the room blurred around the edges and I felt myself float away with it into sleep.

Jessica Dainty

After lunch, Susan's promise of etiquette lessons came true. We lined up in the recreational building, the equipment—balls and racquets and nets—pushed off to the side and took turns walking the length of the room with books on our heads.

I'd been prepared to go into my first group therapy session. To sit and talk my problems out, if I could organize for myself what they were. But Nurse Irene announced that Dr. Isaac and Dr. Rosslins were attending a meeting, that we would instead have etiquette today and therapy would pick up again next week.

We filed into the rec building, the women bouncing along, obviously glad to not be going to therapy. I had been curious and looking forward to it, if just to see what it entailed. I was eager to hear what these other women, not so different than I it seemed, had to say.

We were each handed a book and told to go.

When I was younger, even more a mess of angles and shapes, too hunched over from lack of confidence to balance a book on my head, my mother insisted I practice daily. The moments spent going haltingly across my living room were the most diminishing of my day.

Here the stilted passage from end to end, with an aide's voice announcing "Glide, Glide. Fluidity. Glide," every five seconds seemed almost humorous if not somehow surreal. By definition, weren't we sort of outcast from society? Why did we have to practice belonging to it? And what part of being able to balance a book on my head would ever help me in the real world?

As though on cue, the aide's voice rang in again: "Posture is key to presenting yourself favorably, whether it be to a potential employer or to a potential spouse. Remembering to lengthen your spine will also help keep your back from getting tight after typing!" And she said it just like that, with a finger up, as though to mark the exclamation point at the end of her own sentence.

After everyone had taken three or four promenades down the room, we practiced sitting in chairs and crossing our ankles, smoothing our dresses out at the end, hands clasped in our lap. I had worn my pants, and I could see the aide eyeing me disapprovingly, as though this were for a grade and she were making a note of my shortcomings.

The Shape of the Atmosphere

When we were in Catholic school, my sister Allison would walk in front of me the four blocks to school, her skirt shortened an extra inch on the inside with metal pins from my mother's sewing basket. I, on the other hand, pulled my knee socks up as high as possible, my skirt down as low. I petitioned to be allowed to wear pants, but the Mother Superior had scoffed at the thought and would not even allow me to try.

"Why don't you petition for something more useful?" she'd told me before shooing me out with a look only nuns were capable of, where God Himself could not be more clear.

My public school had no required uniforms but my mother's horrified look at my pants transformed into looks of disbelief on the faces of my peers when I would enter the hallways, the girls around me always in dresses or skirts. I still did not understand what the big deal was.

"Put your legs together, for Christ's sake!"

I turned and saw Susan sitting in her chair, slumped back, her knees wide to the sides. I couldn't help but smile.

Even Susan wore dresses more often than pants. Perhaps someone who did not know her, or who didn't care to take the time, had packed for her, too.

* * *

Wednesday brought still no Elizabeth and I steamed and folded and washed away the thought of her never returning. The heat of the laundry room helped take away the chill that seemed to cling to me after hydro even a day later. I'd begun singing lullabies to myself during hydro. My focus helped distract me until either it was over or I blacked out.

I awoke on Thursday with that feeling of dread. But come check-in and roll call time, they did not line me up for hydro. They instead told me I was going to a different room with Sarah and that Dr. Isaac would meet us there. The room was small, and Sarah was not one for conversation. I had back on the awful cotton paper gown I'd worn during my initial assessment and my stomach churned dangerously at my thoughts. There was no all-seeing drain here though, and if I were to get sick, I had no idea where I hoped for it to go.

The room had an examination table, a sink, counters of medical supplies, as well as a cart with a giant U-shaped contraption with lots of wires and a box that resembled a radio with all its dials and switches.

"What's that for?" I asked Sarah. She had been sitting in a chair in the corner, tapping her heels.

"That's for shock therapy. It's what you're here for. Don't worry, it's not so bad. The consensus is it's better than hydro."

That wasn't exactly a shining endorsement.

"What does it do?" I asked the question just as the door opened and Dr. Isaac walked in. Now that I was more settled here, and my nerves were, given my situation, more at ease, I was able to actually absorb the wonder of Dr. Isaac's face. He wasn't just handsome, as I remembered. He was like a god of some mythical order. Had the ceiling opened up to allow the light to shine down on him, I would not have been surprised. He could no doubt get away with a lot more with a face like that.

"What it does is help you get better." He extended his hand, and I took it, blushing at the hand of a man who had already seen me naked.

He pulled the cart toward us. "We are going to spread a substance called a conductant on your temples and then tighten this little thing on either side of your head." He held up the U-shaped thing, which he grasped by a piece that really made it more of a Y than a U. "Then with these knobs, we are going to send tiny electrical impulses through these wires, to the ends here and into your head. The goal is to trigger different areas of the brain to be active or inactive. The whole thing takes only a few minutes. Ready to try?"

As he asked, he gently pushed my shoulder down so that I was lying before I realized it. They pulled four leather straps from under the table up and across my body. One at my feet, one on my thighs, one around my midsection, and the final across my shoulders.

I was about to protest when Dr. Isaac took a smaller leather strip and somehow forced it between my top and bottom teeth.

The Shape of the Atmosphere

"Bite down. It's to keep you from hurting your teeth or biting your tongue. Because we are stimulating the brain, and your brain controls your body, your body may react in unpredictable ways. Best to be safe."

I tried to speak, but only mumbled sounds made it past the slab of leather. I felt like a bridled horse or a pig with an apple in his mouth. The conductant was slimy and cold, and I shivered in the already damp room. This room was in the basement too, with the same gray walls and water-stained concrete floors as the others I'd been in.

I felt a pressure on either side of my head as though my head were a pimple, and someone with giant fingers were trying to pop it.

I heard Dr. Isaac say "ready?" and felt my head shake and my mouth try to say something, and then I was struck by lightning and my body coiled up into a ball and exploded outward like a firework. And then my veins were full of some sort of sludge and I was water and I was swimming in myself, looking around, thinking how sad it all was that nothing was beautiful.

* * *

My jaw hurt and dinner was the tough pepper steak I saw women sawing through my first night here. I squished mashed potatoes back and forth through my teeth but managed to only swallow one bite. My head hurt and I couldn't remember the name of the woman next to me, though I knew I knew her and her glassy eyes and white hair. I somehow knew she had four grandboys too, but her name had sunk to the bottom of some ocean of information I did not have the breath or ability to reach. And when she said my name, I felt guilty, as though I were Peter denying her, and I excused myself to the commons area where I pressed my forehead to the mesh screen of the window until someone had to pull me away and lead me to my room.

* * *

Routine has a funny way of blurring days together. It wasn't that things got better. Hydro and shock were just as bad each time, the "therapy" of typing and sitting with knees together felt just as demeaning, but I could no longer distinguish what happened when. I was both more calm and more stressed, the former most likely from the higher dose of medication Dr. Rosslins suggested when he returned and he claimed to notice my anxiety over Elizabeth's absence and my annoying strings of questioning. I was thinking that something awful had happened to Elizabeth and I just couldn't let it be true. The higher level of stress came from Elizabeth still absent after two more Sundays, marked by the wave of visitors, none of them my mother.

And then on Monday morning, in early November, there Elizabeth was, sipping her trademark cup of tea, thinner (if such a thing were possible) but smiling when she saw me.

"Where have you been? Are you all right?" My speech was as flustered and speedy as hers usually was.

"I just needed some time. I told you, this time of year, I just need a little extra help. I needed to be alone." She stared at her cup of tea.

"But where were you?"

"I don't know exactly. Same place I go every year. It's darker there though."

I could tell I was not going to get any real information out of Elizabeth, whether she was unwilling or really did not know or remember. She seemed fine though. A little less cheerful, but still Elizabeth. I noticed her hands were shiny, as though covered in lotion. They looked scabbed in places and when she pushed her sleeves back I noticed some fading remnants of bruises along her forearms.

"Well, I'm glad you're back. I've missed you." She smiled at this and patted my hand with hers.

"I've been doing my OT in the laundry room. I hated it at first, but now it's kind of nice to have something normal to do."

"I liked laundry. My favorite is the garden though. They spoke of putting a greenhouse in for awhile, but decided there would be too much glass. I'm hoping I can earn my status back by spring so I can help with the garden. Grounds privileges, even for occupation therapy, are so much harder to earn. But I have never missed the deadline yet." She smiled and put up her finger in lackluster punctuation.

The day carried on with a calm I hadn't felt the past few weeks. I realized, steaming and folding in the hot basement room later, that my worry

The Shape of the Atmosphere

had been overly selfish. Though I cared about Elizabeth, more than anyone else I'd met here, I knew my curiosity, my terror at where she could have been was for my sake too. After all, if she could end up there, who was to say that I couldn't as well?

VII

Time continued to pass, as it does. This had been one of my greatest realizations coming here: time passes. When I was a child, and my routine was taken for granted, I neglected to give time the credit it deserved. Even when I tried to slow it, when my body began to work toward womanliness, I still approached time as though I thought I could win.

Time always won, and now in my second week of group therapy, I dreaded the day when I would be asked to speak, to articulate my problems in no uncertain terms, to prove that I did not need to be here. Instead, I sat and listened as others spoke.

I did not get to hear the details I'd hoped for. Why Susan was here, when it was that Francis first believed she was a reincarnated saint. Instead, we performed breathing exercises, repeated mantras of positive thinking, and received the opportunity to share positive progress from our weeks.

Dr. Isaac presided over these sessions. Nurse Irene, Nurse Peters, and occasionally Dr. Rosslins floated in to listen to a few minutes before floating out just as easily.

My time in Dr. Rosslins' office on Tuesdays remained the more stressful of my therapy slots. Sometimes we did not speak at all, but simply stared at objects on his desk, out-exhaling each other over the course of our hour together. He asked me about my mother once, my father a few times, my sister indirectly, but I avoided these and instead asked him about his family. He smiled at this, showing me a framed photo of himself, a woman, and two children, all dressed nicely, a church shooting up behind them.

"What do you feel when you think of them now?" he asked me at my last session, the first time he had ever lumped them together so sloppily, like a pile of mush set before me.

The Shape of the Atmosphere

I did not have an answer for him. My family's final day together was the first in a while that we'd shared the space around ourselves with each other. Our times at the dinner table, looking back now, seemed just as distant as the rest of our days, drifting around each other, foreign objects that did not recognize each other's gravity. Our sharing a meal around the table had only been an illusion. We had shared nothing but the holding of our breath as my father tasted the meal. Nothing but the silence we passed around with the bowls of food. Nothing but not knowing how to say *Who are you people? And how did I get here...*

And now, I had nothing but time to think about it.

* * *

The aides announced that a new girl would be joining us and the common area buzzed with assumptions. I wondered if this was what had happened when they were told I was coming. Were they disappointed when they saw me? Were cigarettes won or lost in bets on how crazy I would be? I could hear wagers being made all across the room. Susan spread a handful of cigarettes on a corner table and made tallies on a piece of paper from the bridge score pad.

"She's transferring from a private facility in upstate New York. Her family has relocated and wants her closer," Nurse Peters announced. Just not in the same house, I thought. How endearing. "Please make her feel welcome."

Days passed and the whirring whispers about the new girl lost their rapture.

"Did you see her? She came through this morning. Susan is going to lose like twelve cigarettes!" I heard someone whose name I thought was Rachel say at dinner. The buzz started again, and people were on the lookout.

I saw Becca Donelson for the first time in the bathroom during the next morning's routine, naked, absently brushing her teeth in front of someone else's bathroom stall. There had been a girl at our church like her. Some of the boys called her a "retard" and my mother had threatened to wash my mouth out with soap if she ever heard me say such a thing about her. I was angry my mother was so forgiving of this girl's limitations, but so judgmental of mine.

Becca's face announced her illness, but it was not her features, her pouty mouth or squished nose, her heavy, small eyes, that I noticed that day. She was blossomed. Her breasts, her hips, the curve of her thighs were all overly womanly, and I found, looking down my own torso on what I'm sure my sister would call "nubs," that I was overcome. Not with jealousy, or fear to grow up, but with an odd mix of pride and sadness. Pride at my own body that would grow in tune with my mind. A budding sexuality I almost sometimes felt okay with when I thought of Pope or Jonathan, even Elizabeth when she took my hand, brushed against me in the dining hall, gave me her attention. And sadness at the realization that this girl, already there, did not know what she had, would never experience those things that I knew I knew nothing about, but that, unlike her, someday would with all of my faculties.

And, like a kick to my stomach, I thought of Allison, of how this girl had already surpassed her, how I was on my way to surpassing her, that with bony hips and pointy cone-shaped growths for breasts, I was on my way to being more woman than she would ever be.

And suddenly I was jealous of the oblivious way Becca Donelson exposed herself to the world, wondering what type of blessing or curse it could be to look out from just below the surface, unafraid a strange bargain for unaware.

Sarah turned the water off on me, and I left sudsy and wet, still unable to decide.

* * *

The November social came and went with no Pope.

"If you're looking for Clement, he's sick." Jonathan poked his head in front of my searching eyes. "He just started a new treatment and is a little under the weather. I'm sure he'll be fine soon. He wanted me to tell you he said hello."

The Shape of the Atmosphere

I smiled in thanks, but my whole body felt as though it were being pulled downward. I had not realized how much I'd been looking forward to seeing him until just then.

"I'm happy to keep you company, though. I see you have a new girl. What's her name?" I followed his finger, which at least wasn't asking much of me, over to where Becca Donelson stood, shoulders bent forward, hips jutted out.

"Her name is Becca. Just got here."

"Well, why don't you work some of your magic, and make her feel welcome?"

He was right. No one had said a nice thing to her since she'd gotten here. Arlene, who ate hair, received nicer treatment than this girl who had absolutely no control over what she was.

"Becca?" I said, poking my head in front of her as Jonathan had done to me. "I'm Gertie, and this is Jonathan. How are you doing?"

Becca smiled and told us about her family's dog, Rowdy, and how her favorite color was purple. We told her we liked her purple dress, and her blue ribbon in her hair. Jonathan agreed to take us out for a walk, and convinced Nurse Irene it was okay, even though Becca didn't have grounds privileges.

We walked to the tranquility pond, which was closer to the men's wards than any other mutually shared spot on the grounds. I preferred the willow, but I wanted to feel closer to Pope, to chance him looking down and seeing me.

The pond was quite small, but I heard they stocked it with fish in the spring and summer so the men could fish. Sometimes they even cooked them for meals, Jonathan told us. I let myself separate from them, walking along the edge and letting the taller grass tickle my legs through my pants. I'd need to wash them soon, but I hated to be without them for the week it took to get them back. I often wore them a week's worth of days before handing them over to be cleaned. They were becoming shorter at the ankles and a bit tighter in the hips. It was as though my period coming had announced to the rest of my body that it was time to catch up. My bra dug into my ribs, and left painful red marks under my breasts.

Jessica Dainty

I stood on the opposite bank as Jonathan and Becca did, and I watched as he angled behind her and helped her throw a rock across the still surface. It skipped only twice, but Becca's squeal reached me even from across the way, and she jumped up and down and clapped her hands.

Soon we were walking back. I hung behind them and saw the hand on Becca's back which had caused such a stir in me the first time he'd placed it there. I wondered what she thought of it, if anything. If she even registered him as a man, herself as a woman. When she'd arrived, Nurse Irene had told us she was twenty, but that her mind was more like a child's.

Once inside, I snuck off to my room and lay on my bed, leaving the door open, as I was required to do. *Weren't we all children here?* I couldn't help but think.

* * *

The days were getting shorter at a breathtaking speed, and I felt a sort of mourning as I watched the sun disappear before we were called to the dining hall for dinner, and then before free time finished, and when the clocks had no doubt been turned back (as though time could go any slower here) before we were released from afternoon therapy. Daylight Savings Time started the week after Elizabeth disappeared, like she had taken the sun with her to battle the lack of light where she went, leaving us all to fend for ourselves.

I used to love the darkness at four o'clock. The moment when I would look at the clock and think it was late and realize I still had four, maybe even five more hours until bedtime, until the darkness meant night. Here though, the darkness seemed too real, as though this was how it should be all the time, dark and impenetrable. All our treatment rooms, hydro and shock, were dim and dank, made eerie by awful looming bulbs swaying above us. The natural state of everything here was black and these early dismissals of the sun seemed to take my hopes with them.

The grounds privileges were still there in the winter, but not many people opted to venture out as the temperatures dipped below freezing. Not everyone had been packed a jacket, me included. My mother had not packed a coat, this woman who never let me outside without one no matter the time

The Shape of the Atmosphere

of year, even if it was just draped over my arm. I liked to think it was because she'd planned on having me back by now, but more likely, I knew, it was because she had not taken the time.

They had a few extra but despite everything I'd been subjected to in here, wearing someone else's coat when goodness knew what they'd been through in it just did not appeal to me.

It was a Sunday when the first snow hit, and after Elizabeth's husband had left, whom she introduced me to with a gleam in her eyes that was unmistakably pride, she presented me with a lush jacket of purple tweed.

"I know you don't have one. This one was my sister's but she's moved to Arizona of all places! I told Paulie that you didn't have one and he suggested he bring it over. He's such a sweetie. I have two here, and I'm still never warm enough in the winter. But maybe now we can get out for some walks. Once I get my privileges back."

By mid-week, the snow had blanketed everything, the willow's branches so heavy they swept the raised ground with each passing wind, as though trying to clean the snow underneath away. The aides announced that our morning therapies were cancelled and that everyone was welcome outside. We bundled up and bumbled out the door, our frantic feet hitting the snow like children's. Tiny flakes still fell, and while grown women around me made snow angels and threw powdery, unformed snowballs at each other, I lifted my face to the sky and tried to catch a piece of magic, if such a thing existed here, on my tongue.

The men played outside in the afternoon. I watched them out the window during my free time. I could not see faces, but I chose one man and followed him with my eyes, pretending he was Pope. He threw and dodged snowballs with an adeptness and fierceness that astounded me. After a while, he sat off to the side of the action, and seemed to be staring back up toward me. Perhaps he, too, was turning his face to the sky. The snow was heavier now and the aides had turned on the radio. We were expecting an additional few inches overnight.

I entered the dining hall to wonderful smells. I hadn't realized it was Thanksgiving and before me stretched out a full Thanksgiving spread, complete with turkey and three kinds of cranberry sauce. I sat with Gladys on one side and Elizabeth on the other. Elizabeth ate little, and I brought her a cup of warm apple cider and we shared a small piece of apple pie.

Pie was the one thing my mother never mastered, and Thanksgiving afternoons were often spent avoiding the frustrated yells spouting from behind the swinging kitchen door.

"I should be able to make a goddamn pie," she said one year, when I walked in thinking she had left the room, from how quiet it was inside. She sat on the floor leaning against the refrigerator, using a dish towel to wipe her nose. I felt bad now, to know that I had tiptoed out backward, letting the door close slowly so it would not swing and she would not know I had been there. Would it have helped for me to sit with her, to tell her it didn't matter? Would anything I had to give her have made a difference?

"Oh, this is yummy!" Elizabeth said, and I let her finish the slice, even though I'd only taken one bite.

"Do you know how to make pie?" I asked.

"Isn't it practically a requirement?" She said, her voice not condescending but the same chipper as always, her mouth full.

I thought of my mother leaning against the fridge, feeling weighed down with a sense of failure I cannot comprehend, and I felt my first pang of anger toward my father I had ever felt. I wished I could go back and throw the meals my mother cooked in his face, as we sat there, waiting for him to smile, nod, and give my mother the approval that allowed her to breathe again and lift her fork, shaking, to her mouth.

I walked by the chapel almost every night, though I'd only returned inside twice since my first visit.

Tonight, after dinner, I walked in and spat at the foot of the cross. "What about *her* goddamn hope?" I asked, but I did not have the fire to make the words matter and they fell from the air without reaching anything, or anybody.

I'd still choose him. And with that thought, I left my mother on the floor by the fridge and behind her pantry door, resigning from her post at the church, floating away from us into a space I had no desire to reach across. I sat on the kneeling pad and faced away from the front of the chapel. I tried to think of something to offer to the air around me, some form of

The Shape of the Atmosphere

Thanksgiving, but the only thing I could think of was that I was grateful I no longer had to choose.

That there was no longer a choice to make.

* * *

On the first day of December, I received a card from my mother. Mail was always handed out in the afternoon or in the evening with medicine, if the person wasn't present at the first go-round. Saturday mail was handed out Sunday, perhaps to soften the blow of no visitors to those who sat alone. Except most who got mail also got company.

I was handed a letter in the afternoon, and at the sight of my mother's perfectly looped handwriting, I shoved the envelope into my pocket and tried to forget about it until bedtime.

I did not know what she possibly had to say, and I did not want to put myself in the position of having an audience. I ran through all the scenarios in my head. She was coming to get me as a Christmas present. She was sorry. She was moving and leaving me here. Dad and Alison were somehow not really dead and it had all been a big misunderstanding. She too wasn't sure God was there for her and wanted to apologize to me for overreacting. She and Bobby were running away together now that my father was dead.

The list went on and on. Once I sat enclosed in the safety of my room, I placed the letter where the picture of my sister, pieced sloppily back together, sat staring at me day after day. Now both items stared at me, begging something of me that I did not know how to give. What did they want from me?

The note was a single sheet of paper. I didn't know why I expected a longer confessional. Perhaps because I knew I would need more than one sheet to describe my past months.

I hope this letter finds you well. I cannot believe it is almost Christmas time. This house is so big, and this time of year, when your father stuffed it with

Jessica Dainty

decorations, is the only time it ever seemed too small. I haven't decorated anything yet. I am unclear on whether I will get a tree.

I have dedicated a mass to your father and Allison on Christmas Eve. I hope you will think of them.

My mother had never been more obviously lonely to me than she was in that letter. Not the days she locked herself in the pantry, not the nights she must have spent alone while my father slept in the office, not the hours she spent cooking only to wait nervously for my father's approval. Her handwriting faltered on my sister's name, her flawless cursive breaking between the *l* and the *i*, the *o* and the *n*. *Your father* seemed like a fortress, too harsh at the edges as though she was either angry or sobbing as she wrote around his name.

Neither of our names, mine nor my mother's appeared anywhere in the letter. I found this ironic, that though they were the ones who were dead, we were the ones who had somehow vanished. She had sent me away and now she was alone and, as far as I could tell, disappearing in some way I couldn't quite put my finger on.

I thought of throwing the letter away, but I instead slid it back in the envelope and tucked it under my pajamas in one of my bureau drawers. For all I knew, it would be the only one I would ever get.

* * *

A sign-up sheet had been posted for those who wanted to participate in a Secret Santa event. I drew Becca's name.

I spent the next week convincing Nurse Peters to let me give one week of my grounds privileges to Becca Donelson as my Secret Santa gift. The weather was too cold, and while the jacket Elizabeth had given me warmed me intensely, I could not help but see how each night my spot at the window was already taken by this new girl. She was worse than Helen with her *apples* in the other women's eyes. All of Becca's words came out as though her mouth were stuffed with cotton or as though she were slightly

The Shape of the Atmosphere

drunk and people were asking her to say sentences in a language she didn't quite know.

One night, as Arlene and Susan snickered and told her that her shoes were on the wrong feet, I walked right up to her, took her by the hand and hugged her. Arlene laughed harder and moved on toward the dining hall. Susan waited for my eyes to find hers and she smiled a request for forgiveness. I nodded back, as though it were my job to give such a thing. She walked away, and I released Becca who had made no reciprocal motion but who smiled at me when I stepped back, a goofy, gap-toothed sight, and brushed my hair behind my ear. Then she turned back to the window and we stood there together, silent and still, her fingers pressed up against the screen like a child at a toy store, and I knew what my gift to her would be.

Despite the start of December and my mother's letter, I had not thought much about how close the holidays actually were until I started thinking of what to give Becca. I could have cried to know that it was almost Christmas, that time had really escaped me this much, that my father's favorite holiday was to come and go without him here, that my mother had not yet visited me in almost two months, and that I did not miss her but for the need to have her see where I was, where she had put me and to know if what she thought of me really had warranted this.

And then the aides surprised us with carts of hot chocolate and one sat down at the piano and voices both awkward and beautiful filled the room. Elizabeth took my hand, her voice swelled like a nightingale, and I did begin to cry, because this really was as close to a family as I had ever had.

* * *

The aides had posted a countdown in the common room, and we took turns pulling the numbered pages off the wall.

Our monthly social would be a holiday party this month. Planning had started already, and the weeks were flying by with an ease I had not known in my time here yet. Even hydro and shock felt easy and just something I had to make it through to the other side of, and happiness would be waiting for me.

Jessica Dainty

Before I knew it there were only eight days until Christmas and I entered the commons area from the breezeway to find a cluster of women surrounding a menorah. Nurse Peters oversaw, but the women passed the burning taper amongst them until one finally lit the lonely candle already in place. I heard some prayers in a language more phlegmish than Latin and expected to turn to see the women spitting on the floor by the throat-clearing syllables I heard coming from them. I knew they were speaking Hebrew, but I'd never heard the language before in any extended way. Despite its uglier moments, I found the whole of it quite beautiful and soothing, the way it sounded like speech and a song all at once. I lingered on the outskirts, silently observing as they finished their prayer, and then, as though paying respect to the moment, I bowed my head and slid the unattended book of matches off the table edge.

I had not even thought of hurting myself since I'd been here, but the sight of the matches was too much for my mind to resist.

After medicine and dismissal to our rooms, I waited until a check-in to know I had at least twenty minutes. I'd asked for a small cup of water in the commons area which I placed on my bedside table to drown the matches and hopefully with them, some of the smoke and smell. My forearms would be too obvious, as I was naked in front of dozens of women each day. So when the first flame danced in front of me, I lifted my arm and snuffed it out underneath, where no one would even think to look.

I felt the pain right away this time, and after three I had no desire to continue. On the night in my father's office this had been fuel, the sight of my skin melting like plastic in tiny circles before glowing red, the subtle throb rising to the surface before the pain incinerated my arm from the inside out. But now the process was simply exhausting and unrewarding. I felt only pain.

I put the wet, used matches in my sock drawer to throw away tomorrow. The matchbook I hid under my pillow. I'd find some way to return it or leave it around so that when found, Nurse Peters would think she simply had been careless.

I lay down wondering what this change meant for me. That I had grown? That I was getting better? That I had finished mourning? Was that even what I had been doing in the first place?

The Shape of the Atmosphere

I thought of taking the matches back out and using them all just to prove myself wrong. I screamed into my pillow, the noise muffled and far away even to myself. I did not want to owe this place any favors.

* * *

A second letter from my mother, five days until Christmas:

Do you remember whom your father called to shovel the snow in the winter? I'm thinking of making gingerbread cookies for the church party this year. They're always a hit.

My mother's indifference astounded me. Perhaps indifference was not the right word. Her incredible lack of acknowledgment was more like it. I felt as though I were at summer camp and she needed a favor. That being said, I had not thought of the possibility of writing back to the first letter. I knew my address. The hospital provided us with three stamps a week. The first letter had asked no direct questions though. Now, I felt obligated to respond.

My week had exhausted me. Since my first shock session, I'd had hydro on Tuesdays and shock on Thursdays. I knew today was Friday by my sore jaw and fuzzy facial recall. I even had to reach for Elizabeth's name when I sat down with her for tea at night. I was not sure I had the energy to write to my mother. But after dinner, I sat down with stationery from the aide station.

Mother,

The boy on Woodland Lane shovels the drive but he is gone to college now, I am sure. Gingerbread sounds good. I will think of Dad and Allison on Christmas. It will be no different than any other day.

I wondered if my mother would read that the correct way, that not a day goes by that I do not think of them. I couldn't bring myself to draft a new letter

Jessica Dainty

though and so I sealed it and addressed it, licked and pressed the stamp to the corner, my mouth thick and sappy as I handed it off to be mailed.

    I sat in the commons room, watching the bustle around me. Gift exchange would be after the estate social tomorrow. In October, the women had fallen behind in decorating for the Halloween social. The commons instead welcomed the second week of November draped with fake cobwebs and fake spiders hanging from the furniture. The aides had put out craft materials the full week before and everyone who wanted made a mask. The paper was thick, and the scissors were plastic for safety so even the best mask had looked torn on the edges, makeshift and unimpressive. I had not made one, but had taken a feather from the table and wore it in my hair for a few days.

    No one slacked for the Christmas social though. The room already glowed with lights. I had taken advantage of the craft table to make something for Pope. I had constructed a small box out of paper and inside I had twisted a pipe cleaner in a spiral and taped it to the bottom. On the top, I wrote Merry Christmas. When the box opened, the message sprung forward and after my hard work, I wished that I had something more urgent to say, the effect seeming a waste with such a predictable message.

    The next morning, Saturday, the aides did rouse us all on schedule. We had decorations to hang, cookies to bake, the works. I worked in the kitchen. Normally for everyday projects, we used the small kitchen at the end of the short hallway off the commons area where the chapel was. But because we were making cookies for the party, for visitor holiday bags for tomorrow, and for Christmas Eve, we were to use the dining hall kitchen.

    I still pressed and folded on my OT days in the laundry room, and though kitchen duty had been offered to me, I'd seen the stress kitchen life had caused my mother. When my mother folded laundry, hung the billowing clothes on the line outside on warmer summer days, she hummed and smiled, sometimes wore thin white cotton dresses that made me, for fractions of a second, yearn for adulthood. The choice between the two seemed obvious to me.

    Now I found I enjoyed the warm stuffiness of the kitchen. Though it was no less hot than the laundry room, this warmth was fresh and non-

The Shape of the Atmosphere

chemical. Specks of flour seemed to glisten in the air, and Nurse Peters rolled in a radio for us to listen to as we baked.

Only six of us occupied the space. At this point, I recognized everyone's face, but I still did not know everyone's name or trademark sign of lunacy. Susan was there, sitting on the counter, smoking, saying something about domesticity and the irony of how dough is so malleable but then keeps its shape after being fired in an oven. A woman named Juniper, who was new to me, but whom many on the ward seemed to know and embrace as though she were returning after a long voyage, climbed up on the counter to retrieve mixing bowls. Every once in a while, she would grunt and shout, so quickly that the silence returned fast enough that you doubted it had even happened. Helen, despite her limited vocabulary, I knew was excellent in the kitchen. She had done baking duty for the first social I attended, where I'd stuffed cookies into my pockets. Francis was there. The other woman I'd seen many times but did not know. They stood separate from me and each other and did not seem interested in any form of introductions.

"Alright, ladies. Each of you is in charge of mixing a triple batch of one recipe. Helen, snickerdoodles. Susan, chocolate chip. Juniper, gingerbread. Gertrude, sugar cookies. Adelaide, peanut butter. And Francis, oatmeal raisin. All of your recipes and ingredients are laid out, and I see that Juniper has retrieved some larger mixing bowls. Get to it!" On her way out, Nurse Peters flicked on the radio, leaving us with two student nurses reading *Journal* Magazine in the corner and The Everly Brothers mixing with the flour in the air.

I'd never baked before, but as I combined the butter and sugar, the vanilla and baking soda, I liked the increasing resistance the spoon met as I stirred, folded, and mixed. I liked the sweetness that filled the air, that only became more warm and soft over time, unlike the rawness my nose and eyes felt by my third hour in the laundry room, the soap drying my hands to the point of my knuckles cracking. Perhaps that was Elizabeth's problem too, though I never saw her in the laundry room. I spooned my cookies onto sheets and told the nurses I was done. They chaperoned my use of the oven and I wished the front had a little window as mine at home did so I could witness the transformation of the batter, the fluffy rising and flattening I'd sometimes watch when my mother baked.

I cleaned up my work area. Women were laughing and mixing. I was not friendly with any of these women, save for whatever title you could give my interactions with Susan. They did not approach me and I did not approach them. Pat Boone and Perry Como had come and gone from the room and a new voice filtered in. A song I had never heard before but that the radio DJ said was a country man who had penetrated the pop charts by the name of Jim Reeves. Susan's verbal ruminations on "woman as prison" quieted and the motion of the kitchen stilled. Even the flour appeared to hover.

Jim Reeves was obviously singing about love, lost or escaped, but his words, his voice, hit the air and I knew we were all hearing the song the same way. The DJ had called it "Four Walls." The nurses changed the station before the second verse. My timer went off, and I pulled my cookies out of the oven. Women were pulling theirs out of the other ovens, and the sweetness made the air smell edible. But the nurses couldn't get another station to come through in the recesses of the kitchen and we were left with our inescapable four walls and nothing good or sweet enough to fill them.

* * *

Half of my sugar cookies had burnt along the edges and the bottoms ranged from buttery yellow to soot colored. Still, I arranged half of them on a platter next to the others and dropped two each into dozens of tinted party bags and tied them up with ribbon. For the visitors. Here, visitor, who has dropped a loved one off in hell. Have some burnt cookies.

The Christmas spirit was becoming infectious.

Before I could become too much of a Scrooge though, the nurses announced that the men would arrive in less than an hour. The room shouted Merry Christmas in a red and green voice that would not be ignored. A small tree vomited popcorn strings and glitter, handmade paper ornaments. The hustle and bustle sold us as normal. This is what people did at Christmas time. Even here.

The Shape of the Atmosphere

The radio and record player were rolled in, but the nurses did not turn on the broadcast stations. Instead, scratchy Christmas albums spun memories of what we were celebrating, in case we had somehow been able to forget.

This was my favorite time of year. At first for the simple reason that it was my father's favorite time of year. But his boyish excitement, his decorating anything that appeared inanimate for long enough to splatter red and green on it, his insistence on preparing for Santa Claus even after the truth had been told by one of the more bitter nuns at St. Thomas Catholic School because Joseph Carter, an eighth grader in the boys' school, had issued a petition to put Jesus in a sleigh instead of a manger for the annual Christmas Pageant and she couldn't stand the blasphemy—all of this grew on me until it was my own. And despite the telling silence of the kitchen and the sullen mood of those who came out carrying trays of cookies, my spirits lifted unstoppably.

Elizabeth spread new linens on the round tables and set out green napkins. She wore a green and red plaid dress with shimmerings of gold thread woven through, and I imagined someone trying to hang her on the tree, mistaking her delicate, glittering frame for an ornament or some tree topper in angel form.

I wore a dark red dress, more maroon than Christmas cheer, but it was the closest I had. I liked to believe my mother thought I'd be home by now, that she had not planned on leaving me at Willow this long and therefore had packed nothing festive.

I stuck a tree-shaped sticker on the left side of my chest and took the initiative to stand by the door with a cup full of candy canes. When the men filed in, I handed one to each, some taking them with a smile, others scrutinizing my offering suspiciously and turning away. When Pope took his, our hands touched and his eyes were more daring than mine. I turned away first, toward the next person in line.

When Jonathan came in, he winked at me and touched my shoulder. "How's the new girl?" he asked, and I smiled and pointed across the room to Becca in her red and white dress, her oversized hair bow that flopped into her eyes.

Jessica Dainty

The aides and nurses wheeled in lukewarm cups of hot chocolate and people picked at the cookies and fingered the surrounding decorations. Gladys and the elderly gentleman, Samuel, came together immediately and he lowered her to her chair before sitting adjacent. Susan smoked in a corner, scoffing, her eyes rolling repeatedly at the room of men. I wondered if she was what my mother called "queer," but I actually didn't know what it really meant and therefore had no questions to ask. Or maybe she was just like the lady whose articles had been taken and burned, even at the public school. Betty Friedman or something like that. All about how women shouldn't have to only cook and clean and being unhappy isn't a sign of failure. Perhaps my mother should read her.

Despite the hesitancy, the room was soon a blur of red and green in motion. Reindeer sweaters, people carrying wrapped packages, conversations merging and breaking apart as people made their ways across the space. Pope sat on the edge of an armchair wringing his hands.

"Merry Christmas," I said, when I got to him, bending forward to lower my head into his line of vision. "You seem to be too full of holiday cheer. I'm going to have to ask you to calm down. Perhaps I should order you some chlorpromazine? Shall I call the nurse?" I raised my hand as though calling a waiter at a restaurant.

He smiled and stood, motioning for me to have a seat. Once I sat, he wrung his hands again before eventually reaching into his sleeve and pulling out a rolled piece of paper tied by a purple ribbon. "Ow—ow—owt of r—r—r—red," he said, shrugging.

I smiled and slid the ribbon off, uncurling the rolled paper. I stared at myself in disbelief. He had drawn me. My eyes, my ears, my hair, even the slight upturn to my nose—he had remembered it all. The picture was done entirely in gray, charcoal or a soft pencil, I couldn't tell, but it was animated and alive and, if I turned away too quickly, it was as though I moved on paper. Still I looked sad and I became self-conscious to know this was how he saw me, as an unhappy person. Was I?

"It's amazing. How did you"—I searched for the right word—"remember me?"

The Shape of the Atmosphere

He smiled and touched the tip of my nose with his finger before pulling it back and pointing at his head. He shrugged, as though it were really that easy. But I remembered him too. His eyes, his hair that wasn't sure if it was honey or molasses, depending on the light, his hands that were red and chapped and never still. I remembered him so vividly I found it hard to believe I couldn't produce a picture as he did, that my memory would override my lack of talent, and should I try, I could have him staring back at me from parchment any time I wished.

"It's beautiful. The drawing I mean. I wasn't saying that I—you're very talented." I was flustered. My present seemed childish and stupid. But I didn't want to give him nothing, to make him think I was not also thinking of him as he was of me. "Wait here."

I brought back the box. My hands shook as I handed it to him. "I'm sorry it's stupid. I mean, I'm not good at anything, like you are. I just wanted you to know I thought of you."

He smiled. When he opened the lid, the paper caught on the edge of the box. There was no pop, no effect. "And the stupid thing didn't even work. It was supposed to pop up. Here let me see it." I reached out to take it but he held his hand up to stop me. He put the box down, and took my empty hand.

Other people were already on the floor. Elvis' "Blue Christmas" danced around us as he placed my hand on his shoulder and brought his to my waist. I couldn't look at him, my cheeks as though I had put matches out on them, burning and throbbing. I had never danced with a boy before, other than my father, my feet on top of his, our back and forth uneven at best. Pope led me around the floor so that I knew it was not his first time, and I tucked my chin even more, to hide my face and watch his feet. His hand left my side, and I worried the song was over. Instead, I felt his finger under my chin, and before I knew it he was there in front of me. He smiled and feigned a deep breath and exhale. I followed his lead and his hand rested at my waist again. My head found his shoulder.

I looked around. Jonathan danced with Becca, her smile goofy and warm. She left him in the middle to get a cookie, and I almost laughed out loud at the sight of it. Jonathan followed her and they disappeared somewhere out of my line of vision. Pope's hand repositioned itself on my waist, and I could feel each finger, the pressure important and real.

The next song was *Silent Night* and people broke away from each other and settled back into conversation.

Pope stepped back from me but he did not let go of my hand. We spent the rest of the party with me sitting by the window and him watching me. For another picture he had said. To have a setting to place me in. He leaned back in the armchair, his fingers running over his chin, his lips, and he angled his head this way and that, taking me in. I closed my eyes so I could not see him and be nervous, but he was there too, behind my closed lids, his hand on mine, on my waist, his breath tickling my hair. I could hear the music getting softer and then the piano overtook the sounds of voices and footsteps. I opened my eyes and everyone gathered around Nurse Irene to sing.

As the voices broke out and crashed together, some beautiful and harmonious, others clashing and stumbling, I smiled at the world created for me here. This place of awfulness and grace, of torture and joy, and, as Pope took my hand in his, of possibilities of moments like this.

* * *

The Secret Santa exchange was a jumble of handmade cards and crafts, some beaded bracelets. Those who had active resources on the outside gave books and journals. Elizabeth gave Arlene a lovely brass-handled hairbrush, a gesture at which some people snickered. I knew Elizabeth wasn't trying to change Arlene though; she'd just rather Arlene pick the hair out of a brush than a shower drain. Arlene did not take offense, and hugged Elizabeth, her small frame practically disappearing in Arlene's embrace.

Gladys had me and gifted a St. Christopher medal that Samuel had carried with him in the war. She said he was the saint of travelers and since she didn't foresee herself going anywhere, she thought I might like to have it. Religious trinkets had lost their luster to me, but I was overly touched, and as I pressed the foil disc into my palm I actually felt safer.

Becca had to have her gift explained to her by three separate people. Finally, I just went up to her and said. "Becca, you get to go outside." And

The Shape of the Atmosphere

she smiled and bounced up and down in her chair before trying to get out the door. Nurse Peters then took on the responsibility of explaining the limitations of the gift, the main two being "not now" and "not by yourself."

I hadn't remembered seeing her the rest of the social, but I hadn't remembered much but Pope's hand at his lips, his eyes on me even when I refused to look.

"Outside wike what Jonafan does wif me?" she asked, her face still smiling, but her hands clasped tightly so that they burned red.

"Yes, Becca, like when we went to the pond. Outside, wherever you like."

Her hair bow was gone, and I tied some ribbon around her ponytail before saying Merry Christmas and lining up to brush my teeth and use the bathroom before we were sent to bed.

In my room, I placed St. Christopher underneath my pillow before lying down. I pictured myself at home, going to bed on a normal Christmas, eager for presents, both the giving and receiving. I wondered what my father would have bought me this year? My mother? What would I have gotten for them? I had picked out a charm for Allison during the summer when I saw it on sale in a local shop. The charm was a silver lightning bolt because everyone on her team said she was that fast. I'd dropped it into her designated hollow of earth on the day of the funeral.

I imagined she would like to hear about Pope now that I had more to say. About how he held my hand and led me to dance without even asking. She would think that was romantic and dangerous, sexy. When Allison was thirteen and I was eleven, she had told me about George Porter knocking her down during recess and lifting her skirt in front of her friends before finally pulling her behind a tree and kissing her. I'd thought he sounded awful, but her eyes had no idea I was even there listening as she told me, and her voice was like my mother's, full of gold. At the time, I didn't care for Allison's stories. I had no interest in boys or womanhood or love, but I liked that she was telling me and we stayed up until after midnight whispering, my room dark, my sister's voice light and floating.

I turned toward my sister's presence on my side table. "I hope I wasn't too awful of a dancer. Do you like him, Allison?" I was surprised to find I kept choosing my sister to speak to, over my father, or at all. "Well, I

Jessica Dainty

like him." I took the photograph from the table. It had been at Christmas about three years ago and she was smiling, not at a present she opened, I remember now, but at my opening of her gift to me. She'd found a photograph of my mother from when she had been young, about seventeen. My mother had looked like a movie star. On the card, my sister had written, *You in a few years. Don't worry. You're going to be beautiful.*

I had stared at the photo for hours, could hear the rustle of my parents as they stuffed our stockings. I saw nothing of this woman when I'd looked in the mirror, but lately the more I stared, the more our noses looked the same, the angle of our cheekbones. I wished I had that photo now, that my mother had given even two seconds' thought when packing my bag about what may have been important to me. Perhaps she had though. Perhaps she knew even if the mirror increasingly reflected her back to me, that, really, I wouldn't want to see her.

"Check-in!" The voice broke through before the opening of the door registered. "Oh and Gertie, you have a letter. Busy day, we forgot to hand them out at medicine."

Just one sentence:

>*The only thing your father loved more than Christmas was celebrating it with you girls.*

Did she think she was writing to both of us? I stuffed the letter under my pillow, too tired to get up and put it in the drawer with the others, making sure not to move the St. Christopher medal. I closed my eyes and danced, my hand still warm from memory.

* * *

Visiting hours were extended to a visiting day for the holidays. Some patients in Ward 1 even got to leave for the day, a handful for the whole week, to go celebrate at home with their families. The rest of us were stuck here, banking on the overwhelming desire of those who had sent us away to want to come see us.

The Shape of the Atmosphere

I planned to spend the day alone. I kept my pajamas on into the late morning. No one cared. Eventually I went to change, opting for my slacks and a deep blue turtleneck. I kept on my slippers. When I walked back out, I almost ran into my embodied "check-in," and the news that I had a visitor.

I had the thought that my father would be in the common room waiting for me, and a grief so sickening knocked me against the wall. And then the second wave—that it could be no one but my mother.

But a woman I did not recognize sat in a chair and stood when she saw me.

"Gertrude?" I nodded and felt as though someone were shaking me to make my head move.

"I'm Elise Capron. I am a nurse. Your mother wanted to visit. She is well, don't worry," she said as the fear no doubt reached my eyes. I had been cursing her all this time and she could have been at home dying. "I check in on her every few days. The space is too much for her, and she seems a bit forgetful these days."

That's what happens when there's no one around to remind you of anything, I thought.

"She wanted you to have these. Apparently she forgot to put stamps on them and they all came back. She didn't have the patience to re-mail them." The nurse handed me a stack of envelopes as thick as a brick. "She enjoys your letters. Saves them in the front of her Bible." The whopping two I've sent her, I thought, ashamed of myself as I held the first physical weight of my mother's love—or maybe guilt—I'd ever known.

"I wish you the best. Your mother sends hers as well." The woman stood to go.

"Does she plan on—" Coming to get me? Taking me home? What did I want? "—seeing me?" I supposed it covered all questions.

The woman smiled and her face looked like mine in Pope's drawing of me, sad but aware. "I don't know if she could even if she did."

I stood there, confused by the riddle of an answer she had given me, angry at my mother as I held the letters for spending her time and energy on me now, after she had already sent me away. Angry at my father and Allison for the inconvenience of their deaths and how it had to happen when it did, on a day that seemed so good.

    The pressure bubbled inside. I felt as though I were at shock, my arms and legs ringing with electricity. There was no way to escape, nowhere to go. So I screamed. A loud, shattering sound that I would not think could last so long at such a volume. I felt my chest swell and my arm sweep, and I watched tiny puzzle pieces fly through the air. My foot contacted with something hard and immovable, a chair screwed to the floor. It stared back, staunch, mocking me in its solidity. I grabbed my hair and crouched, my voice still clawing out of my throat in scratches and bursts.

    When I was done, the nurses were already on me, the words had already come, a syringe already in hand, and I kind of wished Elizabeth was still wherever it was I was going, so that I wouldn't have to be alone.

VIII

I spent the holidays in a room by myself on what I assumed was Ward 3 or 4. Hydro lasted into the afternoon. I received shock treatment twice each day. There were Negro aides working with the white women here. They were outliers, like planets held in place by the tether of gravity, not quite belonging in the system. I never heard them speak other than in simple one line questions or polite responses with "ma'am" or "sir" tagged onto the end.

The other aides, the white ones, acted more like nurses on this ward than on the others, I concluded because they felt they were above someone here. The Negro aides carried around stacks of towels and sheets, wheeled carts, and floated silently down the halls in a manner no louder than the women who whispered to themselves in corners, heads down, eyes darting, faces always wearing a curtained expression.

I wondered what they were thinking behind their silent lips.

I was wheeled in for shock (I rarely walked anywhere on my own in this ward), braked into a corner while the aides prepped the table, laid out the leather straps, the mouth guard, the bottle of goo that sent the electricity through.

One Negro aide, a young pretty thing with skin like chocolate frosting, must have been new. When she folded open the cloth covering the top of the cart, exposing the crude tools, she commented that shock looked gruesome. I watched an exchange like Dr. Rosslins and Nurse Peters had in his office that first day, a silent communication, a connection of eyes among the white aides. A mutual understanding. A contracted agreement.

They grabbed her and strapped her down while a doctor I didn't know other than this time slot each day looked through cabinets in purposeful aversion.

"Here's your conductant, nig," an aide said, one who had brushed my hair for me the first day after my outburst, when my haze of upped medication

The Shape of the Atmosphere

left me submerged in a shallow muck of disorientation. Now she and the others took turns spitting on the Negro girl's face. I could see the recognition of her mistake in her eyes, but only for an instant. There was a flicker of fear, like a flash of lightning outside the window of a dark room; something was there and then gone and I couldn't for the life of me have said what it was. What remained was the shade of something lost, though. Her face was expressionless and empty, but she didn't blink. They hooked her up to the machine, and her body vibrated, blurred around the edges before it settled into spastic holds, parts of her body levitating at unbelievable angles.

The white aides looked away, but I could not. I had never witnessed it from the outside, and I was horrified but also deeply ashamed at my curiosity, my obvious gaping. I knew I must have stepped forward, must have moved toward her, to help her, but when I looked down, I still sat in my chair in the corner, brakes locked, feet up in rest. I stood slowly. I willed her to look at me. I couldn't be sure, but I felt like her eyes locked to mine, the only still part of her as she writhed and contorted.

This was what I looked like. No wonder they strapped us down. Not remembering people's names afterward didn't seem so bad of an after-effect. I felt myself nodding, trying to convey solidarity. An aide looked at me and laughed, and I realized she thought I was in on the joke, that my nod was my signature on whatever contract their silence had drafted. I moved to the table and slid my hand into the Negro girl's grip.

"Good. Hold her down," I heard someone say.

They didn't give her the protective leather between her teeth. I clenched my jaw as I watched but she clenched harder and I saw the blood before someone said that she'd bitten through her tongue. She kept her eyes on me, and I watched them widen with the ugliness of the world. My hand was a limp, useless thing in her grasp.

This must be what Elizabeth had meant when she said it was darker here.

* * *

Despite the shock incident and the general mental state of the women here, this ward seemed quieter to me. Existence really was a solitary thing. I sat for hours in the small room they offered as a commons area and watched as no one's path crossed another's. Women swayed in corners. One sat strapped to a chair, her head bent forward, hair hiding her face.

I ate in my room here, having to check off a meal choice in the morning. The food came in cold, and sometimes not at all what I had ordered. I ate anyway, hoping my agreeableness would get me back to Ward 2 quickly.

I did not tally the days. A woman named Diana began sitting next to me in the afternoons.

"You look like you'll be prepared when the war starts." Her eyes were large and calm, as though she had asked me about the weather or told me I had something on my face.

"What war?"

"The war of the worlds. I know they passed it off as a fictional experiment, but Mr. Wells wasn't lying, you know. They're up there." And she looked at the ceiling as though she could see through it to the stars.

I followed her gaze. I'd often wondered about heaven, about the satellite that was up there, what it was doing, but never about the possibility of other life.

"I do think it really was just a story," I said, just hoping for some time to myself.

Her eyes narrowed. "So you're part of it, aren't you? You are! You are! Oh God, take her. Nurse! Nurse!" She stood now, her hands in front of her face, as though they could protect her from me. She shook her head back and forth and began pulling at her hair.

"Nurse!" I joined in. "Please, calm down. I'm not one of them, I promise. I'm really not."

She eyed me suspiciously, but seemed more calm as a nurse came out and took her arm, talking to her in a low voice.

After a few minutes, the nurse came back alone. "Try not to shatter any other false realities today, okay?" She smiled at me, and touched her hand to my shoulder, and I went to bed happy to know at least one person thought I didn't belong here.

The Shape of the Atmosphere

* * *

I woke each morning hoping to be back in my old room, the one on Debutante Suites.

Instead I woke up in the small barren room of wherever I was, and this morning an aide and a nurse I did not recognize came in, wheeling a cart of covered dishes.

"Good morning," she glanced at a clipboard, "Gertrude." I sighed and sat up. Even if they used my full awful name in Ward 2, at least they knew me without reading it off a chart. "Your treatment is going to start in here this morning. How is that for comfortable?" She smiled at me as though I should tip her, like the hand towel lady at the town pool, or at least thank her.

An aide rolled a cart in behind her, on which rested a single syringe atop a clean towel. I recognized her as one of the girls who had been in the room when the Negro bit off her tongue.

"I'm going to give you a shot and then Eliza is going to sit with you while you eat. And boy do we have some yummies for you!"

Her voice scratched on the inside of my head. I felt as though I might sneeze.

"What's the shot?" I asked, my silent refusal in my unwillingness to roll up my sleeve.

"Do you know what insulin is? It's basically like sugar, but the type your body already makes. We're just giving you a boost and then giving you food to try to raise your sugar level and reset some of your production levels. Sound okay, dear?"

I knew this was the "give them the simple, crazy-people-can-understand version."

I still didn't raise my sleeve.

"Chocolate chip pancakes," she cooed in a sing-song voice. I eyed the cart, complete with three covered plates, I imagined like room service in a fancy hotel. I missed the choices I had on my old ward, and the pancakes did smell good. I rolled up my sleeve. "Now the rest of the day you may feel a bit off. Dizzy, light-headed. We'll keep you in here through lunch and if you're up for it you can join for some group time later. Oh and sorry my dear, but this goes in the tookus."

    I rolled over and closed my eyes. The prick was barely existent and I wondered if I was falling back into wherever I had been when I came here, a world that lacked feeling. Would I take that over the memory of a bloody mouth and my doing nothing that mattered?

    I rolled back. They uncovered the plates. A stack of pancakes at least three inches tall, covered with powdered sugar, butter, and syrup. Five strips of bacon, a cup of coffee, a glass of orange juice, two muffins, and a bowl of fruit.

    "Alrighty," the nurse cheered. "Eat up. Everything needs to go. Down the hatchet! So better get to it. Eliza will stay with you."

    "Everything?" I asked her as the nurse left. "Are you sure you don't want some of this?"

    "It's not my treatment." Eliza plopped down in a chair she brought in from the aide station and held her magazine high enough in front of her face that I deduced she had no interest in speaking with me. Still, she was kind enough in her absence of meanness, and I wondered how she had been capable of what she had done to that poor girl.

    I absorbed the massiveness of the meal before me. I started with the bacon because it was my least favorite. I saved the pancakes for last. The amount of food thrilled part of me. The fruit was fresh, the muffins still warm. The pancakes, when I got to them, weren't chalky. They were moist and melted in my mouth. I felt full and borderline ill when I finished but I hadn't really eaten much in days, and I leaned back satisfied.

    "Done?" Eliza barely lowered her magazine. "I'm going to clear the carts. You may feel dizzy. Don't try to get up. Just stay in bed. Do you want a book or anything?"

    Her words danced around my head but didn't quite enter. My head rung, like the times I'd eaten the entire bag of licorice laces in one sitting or put gummy bears in my Coca-Cola and drank it down in under a minute. "Thank you," I heard someone say, "but I'm fine. No book. Thank you, no book."

    She was gone before I realized there was no one else in the room but me.

The Shape of the Atmosphere

* * *

Time escaped me and the next time I sat up, fully aware in my bed, Nurse Peters and Eliza were rolling in another cart. Two egg salad sandwiches, two glasses of apple juice, a banana, a slice of chocolate cake, and a bowl of rice pudding.

My refusal to eat lay in my exhaustion. A simple glance at the quantity of food wore me out.

"You have to eat it," Nurse Peters said. She propped a pillow behind me to sit me up. What was she doing here? Did she normally work on other wards, or was she just here for me?

"I don't think I can. I'm still so full." My voice felt hoarse and far away. But it was true. I was still full. I glanced at the food again and thought I might be sick.

"It's for your health. It's part of your treatment. The doctors are here to help you. They know what they're doing." It was Eliza this time, leaning over me, her voice quieter. I wanted to believe her, but her words came out monotonous and empty, like my voice in Sunday School, repeating back statements I did not believe or even understand.

Eliza brought the rice pudding toward me. "No." I shrunk away from her and pushed her hand away. She was tenacious, I'd give her that. She whirred the spoon in front of me like an airplane. The motion disoriented me and I felt dizzy and sick. "I said no!" I yelled, smacking the spoon out of her hand, rice pudding splattering across the floor.

She leaned forward. "You either eat it, or they make you eat it. It's better this way." Her fingers rested on my shoulder and played, just barely, with the ends of my hair.

My bones were heavy and clumsy, like the mats in gym class. They felt too big for my body. I started to cry. "It's too much, though. I can't. I can't."

And then Nurse Peters was there with her fingers on my chin and cheek, opening my mouth, and hers were not so gentle or kind, and Eliza poured the juice in and looked away as Nurse Peters held my mouth closed until I swallowed. How she had to look away for this but could make a girl bite off her tongue, I didn't know. I wanted to point, announce that she was the sick one, for what she was capable of, but my mouth was full and held shut, and I had no will or energy to fight back.

I woke up on my side, my mouth vile with acidity, my quilt smeared with a substance not dissimilar from the oatmeal in the cafeteria. A different aide sat in a chair in the corner reading. I was happy not to be alone.

"Can I have some water?" My words exploded into the room, my head and stomach lurching together at the pain.

"Yes, they'll bring some in to you at dinner."

"Do I have to eat?" The smell of my soiled bed crept into my nostrils every time I spoke. I kept my sentences short.

"Yes, but not as much. You just need to eat something. And have a dessert. They'll bring you something in here."

When my cart rolled in later, pushed by another aide I did not recognize, beside the pot roast and carrots and slice of apple pie, was a neatly folded stack of white. The clean quilt was an ugly shade, yellowed as though from rot, but it smelled fresh and I ate my food uncomplaining, grateful for what I could get.

* * *

The following day was hazy at best. I remember receiving a shot in the morning and being told that I would only need to consume one large meal, which they rolled in and which looked the same as yesterday's breakfast only this time with sausage links and porridge instead of bacon. And that instead of a second large meal, I would receive two other shots spread out throughout the day.

I swam in and out of wakefulness, my coherent self always just out of reach above the surface of some thick, gelatinous substance. I wondered if they had just covered me in pudding instead of made me eat it.

Nurse Peters finally roused me in the afternoon of some unknown day and I woke to find a needle in my wrist and a tall wire rack on wheels with a clear bag hanging heavily from it like a bunch of grapes.

"Today we will take you to meet with Dr. Rosslins. He'll decide whether you're ready to return to Ward 2."

The Shape of the Atmosphere

I had made sure not to scream all week, no matter what I saw. Now I sat across from Dr. Rosslins and we stared at each other for an extended period of time before he placed between us, like a bribe, the news that I was going back to Ward 2. He upped my chlorpromazine dosage, and my Saturdays, even Estate Social days, had an extra therapy meeting with his truly.

I had missed New Year's. 1958 had broken through to existence and I had not even known. A gold and green banner hung above the barred fireplace. Elizabeth told me they'd even brought in a television to watch the ball drop. I wanted to hug her when I saw her, but she started talking before I could say or do anything.

"It was a gift! We get to watch the news at night now if we want, too. But the ball was so incredible. All those people out there. In the cold, nonetheless. Everyone smiling and celebrating. Nurse Peters even brought in sparkling cider and little plastic champagne flutes. We toasted and sang Auld Lang Syne. Oh, and some of the men came over. That boy was looking for you. I told him you were sick and lying down. I didn't know what you'd want him to know."

This was the only reference to my absence in her hurried, breathless speech, to where I knew Elizabeth knew I was, and I was grateful for it. I was sorry I had missed Pope. I thought of having him draw a picture for me to send my mother. Now it might be another month before I could ask him and then another until I could get it from him. But mostly, I was sorry I missed him simply because I missed him. I'd thought of him often in my time of darkness and I wondered if he'd ever been sent to another ward. How they would treat someone who couldn't even get a sentence out fast enough to be listened to.

The black girl who bit her tongue off had come back the very next day, a white bandage looped under her chin and tied on the top of her head like a bow. Her eyes were resolute and fierce, and I yearned to tell her something, anything, to separate myself from the others who'd been in the room. But I couldn't. If I'd been brave enough, I could have done something. I could have ripped the wires out before they could stop me.

But then it would have been me on the table no doubt, grinding my teeth until they broke, and I knew I had nothing worth saying to her. My

Jessica Dainty

hand in hers was meaningless when she had a mouth of broken teeth and a body with a broken soul. Instead I prayed for something worthwhile. For the first time in months, I prayed. That those eyes would simmer and cool into strength and drive and not smolder into anger and bitterness, into hate that would only perpetuate the ugliness of the world.

But I didn't believe it. And having seen what I saw and having been where I'd been, I wouldn't blame her either.

I might even join her.

Since being back, I put forth my best behavior but at night I couldn't sleep. I closed my eyes and saw a giant bloody mouth, broken teeth, a black face with ferocious, angry eyes and laughing white faces with nothing but giant smiles and ugly, red lips.

I asked Jessica when no one was around, "Why aren't there any Negro aides on this ward?"

Her face held surprise. Perhaps she didn't know there were Negro aides at all here. She had mentioned she only works on Wards 1 and 2.

"I don't know. Why?"

"Just wondering," I said, not caring to talk about what had happened to me while I was gone. Perhaps she really was unaware of how bad it could be.

There had been a single black family that joined our church during the previous summer. The first week they came, almost no one else did. My mom, Allison, and I were three of a handful of people. The black family still sat in a separate, closed-off room. When we exited, the family was just coming out, and my mother put herself between us and them. The family had a girl my age, overly skinny but pretty and her legs looked like they could move faster than my sister's, long and lean but with balls of muscles at the calves.

She had an older brother with her that I found handsome in my quick glance at him before my mother hustled us out the door.

"I can't believe people didn't show up today, but still, what is the world coming to when you can't worship in peace?" My mother fanned herself in the extreme heat. It was July, I think, and in the nineties. I pulled at my stockings which felt slimy like a second layer of skin on my legs. "They better use a separate offering plate for them. I don't want any of my money going where it's not meant to."

The Shape of the Atmosphere

I'd seen Alan Smith, a local business owner, take change from the offering plate before. Two older women who always sat together in the back row once got into a fight during the prayer, two blobs of paisley dress falling into the aisle on top of one another. A man my father called Wiley always sat in the side chairs along the wall and tried to give the kids candy as they walked by, never taking Communion or opening his mouth to sing. At the time, I'd taken my mother's words as truth, as a statement to be absorbed and agreed with. They were my first Negroes and the consensus seemed to be just that, a consensus. They weren't allowed places. They were dark by nature. They couldn't help themselves.

Now, when I tried to sleep, it was not the girl's darkness I saw, but the ugly whiteness of those laughing mouths. And I wished I had known then what I knew now and could go back and shake my mother outside of our church and tell her she was wrong.

But being back on Ward 2 made it too easy to forget the darkness of where I'd been, at least during the day. Seeing Elizabeth drinking her tea each night, sitting with Gladys at dinner, even listening to Susan's ferocious ramblings left me with a warm sense of belonging.

Apparently I'd been gone for almost two weeks and on the first Saturday I was back, the aides rushed to the television and turned on the news.

"January 4, 1958, Sputnik falls to earth," the announcer said. "After losing transmission a mere twenty-something days after its launch last October, Sputnik has been confirmed to have been lost off radar and to have re-entered the earth's atmosphere. Most likely the satellite burned up in the upper levels of the atmosphere, the exact thing the satellite was intended to measure. It is unknown at this time whether any pieces made it to the ground intact."

I was one of only four or five people who watched. I sat closer to the television set than my mother would ever have allowed me to at home. My body still hummed and rocked queasily from my treatment, but now it felt as though I could explode, burn up from the inside. I tried to reconcile the idea of something just simply no longer existing. My father and I had watched the satellite, had seen proof of it with our eyes, and now, there was nothing left.

IX

Mid-January brought another snowstorm. My lack of sleep had led to a lack of appetite and a complete absence of energy. Elizabeth thrived in the winter, despite not liking the cold. She bubbled around, talking rapidly about nothing important. I couldn't keep up with her and started spending my afternoons working my way through Willow's limited library shelves.

I no longer fought the coldness of hydro. I succumbed early and the nurses and doctors commented on how my embrace of treatment was delightful to see. I had an overall lack of sensation. My body had cocooned itself and forgot it was supposed to transform into something else, so instead I stayed wrapped up and rotted.

I remembered meeting with Dr. Rosslins and Nurse Peters one morning and they announced another adjustment to my pill dosage, and then the days began to blur together even more. I only knew it was Sunday at one point because I noticed familiar faces escorting nicely dressed people around who looked uncomfortable. They had to be visitors. For all the so-called sickness and strangeness in here, no one ever really looked *uncomfortable*. These outsiders' expressions bore a different type of "let me out of here" than ours did. They simply wanted the fresh air and the open doors to have assurance they weren't one of us. Ours were more screams to ourselves. The walls here were purely symptomatic, I was coming to believe.

I lost track of the days for a while. I felt sluggish and full of lethargy each morning. I almost did not mind the group showers, even stomaching one with Arlene as she bent down to the clogged drain. Each night they gave me my tiny cup of pills. I met with Dr. Rosslins and Nurse Peters these mornings again. They wanted to know how the medicine was doing. If I'd had any discouraging thoughts. Any odd urges to scream or do anything out of the ordinary. I wasn't sure I'd had any thoughts at all. I stared at them

The Shape of the Atmosphere

through a layer of film and wanted to go to sleep and wake up under the willow tree and play in its shadows if I could just get this dark blackness off my back and stand up tall and strong and get one foot in front of the other for a start. That's the only push I'd need, I was sure of it, to start dancing.

And then I thought of Pope and wondered what he would think of me. It was as though his picture had created this new version of me. One sad and lacking in some way. The monthly social had come and gone, and I had been nonexistent. I couldn't even remember his face, though I knew it was there. I had not touched my mother's letters. I felt nothing toward them. Not the anger nor the sadness I felt when I first held them. Nothing.

Then, all of a sudden, I was back in Dr. Rosslins' office, with Nurse Peters to the side of me, the doctor's lips flapping at me like a puppet's.

"Excuse us for a minute," Dr. Rosslins said, and he and Nurse Peters stepped outside of the office and left me sitting there alone, not remembering what we had been talking about or how I had even gotten here from wherever I'd been before. What day was it?

I saw my name on a file on the desk and picked it up. The file seemed thin considering it held everything they'd thought about me since I'd arrived however long ago. When was it again? Or had I always been here? Maybe that was it. Maybe this was my normal self. Maybe everything else was the cocoon, the rotting trap.

> *Gertrude first came to us after the tragic death of her father and sister. She holds a level of resentment toward her mother, having voiced to some degree that it was unfair for them to have died and not her. However, she will not elaborate on this. Her mother contacted us after discovering burns and small cuts on Gertrude's forearms. She feared Gertrude was unable to cope with the death of her family in a healthy way and needed treatment and assistance in this.*
>
> *Gertrude has acknowledged the illogical nature of her condition. She says she inflicted harm because she did not feel anything and wanted to, but admits that these tactics did not aid in her recovery or progress. We have seen no evidence of such activity since her admission.*

Jessica Dainty

She does not exhibit evidence of active hallucination. However, she often talks about stars and space and seems to link her father to these objects in an almost mystical way, which provides evidence of a delusive element.

Gertrude recently needed to be removed from Ward 2 for separate treatment on Ward 3, though she is non-violent towards others. Here she received insulin shock therapy (SEE SEPARATE REPORT).

She is not antisocial but seems to have only one acquaintance with any regularity of interaction, a Mrs. Elizabeth Jacobsen who has been with us for three years since the death of her son (SEE JACOBSEN 115 file for reference). The friendship is calm and balancing and there is no reason at this time not to encourage their interaction.

She has been observed on more than one occasion socializing with a Mr. Clement Marshall (SEE MARSHALL 273 for reference), but again, the interaction seems only beneficial to both parties and should not be discouraged.

She does not have physical contact with family (her mother, Alice) outside of Willow Estate. Recently she has been receiving letters and responding though the content is impersonal and short (SEE COPIES OF RESPONSES IN FILE).

When all of Gertrude's symptoms are reviewed together, she most closely fits the categorization of severe depression not without a delusional and/or surreal quality, though we have reservations with this diagnosis. While we further explore her condition, continued support and encouragement in a social setting (barring development of violence) are recommended. She receives a chlorpromazine dosage, hydrotherapy, shock therapy, and most recently, insulin therapy which seems to have had promising results. See successive charts and pages for dosage and daily orders.

The report spanned a number of pages, different entries having been submitted on different days. But the whole of it read fluently, as though reported all at once. The file was my own and yet I felt I was reading some great secret about someone I wasn't supposed to know about. My letters stared back at me in type. They had opened my mail, transcribed it, read it no doubt, and resealed it to send. Nothing was changed. I wondered what they

The Shape of the Atmosphere

were looking for. Some betrayal of information? Of the terrible things they called treatment?

I flipped to the next page and saw my report from my week of darkness. I was on Ward 3, it turned out. I caught the words *hysterical*, *unfortunate*, and *subdued* before Dr. Rosslins' and Nurse Peters' voices began breaking through my consciousness, getting closer and closer.

I put the file on the desk where it had been and leaned back. For the first time in weeks, I felt a rush of life go through me. Not from doing something forbidden, not for duping the head doctor and nurse, but for doing something proactive for myself. Whether I liked it or not, that was their opinion of me. But I'd seen a number of truly insane women on Ward 3. Women who contorted themselves into odd positions and held them for hours. One lady's hand would travel faster than Elizabeth's speech from ear to nose to chin to nose over and over again. I watched her half a morning one time and she never stopped. Diana had been seven when *War of the Worlds* was broadcast and had dedicated her life to protecting the world from alien attack. After I'd won her trust back, she told me she was in there because she found people like us had the best sources of information and that if the aliens did come, we would be low on their list of priority kills.

I didn't care what these people said about me on a piece of paper. I may not have known entirely who I was and what I was, but I wasn't what they thought. I wasn't any more depressed or incapable than anyone else, especially someone who'd lost someone. More than one someone. Than someone who had been sent away by the only person she had left. And I wasn't delusional.

"I want to get off of my medicine." I stood up as Dr. Rosslins and Nurse Peters opened the door. "I feel sluggish and lethargic. I can't distinguish days, and my memory is foggy. The only thing that has changed is the dosage of whatever you have me on. I'm worse than when I came in. I want you to fix it."

"Okay, well let's have a seat and talk about this." Dr. Rosslins motioned for me to sit. I refused, my arms across my body in silent obstinacy.

Jessica Dainty

"Since your dosage has been increased, have we been anxious? Depressed?" Dr. Rosslins sounded friendly but I could tell he was playing the devil's advocate.

"No, but I haven't been anything. I can't feel anything. I have no motivation. No desire to get out of bed. I don't even remember coming here today. I'd rather be screaming and railing and be sent back to Ward 3"—I faltered, afraid they may take me up on my challenge— "than fit your description of healthy and be miserable." I had no idea where this was coming from. My cocoon had burst open.

"I see." He glanced down at my file, and though he said nothing, I had the feeling he suspected as much that I'd read it.

"How can we be sure we won't have another outburst? You were on a milder dosage when we had to send you away to calm you down."

"I was upset. A nurse caring for my mother came out of nowhere after months of thinking my mom cared nothing for me and handed me a handful of letters she forgot to send. I had to re-evaluate all the feelings I'd had toward my mother since I came in. I just exploded." As the words came out, I knew what I said was true, though I had planned on saying whatever it took to get my way.

"We'll wean you off to a lower dosage over the next few weeks. If we end up with a similar situation as we encountered before Christmas though, I'm afraid we may have a problem on our hands. Are we in agreement?"

Nurse Peters walked me back personally. I felt like skipping down the sidewalk, but when we neared the doors to the wards, Nurse Peters grabbed my arm so fiercely I thought her fingers would meet together in the middle.

"Who do you think you are, challenging a doctor's orders on your health? You're the patient, got it? If I don't see improvement in you from Dr. Rosslins' obvious oversight and kindness, I can make your life miserable in here, do you understand me?"

There was no condescension or patronization in her voice, just pure fire, all goodness burnt away. She clenched her jaw so tight, I thought she might break her teeth, a second mouth bloodied and empty for no reason. Her words singed my confidence at the edges, and I nodded meekly until she released my arm. She motioned for me to enter, and on the other side, she

The Shape of the Atmosphere

shuffled me forward with a "Go on now, dear," and I wished my cocoon had had a stronger hold on me.

Still, I was optimistic. Although my weaning had not yet begun, my body buzzed. When Elizabeth offered a walk, I jumped at the opportunity.

"You've only been back a few days. You don't have grounds privileges yet. Maybe next week," Sarah said, smiling as though denying me satisfied her.

And so I spent the day reading, and when evening came, I joined the growing mass of television watchers. I liked watching because each day, I was reminded of the date and confident that time was moving forward and not standing still.

On tonight's news, a mere three or four weeks or so after Sputnik had crashed to the ground, America had sent its own object into orbit. A satellite called Explorer 1, the man was saying, his mustache disguising his mouth and making it appear as though he may not even have been speaking.

I stayed up by my window, watching the stars. I remembered the night my father woke me, and I watched with amazement. A certainty overtook me as I had watched that circling dot of light, and I knew beyond a doubt that the Russian craft was not the only thing out there, traveling the skies, possibly looking down on me as I was up at it. I didn't think aliens were up there like Diana thought. Just something greater than myself. Now, I pressed my face to the glass, a fog growing and fading as I breathed, unable to see anything but my own reflection and a sea of starless, blackened, burnt night.

* * *

The next day was my first Saturday therapy session with Dr. Rosslins. I sat across from him and we passed the hour passing the silence back and forth. He ventured only a handful of questions, none of which directly concerned my mental health. *How was the week? What was my favorite meal in the cafeteria?* I figured he was checking my handling of simple questions but I stayed silent, insulted by the nature of his inquiry. I'd always viewed myself as weak under the scrutiny of my mother, weak, unable, and insufficient. Being here however, I was coming to find strength in not just myself, but in life in general. In my ability to move through life intelligently and purposefully. The suffocation of my medication still pumped through my veins, hardening me from the inside out, but I'd willed myself into consciousness.

They would not win.

Exorcisms were skimped over in catechism, but everyone knew it depended on the faith of the exorcist. We would sometimes stage fake exorcisms on the lawn behind our catechism classroom, never quite getting to the end once our raised shouts of *vade retro satana* made its way back to Sister Magdalene's over-extended ears. We never pretended to be priests though, but people we knew characterized by varying degrees of seediness—the milkman, Mr. Snarkon; the shady man who cut the grass on the boys' lacrosse field and then ate a sandwich and drank from a thermos behind the bleachers during practice; Mrs. Lancing, the old woman who, like me, took her rosary beads everywhere. The running joke was that the exorcisms worked better the worse the person performing them, but none of us believed that.

It was as though by sheer belief alone, pure faith, Dr. Rosslins thought he could draw out of me whatever he wanted. I sat, stubborn as he, not speaking.

After therapy, I joined Elizabeth in the sewing room. She stitched the seams of a bonnet by hand while I read next to her. The sewing room and the indoor recreational rooms were open now every Saturday since the weather was often too cold to travel out. The rec room where we'd practiced walking with books on our heads and sitting in chairs was a building on its own and held an indoor tennis court, a small alcove with some minor exercise equipment, and a small, rectangular vat of water they passed off for a pool. Winter Saturdays were busy though and only three aides oversaw the whole room. Swimmers were required to wear life preservers, though the water only measured four feet at its deepest.

Hydro tainted my memories of swimming and there was no ladder in this euphemistic pool. Only a slight built-in decline of steps and a metal railing. I'd gone in only once, poised heavily above the water from the life vest. Even without the flotation device, the bottom was too accessible. I missed hiding out on the bottom of the pool. Escaping to the grand

The Shape of the Atmosphere

underwater stage floor. And there wasn't room to swim laps. Here, I had to find other escapes, distractions. Pope and Elizabeth were, by far, my favorites above any activity Willow offered.

Elizabeth tried to convince me to sew.

"You're always complaining how your mother packed you awful things. And look at those pants. You can't even let the hem down to make them long enough anymore! Learn and make something new!"

But I didn't care for sewing and though they offered machines, and even instruction, I declined. I did not know what I wanted to be when I was grown, but my mother was not it. I was slowly realizing that a great deal of the young women in here were of three kinds. The first were the ones I saw during my time in the darkness, that really had broken from reality and their own rational consciousness. The other two were the majority though: those that fit the ideal of a woman, wife, and mother too well and were unhappy for it, or those that did not fit the ideal at all and were punished for it. Susan was the latter, women like Helen the former.

I'd heard this lady that only said *apples* was a former Miss Society, a prize wife of a prospective mayor, and, up until her admittance six months ago, a caring, nurturing mother of three. And then one day, in the middle of an address to the Women's Society of Plymouth, her eyes glazed over and while reading from her note cards, a friend kindly escorted her offstage when she started speaking gibberish and crying hysterically about not having time to vacuum or bake a pie for the county fair. And then there was nothing but apples.

Sometimes I passed by her in the commons room and watched her sit with a cup of tea and book and she sighed deeply, as though she wanted to breathe in the moment and savor it. Outwardly she was one of the strangest on Ward 2, but I would bet, inwardly, she was somehow one of the happiest for being here.

In all my time, being here was never an alternative I sought. I did not belong to my family, save for only my father from time to time. But I did not want out of them. The opposite, in fact. I wanted nothing but to be part of them. For my mother to read to me, to hold me, to open her arms to me, regardless of what I did or did not do. I wanted a sister who came to me and

Jessica Dainty

whom I could go to. For a few scattered moments over the years, with my sister anyway, I almost had that.

But my sister and I drifted away from each other again as all things do without something strong enough to hold them together. And there were no more midnight talks, no more smiles in the school hallway or waves of acknowledgment. However, as we became separate once again, I remember the odd comfort of this stranger, when she came upon me from the dimness of the hallway our separate rooms shared, the slight reprieve from loneliness my mind took as I watched her form float through the darkness to her room.

Once, in the few weeks after our sudden but natural estrangement, when our mother had not come out of the pantry for dinner in three days, she stopped by my room, my door slightly cracked, and I sensed the whispered friction of her nightshirt against the wall as she slid down to sit. She sat there for an hour, as I stood on the other side, present but silent. I did not know now what was between us that we could not reach across. But she sat there running her palm along the fuzzed top of the carpet as we used to with our feet, the rhythm oddly comforting, her presence overwhelming me with a bubbling of love I imagined is what it felt like to have a sister, even now.

When I finally pulled myself away, I heard the rustling of my sister from the floor and could see, from the crack of my door, her lights flash on and off twice, as if she had forgotten something or thought she'd seen something out of the corner of her eye before the upstairs fell dark and quiet and unobtrusive. I imagined, before falling asleep, that she had been looking for me in those brief flashes of light, but concluded, from the quiet dark of the space we so elusively shared, that she had found nothing she could grab on to, relate to, or call her own.

I never saw any visitors here to see Helen. Perhaps she too had come only so close as *almost*.

X

By mid-February my dosage had been fully decreased back to the minimal allowance and my days no longer passed in a fog. My moods still hung low, but I was gaining momentum, pumping myself upward, like I used to on the swings at the playground. Ward 2's free time focused on creating enough valentines for the entirety of the men's wards, even the ones we did not see. As Elizabeth put it, no one should be without the feeling he is loved.

"My little Alexander was always so good at that," and then she grew quiet and sat in a corner while we all worked to fill her request.

Two hundred and thirty-six valentines later, we handed them off to Nurse Irene to send over to the men.

The men had not been as thoughtful and Valentine's Day came and went, commemorated only by tiny satchels of candy hearts dispersed by the nursing staff and chocolate cupcakes with red frosting in the dining hall.

The social that week was themed in pink, and though the holiday had officially come and gone, there was no way the men were getting off the hook so easily.

Francis and Cecelia, a new woman who joined us when Juniper disappeared just as quickly as she had come, hung paper hearts and strew streamers across the room from end to end. Some girls had baked heart-shaped cookies in the smaller kitchen, only managing about three-dozen in the small oven and limited time window. I at first put on a dress but then decided I'd feel prettier being comfortable and put on my slacks and a flowery blouse. I had no idea what had happened last time Pope was here, I had been in such a daze. Maybe he wouldn't even want to see me again. Maybe I had done something awful enough that he too had broken down and been sent away. Maybe I gave his feelings for me too much credit.

The Shape of the Atmosphere

Perhaps it didn't matter what I did. I was just a girl who happened to be near his age and drawable and not too crazy.

The men filed in. I didn't pass anything out at the door. When Pope came in, he waved his hand from down by his leg and smiled.

I had not been forgotten.

Pope came over and said hello to me without stuttering. He commented briefly on the weather and when his drumrolled consonants broke back in, he nodded and shrugged and we played rummy until he had to line up again.

I watched him go in awe, but then a selfish, horrible realization struck me. He was getting better. When he did get better, he would leave. And how could I wish anything different for him, even if it meant wishing something different for myself? After medication, I went to my room fighting the urge to scream. Instead, I threw myself onto my bed, burying my hands beneath me and burying my face in my pillow. I screamed here, where the sound got swallowed up and no one but Saint Christopher and my sister's smiling face were around to hear me.

* * *

Spring unofficially began with a string of warm days, and, as she had predicted, Elizabeth earned back her garden privileges. I, too, was allowed back on grounds for walks and free time, but I opted for kitchen duty rather than garden work. I still did laundry during my regular OT periods, but we were allowed to bake during free time to help out for meals. Volunteers made loaves of bread or cut massive amounts of carrots and peppers for salads. I loved the first punch after the dough had risen. I watched it deflate and then would knead it, working it in and out of itself, both changing and giving it form at the same time.

I breathed in the yeasty, warm smell of the kitchen, stealing pinches of raw dough when no one looked. I enjoyed the sticky feeling my skin came away with after an afternoon in the kitchen. It was a different kind of unclean, natural and earthy, as though I, too, had risen and sweated and fluffed to doneness.

Jessica Dainty

    I still refused the sewing room but took up needlepoint. I liked the specificity of the task and watching the formation of something slowly take place before my eyes. I made one with two doves on it, in thought of Dad and Allison. My first had been a red heart on a blue background. I made it with Pope in mind but it was sloppy and loose because I kept losing my confidence when I thought of actually giving it to him. I instead wrapped St. Christopher in it and slept with it under my pillow.

    Sometimes I took the needlework out to the garden and sat while Elizabeth raked and weeded, her giant straw hat like an umbrella on her head. Elizabeth wore dresses even then, with full stocking and heels, a lace slip I could sometimes see poking out from beneath the bottom hem of her dress. I was unsure she would know how to put on a pair of pants should she be forced. The thought made me smile, and she smiled back, a smudge of dirt on her nose and cheek. She was just as thin, but she looked fuller out here in the sun, even when dwarfed by her ridiculous hat. Her skinny arms took on the look of strength and her frail frame, when she reached to the ground, looked bent with purpose. I still had not asked her about what I had read in my file, about the death of her son. And I didn't dare do it now, when she seemed unaware of anything but contentment.

    "Do you have a sister, Gertie?" She wiped her forehead with the back of her hand, but I'd never seen a drop of sweat on Elizabeth since I'd known her.

    "I did have one. She's dead, though. She died." I focused on the thread, following the snake of blue through to the back side.

    "Oh, I'm sorry, dear. I can't even imagine. Mine's up and gone to Arizona, like I told you. You got her coat, the dear thing. Four months now, maybe more and she hasn't written me a word. Paulie has her address but says he won't give it to me until I'm out of here, by her request." She huffed and placed her foot down firmly in what I guessed was supposed to be a stomp, but Elizabeth was too timid for that. "Can you imagine not speaking to your sister, if she were still around?"

    How could someone like Elizabeth understand a relationship between sisters that never existed?

    "I can imagine it would be difficult."

The Shape of the Atmosphere

"Oh, but here I am being so selfish when she's at least out there. Oh, you must think I'm just hideous!"

"Don't worry. It's fine. Really. My sister and I were never very close."

"Oh, how dreadful. I can't imagine such a thing. Did one of you do something? My sister and I had a time like that. Loss is always difficult to deal with."

"No one really did anything. We had our moments, but it never lasted. I suppose we didn't have the stamina."

"I can understand that." She went back to her work, as though we had not been speaking, and eventually I told the aide overseeing the garden that I wanted to walk back. She sent a student nurse with me, who, the poor thing, tried to talk to me about the weather and how I liked Willow Estate. I ignored her until she clasped her hands behind her back and I noticed her eyes well up. I felt bad, but I only had so much to give.

* * *

The month crept along. Group therapy sessions found me talking and sharing, though I kept my input minimal. I'd decided my story could only hurt me by giving the doctors information they could twist into typed lies and stamp my name on. My file said delusive, which wasn't true, but paranoia might have been fair at this point.

Still, I was doing well off my medication, and everyone seemed pleased. I smiled more and always wore a dress to typing.

The March social arrived and was themed after the blooming world around us. Some women made tissue paper flowers. Elizabeth brought in baskets of real plants from the garden, roots still scraggly and caked in dirt. I helped set up a bowl of punch, laughing to myself as I rested the ladle on the edge of the basin, thinking back to that first social when I met Jonathan and Pope.

As if on cue from my thoughts, the men filed in. Conversation was slow at first, but it was as though everyone had blossomed with the plants outside. People perked up and talked. An aide wheeled in the record player, and I walked over to meet Pope. I waved at Jonathan, who led Becca over to the refreshment table by her hand.

Jessica Dainty

Pope sat on the edge of the windowsill that looked out toward the Willow Tree. The day was beautiful, even though growing dark, and I had already scanned the room to see how many aides chaperoned, to know if asking for a walk was even worth my time. There were only two in the room. One stood with her feet just enough wider than shoulder width to be awkward, as though she believed if she spread her body out, she could cover more ground. Neither of them stood near my hallway.

"Come with me." And I slipped my hand into his. It was the single bravest act I had ever performed. His fingers didn't grip back, but his hand was warm and he let me guide him away from the window, past the placard for Debutante Suites. When we got to my room, I closed the door. Bravery act, #2.

Pope didn't speak, just looked at me expectantly. I could see in his eyes he assumed an explanation was coming.

Stupidly, I picked some words and said them. "I don't know why I came here."

"H—here?" His hand motion posed the unspoken question of "your room or Willow Estate?" and I sat on my bed, unsure of either answer.

"Do you ever feel like you don't belong anywhere?" I asked him.

Pope came and sat next to me. He pulled a folded piece of paper out of his back pocket, leaning into me as he reached behind. He took a pencil down from behind his right ear. I had just noticed it as he grabbed it. He angled the paper on his lap, to get as much flat surface area as possible. I watched him start to draw lines, soft gray beginnings of something I had no doubt would be mesmerizing. I hadn't realized I'd leaned so closely into him. He turned toward me, his cheek brushing my hair which had fallen over his shoulder. He blew on me, with a smile, pushing me away.

I stood and took my mother out of her drawer, the letters heavy for their unread words. Was I willing to lighten their burden to make mine more difficult to bear? Is that what would happen?

"Where would you want to belong?"

The question was so clear and perfectly spoken I imagined Pope had used the past minutes of preparation forming the words before he spoke.

The Shape of the Atmosphere

I turned toward him. "I don't know. The places I used to have aren't there anymore to try to fit into. I honestly can't think of anywhere else I should be. And that scares me."

I carried the letters over to the bed and sat next to him again. "Are you ever afraid?"

Pope's drawing was taking form, what looked like two hands, almost touching. He put the pencil down and took my hand. I kept my eyes on his drawing though, imagining the stillness taking to life, the fingers moving toward one another. I didn't look at him until I felt the buttons of his shirt, the suggestion of his body from beneath where he had placed my hand. His heart was racing.

"I'm always af—f—fraid." He let go before I wanted him to. I lingered beyond his invitation before bringing my hand back to my lap. "I embarrass my p—parents. They had me in special classes, b—b—but the new adm—m—ministration re—t—tested me, and it turns out I'm not s—stupid. There was n—nothing else to d—do with m—me."

Pope rubbed at his jaw like it was tired and sore.

"I d—don't want this place to make me better. B—but I'm more af—fraid of never getting b—better."

"Do you really think you're sick?" We locked eyes as my tone re-echoed in my room. I sounded hateful, judgmental.

He took a deep breath. "I think I can be better than I am."

Pope's hand brushed my cheek, pushed my hair behind my ear. I thought immediately of my sister and her stories, of moments like this she would never have again. I heard my gasp before I realized I was crying, and I felt Pope's chin on the top of my head, in my father's place, before I understood that his arms were around me, that someone was touching me with the intention of making me safer rather than one of the various alternatives I'd been exposed to over the past few months.

Instead of putting my arms around him, I narrowed them in the space between us, leaving my mother in my lap, and brought my hands up to his face. I traced his lips with my index fingers, one on either side arching up and around.

Jessica Dainty

"I think your mouth is perfect." The words embarrassed me. I'd meant that I thought he was fine how he is, that if he embarrassed his parents that was their issue and shouldn't be his. I searched for better words, but I watched the edges of his lips curl up, my fingers still resting on his chin. He licked his bottom lip, and I wanted desperately to know what his silence tasted like, pressed against mine.

"Check-in."

Pope had already released me with the sound of the door latch clicking, and I turned to see Jessica standing in my doorway.

"Clement. Your presence is missed in the Commons area. If you don't mind."

He stood without hesitation, reached up to his forehead as though tipping a non-existent hat, and disappeared into the hallway.

Jessica turned to me once he was gone, brought her own hand to her own imaginary hat, and winked. "Gertie," was all she said, before closing my door.

I lay on my bed looking at Pope's unfinished picture, imagining a finished draft that would bring the two hands together as they should be. Then I felt the edge of my mother's letters scratch at my thigh from where they lay next to me. And I knew some things never came together, no matter how hard you pressed them, that other forces sometimes made decisions for you when it came to where you belonged. I decided, just for today, to be grateful that Pope and I had been forced together in the only place that would have us as we were.

I put my mother back in her drawer, with Pope's picture banded in with her. I must have fallen asleep because when I walked back to the commons area, Jessica was clearing away punch bowls, the men already gone. I was lucky she had been the one to find us, or I'm sure I'd be facing some kind of demerit or punishment. I helped her carry the bowls to the kitchen, an unspoken thank you, the air outside brisk from the absent sun. I shuddered, feeling for a split second that it was winter coming and not spring, that I would have to watch everything around me die again, rather than be reborn. The moment passed, and walking back to the commons area from washing the dishes, I looked up at the stars and squinted. I traced the arc of a pair of lips, connecting the dots. I blew a kiss to the sky. It offered

The Shape of the Atmosphere

nothing back to me, and, for the smallest of seconds, I was fine with it. I didn't care.

* * *

A week or so later, on Monday, one of the aides flipped on the radio and we crowded around listening to official voices. Elvis Presley repeated his oath to serve back to the other voice that filled the room. I looked around. Elizabeth cried, as did Adelaide and the new lady, Cecelia, along with a few of the other women. My sister had loved Elvis, but in our house we listened to classical music or talk radio. The morning after my birthday and Sputnik had been an irregularity, and I'd watched my sister sway to crooning voices as we'd played Chinese Checkers. Elvis had come on only once, but she had closed her eyes and held one hand to her chest. I'd sat biting my nail until she was done and took her turn.

I liked his voice, the way a slight husk worked its way in, especially on the faster songs. I wondered if he would take that passion with him, wherever it was he was going. Or if he needed the rush of an audience to perform. If without them, he would be no different than every other young man out there, afraid to die. And if he were put in danger, would one look at his over-recognizable face be enough to save him?

Pope was twenty-two. All men over eighteen were required to sign up for the draft. I wondered if being in here saved him from the chance. If living in hell was enough to save you from the danger of dying in it.

* * *

On a Monday night in April, the newscaster had announced that Sputnik 2 had disintegrated in orbit. I imagined it knew what would happen should it try to make it home, and saved itself the trouble.

I had somehow missed the news of it being launched in the first place, which happened in early November, soon after I came here. The news reported that this one had housed a dog named Laika. I tried to picture the cone of metal evaporating, the shaking form of a dog inside, or had it died months earlier? Would a living thing disintegrate like a satellite? Or would it be messy and good that it was happening so far away, where no one could do anything about it?

    I'd gone to bed wondering what it would be like to disintegrate, to not simply break apart, burn up and fall to the earth as the first one may have done. But to actually dissolve my existence into pieces too negligible to acknowledge or even notice. When I'd sunk to the bottom of the pool, I'd convinced myself I was invisible to the world. That as long as I was down there, no one could see me. But, of course, I was still there, in my ugly completeness. I wondered what the stars and planets thought of all these recent intruders, all these manufactured things that just didn't belong among them. If when they watched them evaporate, they thought to themselves *finally, it's learned where it belongs*.

    A week later at the April social, Pope didn't talk to or touch me. He seemed distant, pensive in a burdened way, and he rubbed his temples and jaw constantly. I noticed his fingers twitched. When I asked him if he'd drawn anything lately, he held up his shaking hands in a demonstrative no.

    I watched him leave, this boy with a shaking existence—shaking voice, shaking hands, shaking spirit. Some things, like sand, level out when shaken, each grain finding its place, resting on the pieces around it. I imagined the settling of planets and stars after the shaking bang that created them. I pictured Pope as a universe, all inside of him as circling entities, held in orbit by his own conviction to be better. I made myself believe that no matter how hard *they* shook, he might be left whole. We all would. Then he was gone, and I couldn't see him anymore. And it was time for medicine and to be led to bed.

    I couldn't sleep that night. I wondered if the dog from Sputnik 2 had a sense of what would happen to it, if it too devolved to an existence of vibration. Or did the atmosphere have compassion for something alive? Perhaps the layers passed Laika through and laid her down softly somewhere. I closed my eyes, skeptical. Was there a place with so much pity?

XI

By May, I had completed seven needlepoint projects, one of which Jessica hung in the Nursing Station. Every time I stepped up to get my medicine, a giant willow tree, brown and green and gray popped out from the blank whiteness of the fabric. I'd left it plain. The tree stood, alone. I had been going for earnest, but instead, it looked lonely to me, and I felt almost guilty, as though I had done the tree a disservice in my rendering.

I made it out to the tree at least once a week now. Elizabeth always chose the garden, and after the first reaction to my alternative suggestion, I went to the willow on my own time instead of our shared. She asked about it sometimes, as though the willow were a fairy tale, and I always concluded that I had no idea what that head of hers held. We'd both been docile for months now. No syringes or outbursts and with summer pushing its way in early I felt confident that Debutante Suites would be my home for the foreseeable future. Elizabeth's mood prediction did seem to hold up; the fall had not been her time of year. Every other season seemed fine though, and we took our walks and tea together and for the most part formed a normal friendship. The only friendship, really, I'd ever had.

I had been optimistic once before, when my switch to public school had been announced. That was a clean slate.

My teacher's name had been Mr. Drakinson. I'd never had a male teacher before. The priests at my old school roamed the halls but kept to the boys' classrooms. The closest they came to teaching was sitting behind the desk, while one or another of the nuns ran an errand, went to the bathroom, or as I imagined, went into a small room to scream.

Mr. Drakinson's classroom was depressingly white, with ugly orange blocks of color sporadically punctuating the walls. Our cubbies were already labeled, mine with the hated *Gertrude* spelled out in all of its awful fullness.

The Shape of the Atmosphere

We stupidly called him Drake the Snake, giggling as we chanted his name on the playground and doodled with still untamed script his name on our notebooks. We flocked to those sorts of things, those experiments with what we thought to be adulthood. And I'd joined in, eager for the opportunity that one of these girls, maybe more, would be my friend. But from the first day, I often spent my time on the playground alone, under the far jungle gym, braiding friendship bracelets that always made their way back to my desk after I gave them away, along with the sound of unsuccessfully stifled laughter.

But my teachers, for the most part, liked me, at least objectively. I spent hours, days on projects other kids probably spent a fraction of an evening on. I soaked paper in coffee for a day and had my father help me singe the edges to make the pages look aged for a project in Social Studies; actually made a book binding for a project on koalas and Australia when I could have just bought a flimsy folder. I got "O"s in all my subjects on my report card. Only in the areas reserved for *Peer Interaction* and *Communication* did I get the disappointing "S" for satisfactory.

Then the first term report card for Fall in seventh grade held the dreaded *U*, and I excused myself early from dinner and cried silently into my pillow, hoping to suffocate my own gasps so my father would not climb the twenty-three stairs to ask me what was wrong.

I hated group projects, and often did all the work myself, to avoid the interactions. My peers never minded, of course, and they sat back and threw spit balls at each other, wrote notes, and made fortune tellers, those paper finger contraptions I, too, wasted hours of my life on. Now when I thought of such ridiculous simplicity, such free time, I couldn't remember what it felt like. Here free time was always bookended by things that held too tight, squeezed until you couldn't breathe, so that you could never quite relax.

But then, I grasped as desperately to triviality as anyone. When group project time overflowed out of the classroom, I yearned for a sense of normalcy and invited kids over. They sometimes brought friends along with their materials, and the boys wound up playing roller hockey in the basement with my sister, the girls occupied by her makeup and perfume bottles, while I cut poster board and tried against logic to reposition rubber-cemented paper.

Jessica Dainty

Before I knew it, people were flooding my desk when group projects were announced. Wistful eyes were silently pleading *pick me pick me*, and, even though I knew it wasn't me they wanted, not me for a friend or any sort of companion, they still wanted something from me, something only I could give. As Gladys had said, wasn't being wanted, for whatever the reason, something?

I shocked everyone one day by choosing a skinny blonde girl named April, the only other person in the class who was probably less popular, less desired as a friend than I was. She ate paper during lunch hour, rolling the sickening heavy wetness around in her mouth.

I realized too late that she had been my chance. She was nice, quiet, and way smarter than anyone else in our class. She had a quirky sense of humor and, at twelve, a maturity that astounded me, especially in spite of her odd behaviors. I blew it though. I passed up the chance for an actual friend whom I liked for the chance at multiple friendships with girls I couldn't stand. They made fun of her. I was put on the spot. I joined in. For three brief weeks I was not the focus of ridicule. She was, and when she stopped coming to school in the weeks before Christmas vacation, no one knew where she was. The rumor circled that she had lost it, broken down and been sent away, taken by force as she pulled out her own hair. The cruelties returned to me, but by then I felt it a fair enough punishment.

Now I wondered sometimes, late at night, if maybe she was here, behind these same walls. If the rumor was true. I saw Arlene with her handfuls of hair and I thought of April, how nice of an exchange they could have with one another.

But when I thought of April, I really thought of myself. I'd trade the hydro baths, the shock, everything in a heartbeat, but, were I able to go back now, I'd take great peace in knowing that both April and I would have had at least one friend to confide in, and perhaps now we would both be in very different places, behind very different walls.

That was an old life, though, lost, and not worth dwelling on. I had what I had now. And Elizabeth was the first person who never asked anything of me. We just fell together easily, as though by mistake. Becca Donelson, on the other hand, I made a conscious effort with, saw her as a second chance, a new April. I wanted to hold her hand, what with the way

The Shape of the Atmosphere

she pressed her cheeks against the mesh screen so that she walked around with red marks on her face half the day. But somehow around the start of May, it became obvious that Becca Donelson was pregnant. She'd had no visitors, no obvious interactions. She attended none of my treatments so I did not know what hers entailed. And yet there she was, bulbous and glowing, resting cookies on the growing mound of belly she seemed fascinated with.

I helped her in the cafeteria and tried to bargain with the nurses when she started needing the bathroom more frequently.

"Do you know what's happening to you, Becca?" I asked her one day, her hand resting on her stomach, as though she must know, was already, somehow, a mother.

"Gowna haf a baby," she said, her speech sloppy.

"That's right. And what will that make you?"

"A momma," she said, giggling. "A good momma."

And in that moment, I had hope. I did think Becca Donelson would be a good mother, unassuming and always kind. Blind love.

But by the end of May, Becca's family had come to get her, and she left to as much gossip as she had come. And she cried leaving, wanting to stay and play. But no one reached out to save her, to keep her here where at least someone had claimed her in some way. Not even me. I just watched her go.

* * *

June was a hot month. Ward 1 got to go off the premises to the local ice cream parlor and Nurse Peters set up a point system where five Ward 2-ers could earn the chance to go with them.

This was my first introduction to the honest ruthlessness of women. Compliant behavior, volunteering, general attitude and disposition, as well as psychological progress were the vague parameters of our earning categories. Women pinched each other during free time to make them cry out and look unstable, stole things from each other's rooms and replaced them conspicuously once they'd announced emphatically that something was missing, turned the oven up on loaves of bread so they would burn. I didn't participate, but I also wasn't proud of my role as silent observer.

I was not about to rat anybody out and make myself a target. I wanted the ice cream trip as bad as anybody else, but I wasn't about to degrade myself to get it. I left that job to the general practices of Willow Estate.

They'd posted our rankings halfway through, which only fueled the animosity. I stared at my name. Number three. The next morning, though, my towel was unaccounted for when the call for water-off came. The bathroom cleared out faster than most mornings and I was left dripping, with Sarah's unsympathetic eyes ordering me out.

By this point, I had stood naked in front of men twice and three times my age, men I found attractive and those whose eyes made me feel disgusting inside, like a bug crawling beneath my exposed skin. But regardless of the situation, the setting had mostly been private—the bathroom, an examination room, the hydro room.

"Sarah, please. You had to see someone take it. Can I please have a towel?"

She practically laughed in my face. "One towel per patient. You know the rule."

"You handed me one in line for Christ's sake! You know I had one. It's not my fault."

Sarah's face hit me full force for the first time since I'd been here. Her eyes were hazel, fierce, on fire. "Watch your language, you little cunt. Now get out of here."

I was amazed that my body had not been physically moved by the force of her words. I was aware that Sarah and I were not friendly but I did not understand why she so obviously now not only didn't like me, but seemed to hold something against me.

"Please." I sounded pathetic, like I did when I begged my mother not to send me to public school, to confession every Sunday. Away from the table before I'd eaten when I refused to wear a dress to dinner.

"Out."

And so I walked the length of the hallway and into the commons room, mostly empty of patients but punctuated by staff who stopped in their tracks to watch the naked girl. I kept my eyes forward and my chin up. I did

The Shape of the Atmosphere

not pass the blame. I did not offer an excuse. When I made it to my room, I sat on my bed naked. I sat there past three faltering "check-ins" though each less surprised than the former. I finally dressed in my mother's favorite dress. I wore no stockings and put on the highest heels my mother had packed.

The next week, my name was not on the list of top five point earners. Elizabeth said that they had gotten to taste more than eighteen flavors. That the milkshakes wore towering hats of whipped cream, the cherry like a little button on top. She'd smuggled in a small sample cup, but by the time she got it to me, it was melted and warm and tasted a bit sour. Still some sweetness had been left, though, a cinnamon aftertaste, and I was grateful for it.

It was my mother's birthday, and I had sent her a short note earlier in the week. Today, I made my way into the estate chapel for the first time since I'd come back from Ward 3. The chapel offered services every Saturday and Sunday, both Christian and Jewish varieties. But I only ever went in during off times, when the room was open for however I wanted to use it.

I went to light a candle for my mother. I could imagine it would be something she'd have liked on her birthday, regardless of my personal interest in the act. Elizabeth was in there, and a young aide I'd never seen before sat in a corner reading, holding down the job of fire overseer.

Elizabeth came to the chapel, I knew, at the same time, before our cup of tea, each day. I knelt beside her but did not speak. I lit a candle and thought of my mother but could not bring myself to pray. What could she want or need from me anyway? I hoped she was well, but that was all. She was a stranger to me, more than ever, if such a thing were possible. Less human even than the days I knew her only from behind the closed pantry door. At least then she had some layers and dimensions. Now she was a woman I knew mostly via one-line letters that carried no voice but a possible loneliness that did not humanize her but made her more exhausting in a sense. She exasperated me, and I had not seen her in months.

"You see the girl watching us?" Elizabeth's voice was so quiet that at first I thought I was hearing a message from beyond. Her mouth barely moved when I turned slightly toward her as she continued. I nodded.

"She's one of us."

I glanced at her. "What do you mean?"

Jessica Dainty

"When I first came here, I was on Ward 3, and then for a brief month or so, they moved me to Ward 4. She was there."

"So she's worked here a long time." I glanced back at the girl, who seemed oblivious in her reading.

"Not as an aide. She was there as a patient. I've heard rumors that they're using converts though I hadn't seen it yet. "Recovered" patients are cheaper than training. After all, we've seen and done it all. Never would have thought she'd be recovered though. A Ward 4-er who was convinced she smelled like sewage. Wouldn't talk or get within three feet of anyone. Thought it was some sort of judgment from God. They must be really desperate for help around here."

I eyed the girl from over my shoulder, trying not to turn my head. "She looks normal enough."

"Yes, but don't we all!" Elizabeth's voice rose and the girl dropped her magazine.

"Shhh!" Her finger shot to her lips. "This is a sanctuary not a vestibule for chatter."

Elizabeth and I giggled and rose from our knees. I scanned her carefully as we exited. She did look normal. But as Elizabeth said, *don't we all*.

* * *

The estate social had been cancelled in June because the men were watching the World Cup instead. A few women gathered around the television set, as a way to be with the men on at least some level, but I stayed away. Allison had always liked soccer, and had our town offered a girls' team, she would have played that over field hockey any day. She wasn't happy with being great in a girl's sport. She wanted to be great in a guy's sport too.

The men were fast though, from the brief snippets I saw in passing. And I wondered if Allison would ever have stood a chance in the world she didn't get to live in. Perhaps, for her, it was better that she was gone. She was a girly girl too, don't get me wrong, but any girl trying to break into a man's world didn't seem to get very far, and never got anywhere easily.

The Shape of the Atmosphere

The Susans of the world, the Junipers, and Helens too, ended up in places like this, where they weren't a threat to anybody.

XII

Since my decreased dosage worked, Nurse Peters acted toward me as though our little exchange had never happened. She praised my good behavior and even used me as an example in group therapy one day as someone who was taking both responsibility and initiative in her own treatment. I wanted to slap her.

Sarah, on the other hand, only got worse. Elizabeth knew about the towel incident and was convinced no one on the ward had taken it. Now, whenever I passed Sarah in the halls, I had to move to the side to avoid her running right into me. She did not waiver. She did not budge. I had no doubt that she had been responsible. What she cared about the ice cream outing, I couldn't imagine, so I had to believe, whatever her problem, it was more personal than a point system.

Soon, the weeks she worked hydro, I was left in the water for hours, like my time on Ward 3. I ended up with pneumonia in July and four heating blankets over me on a ninety-five-degree day trying to sweat out the fever. When I was finally cleared for regular activity again and strict hydro time limits (which left me thanking my lucky stars for my bout of pneumonia), she refused any of my requests for walks, bathroom breaks, or aid of any kind.

I was convinced she too was "recovered" and simply crazy. But the rumors said no. Arlene said her father was an experimental psychologist at a public institution and he made her work here for information. Susan claimed she had pent up sexual issues from being around naked women all day. Elizabeth's theory made the most sense, though. How else do you get through hell? "Make yourself impervious to the fire. She's a tramp because she has to be."

I didn't care which was true. I was going to kill her with kindness if that's what it took. I smiled. I said good morning. I thanked her for my

The Shape of the Atmosphere

medication, for my hot water and warm towel after hydro. I complimented her hair, her makeup which made her face too angular and ugly. She didn't reciprocate but she did stop calling me cunt, and my towel didn't disappear anymore. Still she followed me with eyes that spewed hatred, the way the white aides had stared at the Negro girl before they'd pinned her down and shot her body through with fire.

* * *

In July, all the women had written letters to Elvis. I even saw Susan sprawling something on pink paper and stamping it overseas. By September though, no one seemed to care anymore, and the stationery table was cleared off for bridge games. My mother had not written in a while. The last letter I received from her was in June, saying something about the church fair and switching it to day because of how there were three Negro families now at the church and nobody wanted to be out at night with them attending. I hadn't written back.

The men had not come in June, I'd missed the July social because of my pneumonia, and then at the August social, Jonathan had put his hand on my back and told me Pope would not be coming, that he was not well, and couldn't make it. His eyes were heavy things of concern, but his mouth went flat and empty after that, and he took his hand back and walked away.

It had been three months since I'd seen Pope, and I woke up on a Sunday in August to still no visitors. When I was done, the letter to my mother tallied thirteen pages in length. I told her everything from the moment I thought she was beautiful in church to shitting myself in my first hydro session. I told her about Dad looking for his watch which she had worn on her bony wrist and that if he'd been able to find, he might not have died. Neither of them would have. I told her that I hated her. And that I thought I could love her. That I was angry with her. That sometimes when I thought of her voice instead of my own singing me lullabies, it helped me sleep or get through hydro. That I couldn't remember anymore the exact color of her hair.

Jessica Dainty

When I was done, I went to the chapel and lit the corner of the pages. Half the sheets had fallen in ashes before the aide even noticed what was happening.

* * *

I lost my grounds privileges for two weeks after my spat of delinquency in the chapel. But they left me on Ward 2, which I was grateful for. The possibility of being sent back to Ward 3 hadn't occurred to me, and when the aide's voice heightened to a yell and she threw the papers in the incredibly small fount of holy water to the side of the candles, I panicked at my potentially very stupid decision.

Nurse Peters had seemed unconcerned though, and even Sarah's behavior to me remained stagnant. Nobody made a big deal about it. Elizabeth said everyone was given some leniency around the one-year mark. People had taken the fact that they've been locked away for an entire revolution of the sun pretty hard.

A whole year. The reality had not yet hit me. We had not had our September social yet, but the leaves de-greening outside screamed October was coming. A whole year.

A whole year and how many space ventures later, I was still in Willow Estate, my father and sister were still dead, and my mother still could not bear to see me. A whole year and I was in a place where they drugged me, electrocuted me once a week, froze me once a week, and humiliated me at least once a day. A whole year and I was in a place where I had a friend in Elizabeth, a relationship with no judgments, a friend and maybe more in Pope, an immediate support system that did not come in only once a night or lock itself behind a closed door. The scale tilted, but I hadn't yet decided in which direction.

* * *

The day of the social, I sat in Dr. Rosslins' office for an interminable amount of time. Then they let me walk to the willow tree after the session to

The Shape of the Atmosphere

sit underneath the covering. The weather was markedly cooler, and I pulled my sweater around me. The covering had begun to wilt, and some of the leaves lay on the ground beneath the branches. The ones that remained ranged from still-vibrant greens to blazing yellows and soggy browns. The sun was out, but I didn't find this visit comforting. It seemed too early for things to be dying, and I felt too exposed. But when I told the aide I wanted to head back, she became flustered and suggested a trip to the garden or to the pond instead.

I did not care to go, but agreed. The air was not cool enough even to frost the top of the water but my hand burned with cold when I swirled the still surface. My fingers numbed and I moved them around, trying to return some warmth. The air bit at my ears and the exposed skin at my neck. I had no scarf and though some women knitted, I was not friendly enough with any of them to ask for such a time-consuming favor as them making me one. Maybe my mood was chilling me. Could it really be this cold in September?

"Can we please head back? I'm cold." The aide's eyes were big and doe-like. I went in for the kill. "And I am still getting over my pneumonia. I really don't feel as though I should be out this long." I added in a meek cough for effect.

She led me back but we entered through the backside of the dining hall, into the kitchen where we had baked the Christmas cookies and where I kneaded dough and dusted flour on an assortment of things one day a week.

"You wait here. I'll be right back." She exited into the dining area and out the door toward the commons area of the main building.

I was alone. Left alone with no one coming to do a check-in until this aide should decide to return. I didn't know how much time I had and I had no idea how to spend it. I could throw flour around the room and cover everything. I could exit back out the door I came from and run. Somewhere. Where though? Instead of doing any of these, I opened the refrigerator. There were three cookie sheets full of cupcakes. I took one and licked the frosting off, shoved the spongy cake into my mouth. I did this with a second and a third. When I heard returning clicks on the tile floor, I closed the refrigerator and washed down my transgression with water directly from the faucet.

Jessica Dainty

"You can follow me now." The aide's voice echoed from the other side of the hall. I wiped the front of my dress to ensure there were no crumbs and followed.

The commons area quieted as I entered, but my eyes absorbed that the men were already present, the party already begun. The jumps and shouts of "Happy Birthday" reached me the same time my eyes caught sight of the banner.

They'd thrown me a surprise party. In my year here, they'd never actively celebrated anyone else's birthday. "It's because you're young," Elizabeth explained to me later. "Nobody else here wants to celebrate getting older in this place. You've still got a real chance though."

There were balloons, streamers, and soon Arlene and Susan were carrying in the trays of cupcakes from the kitchen. I'd hijacked my own birthday cake.

I swam through a sea of well-wishers. Pope waited patiently on the other side, sitting on the window ledge. He stood up when I approached.

"Happy birthday, Gertie," he said, his voice steady and strong, though closer to a whisper. He had disappeared for three months and reappeared whole. Nothing else in this broken world had been able to do that. He held out a rolled paper, tied with a ribbon, like the first drawing he'd given me. "Go on now. Open it."

The picture was of the willow tree and me sitting beneath it. This one was not black and white, a study of shadows. Here, the willow leaves burned an intense orange, the sky exploded in shades of blue, the grass glistened green like the city of Oz. The only part done in pencil was my person. I sat, colorless in the midst of all around me. And yet, he managed, despite this, to capture a peacefulness. I was not unhappy; I was not sad. It was as though I had given my light to everything else around me, and I was glad for it, sitting back and enjoying what I had done.

"Thank you. It's beautiful." And I meant it.

"I can see you sometimes from the windows over there, you know. Only once or twice, but it's happened."

I smiled at the thought of him watching for me, perhaps sitting at the window for hours, just for the chance of it.

"Want to take a walk?" I asked.

The Shape of the Atmosphere

Outside, I knew I was not being led anywhere but where I wanted to go. The sky was bright blue directly above us but just starting to yellow at the edges. Two clouds morphed in and out of shapes and sizes as though they could not decide what they wanted to be, and were mocking me, playfully, with the fact that they did not have to. I'm sure if I told someone I looked like a frog one minute and a dog the next, they'd never let me out of my bed. I'd probably not even be on my ward. No inhabitant of the Debutante Suites could be that crazy.

"Do you see shapes in clouds?" I hoped it did not sound as crazy as I felt it did.

"I haven't looked in a while. I remember doing it when I was kid though."

"I'd like to go to the willow tree, please." At my words, the aide with us veered off the path onto the grass.

When we got to the tree, I no longer saw the soggy brown. The yellowing sky lit up the yellow and green left in the leaves, even a touch of orange. We walked through the shedding branches. The aide stayed just outside.

"Your speech." I started my sentence. Pope nodded, and looked down as though he knew my train of thought, knew what recovery meant. "It's gotten better."

"Well, I certainly wouldn't have believed shock could have helped either, when they first told me what it was."

"Shock did this for you?"

"I can't imagine what else it could be. They told me the nature of my problem could be greatly helped by the process. But this?"

The ground within the willow tree was surprisingly free of leaves, as though they did not want to disturb the tranquility of the inside. "Wow, that's great. I'm really happy for you. Does this mean—" My stomach lurched. The cupcakes rebelled against me. I leaned forward and vomited, the sugar a film on my tongue and teeth. "Oh my God! I'm so sorry," I said with my hand over my mouth. I looked down to see the swirls of white cream on his brown shoes. "Oh, I'm mortified. Just leave please."

But he didn't leave. Instead, I heard a softness in his laugh and felt his hand lower mine away from my mouth. He hugged me to his chest, and I missed my father stabbingly, having the smell of a man so close. "I'm not going anywhere," he said. He pulled back slightly, too soon, I thought, but he didn't fully let go. Instead he lowered his face toward mine. And before I knew it, his lips were pressing into mine. My body vibrated with an intensity greater than any voltage the nurses could charge through me. My mind raced between joy and fear, excitement and dread at my foul mouth, the vomit on his shoes.

One of his hands found my cheek, and gently, pulled my face closer, and his tongue made it past my filmy teeth. I met him a little less than halfway but soon we were equal partners in this moment, and I wished my sister were at home, waiting for every detail.

When we finally separated, his face still close to mine, our foreheads resting on each other's, he sighed. I searched for the right thing to say, but he beat me to it.

"W—w—w—w—ow," he stuttered, the word insignificant, his stilted speech the best compliment he could have given.

"Time to go." The aide smirked as we bowed under the hanging twigs, but she walked ahead of us.

The sky had changed, the blue now fully overcome by the impending sunset, the clouds no longer morphing but stretched out in wisps, like a blanket as though they knew night was coming and thought they could cover us all.

XIII

The rest of my party was a daze. The rest of my week was too. I went through hydro and shock unfazed. Even Elizabeth's sudden increase in episodes of stillness wasn't enough to jar me out of my good mood. They increased her medication and sometimes she stayed in bed all day. I only met her for tea one afternoon, sometime in mid-week. It was getting too cold for the garden, and the last time we had walked there together the dullness of the colors, the drooping leaves, left her greatly affected and she did not eat anything at dinner.

I wrote my mother three letters in the few days after my surprise party. None was overly personal or informative, but I figured I'd let her benefit from my good mood, should she be interested in hearing from me. I told her about the willow tree and how the colors were fading, in one letter. I mentioned the surprise party in another and my three cupcakes. The third contained only the single line *And how are you doing?* once I realized that my birthday also marked the day of the accident, and the anniversary was approaching unstoppably.

I made this realization replaying my time with Pope under the tree. Even though my actual birthday was still over a week away, I linked the two together now, inseparably, unwittingly. At first I was angry that such a moment had to share the same span of days in my memory as Dad and Allison, but then I was grateful for it. I had gone through almost the entire celebration without thinking of loss, without thinking of my mother sprawled at Bobby's feet, without thinking of my vomit on my mother's dress and our tiled floor. I'd barely passed a day without thinking of these things, and now, on the days it should matter, the memory had not even penetrated my mind.

I was relieved but also guilty. And I did care how my mother was doing but also did not want to address the accident directly, to make her

The Shape of the Atmosphere

think of it, should she have been as lucky as I and had something lovely distract her.

When I was done writing my mother, I began a letter to Allison. I recounted my walk with Pope from the drawing to the hug, to missing Dad, to Pope's lips finding mine. I addressed it with a made-up address and sent it to be mailed, not knowing who would receive it. I imagined her getting it somehow, somewhere, and opening it, giggling and giddy as she pored over the contents. I did not know how she had become more of a sister to me now than she ever was before, but I liked these imaginings. This idea that we could talk about such normalcy as first kisses and trinkets from boys, as walks and holding hands. I found myself really missing her for the first time, though in a way not even her, but this new idea of her as someone I knew and confided in.

That night I dreamt I was floating on top of the ocean and sank to the bottom. Instead of fish and coral and flowing plants though there were stars and night, glistening orbs of light. I breathed in and exhaled planets and galaxies, swirls that exploded into existence. I breathed out my father and sister and then they sped away. I shot after them, from planet to planet, star to star. Every planet had water and I dove from lake to lake, ocean to ocean across galaxies. No matter where I went though, how far I dove beneath the surface, I never found anyone. After looking everywhere, I breathed back in the worlds I'd created, the life sucked down like through a funnel, watching for them, but they did not come. Soon I was floating again in a starry sea. I woke up holding my breath.

The next day Elizabeth tried to cut her wrists with a plastic knife in the dining hall. They dragged her away. The sky looked like it might snow, but it only rained instead. The rain froze to the windows in hard streaks. When her husband showed up for visitation, they led him away by the arm and he followed. He had done this before.

* * *

I waited patiently for Elizabeth's return. All of October passed, the willow tree shedding its leaves like the tears I refused to shed because I

Jessica Dainty

feared it meant admitting she wouldn't be back. Pope and I had played rummy at the October social, and I hid behind a paper mask.

The first snow came and went, barely a dusting in early November that left the ground looking sweet like someone had sprinkled it with powdered sugar. The next day was unseasonably warm and I walked with no shoes under the willow tree, letting my toes numb against the still-cold dirt.

My mother did not respond to my letters. Instead I got a note from the nurse who had come to visit before, saying my mother was happy to hear from me but was not up for writing. That she sends her love. I knew my mother had nothing to do with that letter, that the nurse was offering words she thought would fit but that my mother would never give. How could she know she'd given herself away?

In the midst of this, one Sunday afternoon, Becca returned, brought by her mother who did not stay. Her stomach hung empty, a little looser around the middle. *How her mother could bring her back here when she knows what must have happened...*

"Hi Gewtie," she said when she saw me. She smiled easily but did not hold it as long as she could have. I imagined she could not have given birth more than a month or two ago and I wondered if she mourned the loss of something, even if she did not fully understand.

"Hi Becca," I said, embracing her and holding her tight. "It's nice to see you. How are you? How's your baby?"

"Oh, she's bootifuw. A bootifuw guwl." She beamed and I wondered, as I stared at her back in this place, congratulating her, if she understood what had happened. That her family had traded her in, kept only the part of her that worked for them.

* * *

I had stopped taking tea in the afternoons. I had never cared that much for tea, only for my time with Elizabeth. Without her there, my water got cold and I just wound up tossing it out. I read instead, or joined the jigsaw table when it wasn't too crowded. Sometimes, the aides let me go into the kitchen to do extra preparation for meals, and I passed my time chopping

The Shape of the Atmosphere

carrots and celery, surrounding myself with the yeasty magic of rising dough under moist towels.

Pope's recovery motivated mine, and while I hesitated to categorize myself as needing to recover, I knew that if I lost both Elizabeth and him, I could not bear to be here alone. The color and shape of my evening pills had changed, and I wondered if the doctors and nurses too had noticed my "improvements."

"Therapy" was the same and the days involving group therapy were exhausting. I no longer volunteered to join the discussion. I let Arlene talk and the newer girl Cecelia explain how she'd managed to stop pulling her hair out on the left side of her head by imagining God's hands shielding her from herself. And yet this was progress.

I went to chapel each day in Elizabeth's place. I could not do it for my mother, but for Elizabeth I found it increasingly easy. I eventually even found myself praying vaguely about strength and forgiveness. About bringing Elizabeth back to herself, from wherever it was she'd been taken.

And then, as though in an epiphany from God, I realized I knew exactly where she was. In the darkness, waiting out the cold. And I realized too, that I'd been there, and knew how to get her back.

* * *

I eliminated a screaming fit like the one that landed me there the first time. Eventually I ruled out every option that would place me there as a patient. I knew instead, I had to enter as a visitor, a refugee. A spy. I was so preoccupied at the November social, Pope had gone to sit with Gladys and Samuel, returning only to give me a hug and kiss on the cheek before he left with the other men. Now the calendar marked Thanksgiving as four days away. Other than Christmas it was the lightest-staffed day in the estate. Aides and nurses went home to family; the patients ate enough turkey to knock them out good for the night. Everyone was calm and looking forward to the holidays, not yet riled up with excitement.

The day before Thanksgiving there was a wind storm, and ice weighed down branches and the main building went dark for most of the afternoon. I got to accompany Jessica down to the basement room where the breakers were. I held a flashlight while she flipped switches until someone yelled down the metal staircase that the lights had turned back on.

"So where are we exactly in relation to all the other basement rooms? Like hydro and shock?" I asked.

"Well, this is the maintenance side, but these hallways basically all connect down here. You can get mostly anywhere from down here. These hallways even stretch across the grounds to the men's side, but you didn't hear that from me. I wouldn't even know how to get there, but I do know it can be done. There are stairways like this one," she said as we climbed back up to the main floor, "scattered all around here. We got a map when we started but I never really studied it. More for emergencies or escapes than anything."

"Escapes? People have escaped before?"

"Tried anyway. Knowing the layout, someone always manages to cut them off. We find them before they find themselves. It's too easy to get lost down here. I once got stuck for over an hour with a group I was supposed to take to hydro my first week as an aide. We wound up somewhere near the furnace room. I tried getting back there one day and I couldn't even find it again."

"What about the wards?" I asked. "Do they connect from down here?"

"The wards? Um, well since Wards 3 and 4 are on another floor, they're all the same. These stairwells keep going. Just depends where you get off." When we entered the common room again, she blew her hair off her face with a quick upward puff. "You're awfully chatty today. New medicine treating you all right I see." She squeezed me on the shoulder and walked away, tapping Susan on the nose. "Check!"

We had come in from a door Jessica locked behind her. It wouldn't open and I didn't know how I was going to find a way up to the second floor or the third. Where I had been stuck to me, the heaviness of that place hanging from my memory each day. I had a feeling the darkness for Elizabeth was more literal. She had to be on Ward 4, somewhere I had never been.

Once there, I wouldn't even know where to look, and I possibly only had twenty minutes to search. If the student nurses were doing night checks, I could probably just arrange my pillows under the covers and they'd think

The Shape of the Atmosphere

nothing of it. But the seasoned nurses knew you had to not only see but touch for night checks. I'd heard how one time, an entire hallway had snuck out to the kitchen for a late night snack and had somehow managed to get ahold of a bottle of gin. Juniper had been one of them but no one else on Ward 2 now claimed involvement. They'd been dragged back and given extra shock for a week. No one snuck out again, but the nurses didn't take chances anymore.

I couldn't count the times I've been shaken awake by a nighttime check with no apology. I'd have to be savvy.

I was antsy the whole rest of the day. After dinner, Jessica swept the commons area, a job normally done by Elizabeth. I took a deep breath. I hoped I wasn't wrong about her.

"Jessica?" She turned and looked at me.

"Yes, Gertie?"

"I have a favor to ask you." I hesitated. "It's Elizabeth. I've just got to know if she's all right."

"I can't tell you that, Gertie. And plus, I don't go on those wards. My rotations are strictly limited to you all."

"I know where she is. And no one would ever know that you knew I knew." I waited. Jessica's face held, neutral, thoughtful. "Please."

Finally, she leaned on the broom handle and smiled. I knew I hadn't made a mistake.

* * *

"You on the rag or something?" Susan asked me the next morning. I sat wringing my hands, my knee bouncing.

"The what?" I said.

"The—never mind. You okay?" And I shrugged her off with a smile and a nod and she went back to coaxing Helen on using her voice for empowerment.

I remained distracted even during shock, forgetting I'd even gone until dinner when my sore jaw reminded me.

Jessica Dainty

At dinner, I ate little and left early. The Thanksgiving meal resembled last year's—turkey, cranberry sauce, corn, mashed potatoes, gravy. I avoided the pie.

After medication, I lingered to watch Jessica, Sarah, and two other more seasoned aides put on their jackets and wish each other a happy Thanksgiving. Jessica smiled at me as she left. A quick wink and she was gone.

The "recovered" girl from the chapel as well as a handful of student nurses remained. Nurse Irene came in to relieve Nurse Peters. The recover-ee would be ruthless, I had no doubt. Anyone who'd made her way out wouldn't risk screwing up and winding up back in. Nurse Irene and Nurse Peters never ran checks unless someone was under ordered surveillance. I could only hope I'd wind up with one of the student nurses checking in on me.

"Excuse me, my neck has been bothering me. Would it be possible to get an extra pillow just for tonight?" I asked.

I could see Nurse Irene watch from the corner of her eye as the student nurse turned to chapel girl. "Samantha, is that okay? Are they allowed extra pillows?"

"Ward 1 or 2?" Samantha asked.

"Two. Debutante Suites. I have full grounds privileges and have no demerits for the month. I just haven't slept well the past few nights. I'd really appreciate it."

Samantha flipped through her clipboard.

"Just give her the damn pillow, Samantha. There's nothing on that stupid clipboard about her anyway. It's check-in lists." I'd never heard Nurse Irene so harsh before. She sounded more like Nurse Peters.

Samantha glared at me but handed me a pillow from a closet behind the desk.

"Is this the firmest one you have? I think mine is too soft is the problem."

"It's the only one in here. Goodnight now." She spoke through her teeth and her nostrils bloomed at the edges.

In my room, I reached into the case to the bottom and felt a piece of tape and then something cool and smooth. I changed into my pajamas and then put on my white robe and slipped the key into my left pocket.

The Shape of the Atmosphere

"Check-in!"

I waited through four more check-ins, until the room lights were ordered off and the hallway was dimmed to just above dark. Then I waited three more. I lay in bed. For the first two check-ins, Samantha came in and pushed my shoulder down with each check. On the third, a student nurse entered and I could feel her looming over me but she did not touch. By the fifth check-in, she no longer fully entered. I could sense her eyeing my form through the filtered hallway light and leaving satisfied.

When the door latched after my seventh check-in, I arranged my pillows on my bed so, through the dark, it would appear I was still there. I waited near my door until I heard the footsteps walk back past from the other end. The nurses always worked their way in so that they could do a second check on the way back to make sure all doors were still closed and nothing suspicious had transpired.

I turned the handle slowly and cracked the door. The hall was dim but not dark. No one could see down Debutante Suites from inside the nurse's station, but if someone were out and about in the commons area, they could easily catch sight of my shadowed form or hear my bare feet on the floor. I squinted down the hallway and saw nobody. I closed my door soundlessly behind me and tiptoed away from the commons area to the end of my corridor. I'd never walked down this way. I did not have any close acquaintances on my corridor and did not visit many rooms other than my own and occasionally Elizabeth's, which was two hallways over on Society Lane.

The walk stretched on and I thought the hallway grew as I tried to reach the door on the far end. I slipped the key in and turned it. Jessica had come through. The key worked flawlessly and I found myself in a dark stairwell. Now that I was here, I didn't know what I had been thinking. I had no idea where to go once I'd climbed the flight of steps up to the next floor, or even that Ward 3 and 4 were on the next floor.

Luckily for me, the door on the next landing read W.3. I ascended one more flight to W.4. I took a deep breath and snuck in. There was nothing dim about this hallway. The place shapeless and colorless, pitch black. This was probably more what Elizabeth had been referring to when she said it was darker here, and I at least felt confident I was in the right place. I did not remember Ward 3 being so black, but I did not remember much other than a Negro girl being set through with fire.

There were numerous doors on this hallway, all closed and unmarked. I slipped out of this hall through the only opening and down into another. This corridor had no doors at all down the sides but opened up at the other end to a set of three. The first was a storage closet, the second was locked, and the third stretched out into another hallway, too quiet to contain anyone. My key worked on the second hallway, so I followed it. Single suspended bulbs hung from the ceiling. None was lit except one about halfway down and that one did not sustain itself but rather flickered eerily.

On either side of me were cells more akin to a jailhouse. At first glance, each looked empty, but as my eyes adjusted I could see human shapes taking up corners, crouched and blurry. As I neared the flickering light, I could see more. Some women were naked, some were covered in what could only be their own feces by the smell and color. The cells did not have toilets or sinks, but only a single mat somewhere in the square room.

I had passed at least fifteen cells and was nearing the end of the hallway. It became harder to see again, and I squinted into each as I passed trying to catch a glimpse of Elizabeth's slight form. I couldn't have much time left before my next check, before it was possible they'd know I was missing. Plus, did they do checks here too? More often? I had no idea how much time I had. And then I saw her. Standing, slenderer than ever in the exact center of her barred room.

"Elizabeth!" I tried to whisper but my voice came out shrill. I rushed to her cell.

I heard rustling from the other cells and caught the outline of faces pushed between bars.

"Elizabeth, can you hear me? It's Gertie. Are you okay?" I pressed myself against the bars and reached my arm through. She made no reaction.

The only sound she made was a melodic rasp, like music coming through a bad speaker, in and then out. It was a lullaby, something about roses and thorns and sunshine. Her voice was far away.

The Shape of the Atmosphere

After a few minutes, I slumped against the bars and sat on the floor. The hall smelled and I retched for a second at the thought of what I could be sitting on, but in the end I didn't care.

"Gertie. Is that you?" Elizabeth's voice crackled, a voice struggling through static. I'd barely registered she'd stopped singing, and I wondered if for a moment I'd managed to float away on her song. I turned suddenly. She startled.

"Oh, Elizabeth. You've been gone so long. Are you okay in here? I've been so worried about you. How are you feeling?" My words came out in a rush and I could see I'd overwhelmed her.

"It's the time of year you know. How's the garden? Always this time of year." Her words were almost singsong, like her response was part of her lullaby, and she did not look at me, as though she didn't believe I was really there.

"What are they doing to you here? This is awful." I scrunched my nose as a patch of stale air hit me.

"I don't like the darkness. I've tried to get to the garden but they won't let me. It's too dark to see colors here. Are there colors where you are?" She had wandered over to one of the concrete walls and was running her finger along it. My stomach turned watching her. I should not have come.

"My Alexander loved the garden." She pressed both hands against the wall now, palms flat.

"Tell me about him." My words were desperate but non-threatening. I sat Indian-style and put my chin on my fists. She smiled and sat in front of me, mirroring my pose.

"Oh, he was a lovely boy. My husband, too. We would go to the park together and see the tulips. In Boston, have you ever been to the Gardens in Boston, when the flowers bloom? You can't ignore them, that's for sure! Even when he was a baby, Alexander would turn his head to try to smell them when I bent down, like he knew they were something special. First year he could walk, he tried to eat one!" Her voice lilted, and a laughter I'd never heard from her bubbled out. It seemed odd, but I had the immediate thought that maybe this was her real laugh and all the others some cheap facsimile.

I hesitated. She hadn't continued her story.

"I bet there are flowers everywhere where he is now, Elizabeth. Every single color."

Jessica Dainty

"I think so, too." She pounded the top of her knee with a fierce ball of fist. "God dammit, I hope so." I'd never heard her swear before, didn't think she even knew the words, and yet it seemed like the most real and honest sentence she'd ever said. She rose, with some effort to her feet, pushing her negligible weight onto one of her knees before managing to stand. She walked back over to the wall and placed her palms once more against the surface. I noticed there were scratches in the concrete. I couldn't remember if her nails had looked bloody. Too many things made too much sense.

"I know so," I offered. The words came too late and hung awkwardly in the space, connected to neither the words before nor after them. "Elizabeth, there are colors out there, tons of colors. You always make it back."

"I don't want those colors anymore. I don't want to go back." The darkness and her breathing suggested some kind of low-lying beast in the dim, building up to strike.

"Elizabeth, maybe I should go get someone?" I took a step away from the bars. The light flickered and she disappeared and reappeared from view. I thought of the satellite, disintegrating into nothing. With urgency, I stepped back and reached through toward her. "Come take my hand. It's all right."

She turned her head, her fragile neck, and looked at me. My eyes were adjusting, and I focused all my energy on seeing her. I could see the corners of her mouth turned up through the dim, but she was not smiling. She was in pain, and before I could say another word, before she could get to me or I could get to her, she had turned back to the wall, reeled her head back and slammed it against the concrete. I was surprised her slightness survived one blow, but she followed it with a second and a third and I could barely hear her say something about the darkness over the hollow thumps of contact.

The sickening thwacks even drowned out my own screams and the heave of vomit that somehow ran down my hands and arms when a moment ago it had not. I counted seven smacks in all and then a final, more hollow slump of her body to the floor. By the time I felt hands on me and heard the questions and panic fly around, Elizabeth stared up at me from half a skull, and I didn't know how I'd ever be able to see anything but this when I closed my eyes.

XIV

I woke up strapped to a bed in a room not my own. I heard and understood everything being asked me but I could not formulate my responses. I would simply start crying or begin to vomit again and they had to roll me onto my side so I did not choke and they had to dispose of two dead bodies, instead of just one.

At some point, I felt a sharp point in my arm and saw a glint of syringe and then things muffled and I slept.

I dreamt about my mother's pantry but it was full of her liquids, like a pool. I floated, trying to open the door, swimming toward the crack of light at the bottom. When I ran out of air, I breathed in and swallowed, drinking it down. The door opened. My father came in, carried me and put me in his and my mother's bed. My sister came in and curled up next to me, humming something like a lullaby in my ear. She was young, and her hand, when it reached for me, was smaller and fit inside mine easily.

And then no one was there, and I lay in my own bed, alone, my telescope spinning, my head dizzy, a sudden fierce pain in my side. I woke up screaming to a second round of unfamiliar hands on me and another glint of syringe.

This time I did not dream. If I did, it was only me, in a dark room, alone.

When I woke up the next morning I was in a room I did not recognize but it at least did not look like a basement. The sun came through my blinds and for the briefest of moments, the dream won out, and I almost thought all of it could have been a dream, the hidden key, the sneaking, Elizabeth. All of it. But my white robe hung on a chair to the side of my bed and held bloodstains like hardened confetti and my hands were freckled with rusty red. My mouth tasted like the night of Bobby and my mother on our foyer floor and I hated to be reminded of both of these tragedies at once.

The Shape of the Atmosphere

I was wearing a white dressing gown like my awful first day in the basement and my days at shock. I had no time to process, to mourn. My door opened. An aide opened my blinds and stormed out as disinterested as she had stormed in. A moment later, Nurse Peters came in, smiling.

"How are we doing this morning, Gertrude? Are we feeling alright?" Her tone held a hint of annoyance, as though I had brought whatever this was on myself.

"My head hurts. It's uncomfortable." I shifted my body. It ached and my head pounded as though I were the one who had smashed it against the wall. As I tried to sit up, something pulled at my side, like I was being cut open. I gasped.

"Lean back. We had to do a minor procedure on you. You were so hysterical after what happened, and over the past seventy-two hours you were not able to be consoled. Dr. Isaac proposed an oophorectomy, a procedure that is slowly being replaced by other methods but that in the past has shown very positive results. And by your calmness this morning, I'd say we made the right choice. Welcome back!"

I fingered my side. The tenderness astounded me, and when I lifted the dressing gown I saw black stitches stretching vertically across each side of my stomach.

"What is it?" I asked.

"Hmmm? Oh that'll heal up before you know it. A few weeks and you'll be back to your old self. Even better."

I leaned back on the bed, too fast and I sucked my breath in quickly, not willing to announce my pain in words. "Is Jessica here today?" I asked, afraid for the first time that, because I had been caught, she would be implicated somehow in what had happened.

"She has the holiday weekend off. She'll be back."

A weight lifted for the first time this morning, and I lay grateful that at least somebody had come out of this whole.

"We'll try to get you sitting up and out of this room in a wheelchair within a few days. For now, just relax. We'll take care of you."

I wanted to believe her. Right now, I did not have the strength or conviction not to. I squeezed my eyes shut, but Elizabeth was there with her broken head and gaping face, and I stared at the ceiling instead, until the room darkened once again, and I was gone.

*　*　*

"Sarah said you had the weekend off."

I'd woken up groggy eyed and drooling, but with Jessica sitting by my bedside. I was still in the unfamiliar room I'd been in since Elizabeth, but I sat, lucid enough to wonder where I was.

"I did, but I heard what happened. Oh, how horrible this must have been for you." She would have gone on, I could tell, but Nurse Peters came up behind her.

"Eat up now, dearie." And Nurse Peters was gone as quickly as she had come, like my mother dropping something off in my father's office. I squinted at the tray. Oatmeal, lumpy and no longer steaming, a cup of coffee similar in its lack of heat when I touched the side of the mug. As opposite to the breakfasts I'd had in Ward 3 during my insulin treatment as it could possibly be. While the other meals had been part of the torture of that treatment, this was more threatening. It said, *we no longer care what you get, but you will take it*.

I rolled my eyes back to Jessica. I hadn't liked her on my first day, possibly because as the first person I'd interacted with she represented this awful change of life to me. She was the face of Willow Estate and my standing naked in a cold basement room and of that glaring eye of the drain, of Arlene eating her hair in front of me. But now she whispered to me, and her eyes were a soft brown, like the fur of a small copper-colored animal, and she called me Gertie. And she'd come back for me, the only person so far in this place who had come back for me.

And yet a funnel of pain swirled in the recesses of my chest, and though it was not quite sadness or loneliness or fear, a forcible grief consumed me. I wanted my mother. Not my father or sister. They were gone, I knew and there was no hope for them. Nor for Elizabeth. Jessica was comforting and nice, a friend in a place I'd had only a few, but she was not family. My mother was left. She was real. She was alive. Her blood was warm

The Shape of the Atmosphere

and flowing. Her heart pumped and her arms could envelop me. And my urge for her was greater than any of the awfulness I'd experienced here.

But she was not coming. She did not want me.

I leaned back onto my bed, turning my face toward the ceiling. "Would you sing to me?" I did not look, but a broken hum crept along the space between us. It was not a song I recognized and it only lasted a few seconds before the silence took over again.

I rolled onto my side and could feel the pull of my stitches and I could smell the sourness of my bedding, from being stagnant however many days.

"Will someone change my bed before lights out?" I asked. I could sense her body moving, that she would be going soon.

Jessica did not say anything, and I knew she had gone. I began to doubt whether she had actually been there at all. Time was a swirling funnel, and I did not know how far I'd gone or how far I had yet to go to be done. If someone offered me my freedom if I could say what day it was, I'd have failed, re-sentencing myself.

"How are we feeling today?" Nurse Peters came back in, blocking my swirl downward. "Would you like to try a trip around the ward in a chair? We'd like you to get up and around today, Gertrude. Sarah will take you for a walk outside. Perhaps you'd like to visit the garden?"

"The hanging tree," I said, instantaneously. "The one that hangs down and hides. That's where I'd like to go."

I didn't think I'd been awake more than a handful of minutes at a time since they'd brought me back here, done to me whatever it is they had done. My thoughts were murky and my head felt heavy and swollen, like a full round pumpkin, so that I imagined I could simply pluck it off and carry it. That that would be easier to manage.

I was about to ask if someone could help me pull it off, but I realized in time the absurdity of this, as the room came back into focus and the faces firmly placed me back in my current setting. My hands trembled and I wanted something to stabilize them, to distract me from how close I'd really come to insanity, thinking my head was a pumpkin. I remember my mother coming out of the dentist's office once convinced my sister and I were pineapples, her cheeks puffy with gauze, her eyes glazed over just enough for us to know she was not quite herself. That she'd had something akin to her pantry liquids. I breathed deeply, satisfied to think that whatever flowed into my arm, whatever effect the medication had on me caused my confusion. Not myself.

    I cocooned myself in the ugly sour blanket and slipped on my loafers.

    "Do I have to take this with me?" I pointed at the bag which hung attached to my arm by a twirling translucent wire that almost looked like pure liquid spiraling down in midair.

    Nurse Peters smiled, and, taking my wrist, pulled the needle out painlessly. "Have a nice walk, dear. Some fresh air will be just the thing." She patted my cheek in a way that was meant, I'm sure, to be affectionate, but it reminded me too much of her enforcing grip after my insulin treatment, when she had held my mouth open and then shut against my will.

    Nurse Peters helped me into a wheelchair and left me in the hallway. Sarah eventually came and she pushed me onward without speaking.

    As we walked, with no one in front of me, I imagined I really was leaving the building behind, wondering what it would be like to walk out and know I did not have to go back. Instead, I felt tethered, like I pulled against some unseen rope, or as though the needle had thread all the way through me and I was tied to this place, from the inside.

    The air nipped at my ears and I was glad that I'd brought the blanket. The grass browned in places and a slight frost whitened the tips at the top of the hill, but otherwise, the grounds were pristine, as though someone had cut each blade by hand, to be exact. I imagined such a thing would be a never-ending process, as by the time he or she got to the end, the grass at the beginning would already be longer once more than the grass at the end. He would have to cut the first blades shortest and leave each section gradually longer so that, when he finished, they would all be the same length. I exhausted myself just thinking about it.

    The ride up the path jarred me, and I clutched my sides trying to steady myself so my stitches didn't rip.

    The tree looked hungry, its branches bare and skinny like Elizabeth's frail fingers and bony shoulder blades. There was no wind today, and the branches hung eerily still. When they moved it was as though they were

The Shape of the Atmosphere

shivering of their own accord, rather than being moved from some outside force. As I got closer I saw that a few stubborn leaves still clung to one or two of the branches. I stood cautiously, one hand on the wheelchair, and plucked them off, the ones I could reach, one by one and watched them fall to the ground.

I wondered if Pope could see me today from the window in his ward, but I did not look for him. Elizabeth had left me and soon he would too. And then I would have nothing but Sarah's detachment, Dr. Isaac's career ambition, and Nurse Peters' iron grip. Jessica was kind but her interaction was limited by our positions to each other within these walls. She would never be to me what others had been, though I was still grateful for her.

"What day is it?"

"It's December, if that tells you anything. You've been out of it for a while."

I nodded and looked up at the leaves I hadn't been able to reach. There were so many things I hadn't been able to reach.

"I'm not going crazy, but I am going to scream now. Just thought I'd let you know."

Sarah blinked at me but said nothing and I reeled my head back and pushed my voice out from as low as possible. Then I took another breath and did it again. My voice was not high pitched and sobbing but full of a gravity I could not claim as maturity or wisdom. Possibly pain, but it felt too heavy for even that, and I wished Elizabeth had screamed when she was killing herself so that I could know she was releasing the awfulness inside of her. But she pounded her brains open silently, the wall's unforgiving brick offering the only noise, hollow sickening thwumps that I never thought could have been sustained for as long as she was able to.

I sat breathless and hoarse, my sides aching, my throat burning from the cold air and sharp intakes of breath between releases. The tree could not hide me today and I did not make it. I sat unconcerned of my surroundings. I stood fully up, releasing the support of my wheelchair. I did not care about the ripping pain at my sides. I kicked at the trunk. I scratched with my fingernails until two of them bled. I could not keep it inside anymore, and I cried selfishly for myself because I knew crying for anything or anyone else would change nothing.

Jessica Dainty

"Time to head back." Sarah's voice was soft, and she had said nothing the entire time we had been out here. Sarah had enough kindness or detachment, I didn't really care which, to stand just outside the inner sanctuary of the tree where she could see inside without fully intruding. For the first time, I'd felt as though I'd been left alone, in a good way. I had been me, and even though I was not entirely sure who me was, not anymore, if I ever had, I knew somehow then that I would eventually know. That this place could strip me of my clothes, my physical rights, even take something from inside of me without my knowledge or permission, but that they would not strip me of me.

I'd witnessed two more of Elizabeth's still spells right before she had been taken away, and watched her body slump down heavy at the end. For the first few seconds, before she fully came to, I could see this amazing thing in her eyes, before she absorbed the white walls and the doily draped tables of the commons area. This amazing thing, I was almost certain of it, was life. I could not remember if I'd seen any flashes of it that last night, other than maybe in the brief seconds she sat in front of me like a schoolgirl, talking about Alexander. The end events overwhelmed my memory and I hated that they would forever be what I saw first when I thought of Elizabeth, of my adolescence, of what had become of my life. But I knew she would want me to charge forward. To take those pieces of life she may have dropped along the way. And make something of them.

* * *

Finally, after about two weeks, they sent me back to my room on Debutante Suites. I could walk short lengths at a time now before needing to sit back down, and I rarely used the wheelchair. I stayed in the white robe though, a clean one, as pulling clothes over my head and bending over were too painful still. I often sat in the commons area most of the day. I'd been given a pass on group exercise and recreation time. I instead looked forward to the coming social, when I could talk to Pope.

At the next social, though, Pope was not there. I had regained my lucidity enough to know shapes and colors without fail, the formation of

The Shape of the Atmosphere

particular faces, and I did not see his. His face of soft angles, if such a thing were possible, like a knife edge sticky with dough.

The next day though, while I sat looking out at a powdered naked willow tree, visiting faces scattered around the room, the ground outside dusted as though through a sifter, I heard a stutterless voice and part of me elated to know he'd be there when I turned around, but the other part of me broke in a way that I knew was irreparable because now I was truly alone in this place.

"Hi, Gertie. May I have the honor of visiting you on this fine day?"

I couldn't help but smile. He wore a pea coat and a hat like a newsboy and like my father wore the early mornings when he played golf. He looked healthy and happy. And he had voluntarily come back to this place, for no other reason than to see me.

"I'm not much for company these days. But I'm glad to see you."

We walked out on the grounds. I shivered coatless. The coat Elizabeth had given me scratched at my skin like it would burn right through. Pope gave me his, but I was too cold to regain any sort of comfort. Still, the walk was nice, and the grounds, though more gray than white, felt light with the snow, and I had a sense of spring coming, though it was still months away.

"I don't want to be here when the garden blooms. I need to be out by spring."

"Has your mother come—" Pope stopped short at my shaking head.

"I know I won't be. I just want to be."

We walked in silence. Our assigned aide dawdled a few dozen yards behind us. We weren't two crazies after all. One was a mature, healthy male now.

"Did you hear about Elizabeth?"

"Vaguely. I heard you saw. And that she—well. You saw. I'm sorry."

The sky was swirled with clouds like bands of heavy cream, and I wondered if it rained if it would be thick enough to swallow us whole.

"I'll come visit you every Sunday, Gertie. I promise I will."

Fifteen minutes later, he left and I returned to my window, the willow tree both still and trembling and me mesmerized by how it could be both at once.

XV

To my surprise, Susan began eating lunch and dinner with me. She stood in front of my stall in the mornings, blocking me from others. She faced away from me in the showers, but always took up enough space so that no one else wanted to share our trickle of a waterfall. She pulled a chunk of her hair out on purpose to be placed in my new therapy group for those with any connection to violent outbursts. Elizabeth was my connection.

After two weeks, after Christmas had passed to my purposeful avoidance and 1959 became a reality in my world of uncertainties, I couldn't resist anymore.

"Why are you being so nice to me?" She sat near me, in an adjacent chair, though facing away, as though following me but not wanting me to suspect.

She closed her book and rested it in her lap. A gilded face stared out at me from the cover.

"I'd want someone to be nice to me. Had I been the one to be there." She paused, bracing to continue, but then just shrugged, as if to say *sorry, that's all I've got.*

"You thought Elizabeth was flippant. You didn't even like her."

"I loved Elizabeth." She spat it out like flame, the words burning a truth between us, and I knew my mother would have been right about Susan, had she met her. Susan's head was down now, her hair shielding her face but not enough to keep the sound of sniffling from passing through.

I moved toward her, this woman carrying a grief not entirely unlike my own, and sat on the arm of her chair. I took her hand in mine. Her fingers were skinny and bordered on cold. I lifted her chin, through her barrier of hair, with my finger, as Pope did to me. Her eyes were velvet purple, normally blue but deepened as though by the richness of grief, and I decided right then that Susan was beautiful.

The Shape of the Atmosphere

"I loved her, too," I said. And we sat there together, our hands keeping the other's still, until the room shadowed into itself and we were called to bed.

* * *

That night in bed, I did not think of Elizabeth for long. I closed my eyes and saw Susan's eyes, her pain. I thought of Helen and her *apples*, of Juniper and her five-day stays. I did think of Elizabeth and her topical cheerfulness and what must have been a suffocating inner turmoil. But mostly I thought of the ones who were left, of the women I passed day by day. Of the Gladyses whose families could not be bothered, of the Arlenes who were just too different to stomach in public.

We were offered etiquette and typing lessons under the title of therapy. They framed us. We were encouraged to speak in our talking therapy sessions, group and private, but the listeners always held their molds up between us and them, sifting our words through and pressing them into shapes they liked to look at before throwing them back to us. We sat confused, unsure of what to do with what we now held.

I woke up with a plan.

"Nurse Peters. I'd like permission to start a ward journal. A newspaper of sorts. I don't want to sew. There's no more room for my cross stitch in the nurse's station. I know there are typewriters here. Pope—Clement—says that the men receive a newspaper page of all the sports news once a month. Is there maybe even a press?"

Nurse Peters eyed me like a suspicious mass in a corner, as though she were too far away to discern whether I was a teddy bear or a rat.

"There is a press, though I'm not sure it works anymore. The typewriters are open for your use during free time however. We encourage self-expression and creativity. We have the supplies, but don't expect any help. You want to do it, you're in charge." She rifled through a stack of papers and pulled out a clean sheet. "Get at least fifteen signatures of women who would be willing to help you, and I'll approve it. Now leave me alone. It's my lunch break."

Jessica Dainty

I clutched the white sheet like the grail. It glowed in my hands.

The week before Christmas, we had sat around the radio and listened to President Eisenhower talk to us from outer space.

"This is the President of the United States speaking. Through the marvels of scientific advance, my voice is coming to you via a satellite circling in outer space. My message is a simple one: Through this unique means I convey to you and all mankind, America's wish for peace on Earth and goodwill toward men everywhere."

Goodwill toward men. I had looked around me. At the Beccas and Susans and Helens that were no doubt hidden behind walls all over the state, the country. The world. What about their goodwill?

I hadn't even spoken to fifteen women in my year-plus stay here, but now I knew where to start.

"Susan." I approached her, breathless. "I need your help."

* * *

By the end of the next day, we had thirteen signatures. I'd been gone so long and, since I'd been back, so consumed with Elizabeth that I did not know Gladys had been moved. Jessica told me she was on Ward 3, only because she needed more constant attention. She had fallen ill before the new year, something in her blood. There was no way to get her signature, I was told.

I turned away.

"I'll sign it." The words kissed my cheek as they floated past, toward my ears. "After all, make your paper too biased, and no one will ever take it seriously." Her signature smiled at me from the page.

* * *

Helen did not say anything as I spoke, nor did she say anything as the pen proclaimed commitment on her behalf. I expected to read *apples*, but a remarkably regal script whispered to me, that, yes, she did in fact have something else to say.

The Shape of the Atmosphere

* * *

Juniper, on one of her return visits, was the one who gave us the name.

"How about Suite Women," Arlene said, sucking on the end of her hair like she could get marrow out of it.

"The Debutantes?"

"Listen!? With an exclamation point?"

"Stories from the Inside?"

The words built slowly like a rising tide.

"Remember last Christmas in the kitchen?" It was Juniper this time. "That song. That Jim Reeves guy song?"

* * *

Juniper wasn't here anymore when a week later, the first issue came out, *Four Walls*, in giant letters at the top.

The first issue was dedicated to the memory of Elizabeth Jacobsen. Women wrote letters, apologies, some signed in openness, others left their submissions blank in anonymity. Susan left hers unsigned, but the flowing rhymes, the poetic professions, the mention of her form—*her pale skin, our minds akin, alas she never knew me*—could only have come from someone who watched her, loved her. Jessica's was also anonymous, for obvious reasons, though she laid no claim to her part in the night's events. Hers simply read, *What would have become of you if no one had been there to watch you go?*

I did not submit a letter but instead concerned myself with the facts portion of the publication.

> *Elizabeth Jacobsen, overcome by her situation, took her fate into her own hands. After the death of her son, Mrs. Jacobsen could not sustain herself in happiness. This woman, light and airy like a bird, took wing and flew away. She loved the garden, sewing, and tea. We will miss her.*

Jessica Dainty

The day after the first issue of *Four Walls* came out in early February, I found a copy of Elizabeth's file under my pillow. I pored over it through enough check-ins for the sun to both darken and peak out again, as though watching from behind a curtain for me to finish before showing itself fully.

Elizabeth had been in and out of hospitals since she was thirteen. She was married at sixteen, had her son, and when he was not quite two, while he splashed and sprayed and bubbled and laughed, she went still, the bathwater rushing like a dream. When she came to, the roles had shifted, and he was the still one, eyes open and staring. The file did not say all of this, but I could not envision it any other way, how awful it would have been to flicker to consciousness only to have the world blind you in such a way.

People carried her away but men were sent to jail, women to hospitals and she spent a year at a state institution where they bled her to the point of needing to be revived. She had not been without drugs, shock, hydro, guilt, or more than ninety pounds on her frame since she was a teenager. Since before the atmosphere had been penetrated by man, since before we could do so much outside of this world, but never enough inside.

When I went back to my room that night, the file was gone, no doubt back where it had come from. I read and re-read the pages in my mind, the words a glowing stretch of shapes on the insides of my closed eyes. Elizabeth's story was only one. And she was gone. I needed the others to tell theirs before it was too late.

Susan was the first to volunteer. The next issue a month later, in March, whispered nothing like the dear departings the previous had. This one instead screamed atrocities, rape, abuse, and then quieted to the warmth of friendship, of hope, before crescendo-ing again into a bellow of hydro, shots, and shock.

There were only five copies of the first issue, which we had passed around the commons area. I had typed them all myself, during free time, leaning over the scribbles the women around me had handed in. This past month, Susan and Helen, along with a revolving handful of others, typed out our confessions, and the clicking filled the air like its own language. We managed over twenty-five copies before our "release date."

The Shape of the Atmosphere

The bridge table begged for players. The jigsaw puzzle mourned in pieces. Women punctuated the room in quiet balls of intensity. Nurse Peters' face burned red for a week. We had extra time in the bathroom. Women enjoyed privileges they didn't have recorded as theirs. Nurse Peters' nerves benefited us. She couldn't shut us down, not this soon. She would be the one surrendering, recognizing something dangerous in what we were saying, and since we were not the ones incriminated in the end, she couldn't take that chance. My intent had never been to indict Willow Estate or the staff. Just to let these women speak.

Jessica fawned over the paper. She promised to talk to Dr. Isaac about getting permission for edited versions to be sent out to town newspapers, larger news sources. Other hospitals around the country were doing similar things and the stories were helping with funding as well as research. But Dr. Isaac's eyes were as red as Nurse Peters' cheeks, and our words remained inside our four walls.

I decided to make a poetry issue next and the one half shelf of Shakespeare lay in disarray for three weeks. Drafts desecrated the trash cans, the floors immediately around their perimeters. Crazy women spewed their words out in shattered sentences hoping for beauty, and when the next issue came out, each line-break, each not-quite-right rhyme, glistened with something lovely.

All during this time, Nurse Peters' face took on a permanent likeness to a raspberry. She never spoke to me during this time, except for once.

"I underestimated you, Gertie." The fire oozed from her pores so that I found myself sweating even after she had walked away. This was the first time she had not called me Gertrude. And yet she was not entirely angry. There was an implied nod of respect in her words, and I couldn't help but hold my chin a bit higher the rest of the day.

Susan hounded me during these times. She was with me in the dining hall, in my room during the day, in the common area. She even followed me out to the willow tree a couple times.

"We can do more. This is good," she'd say, slapping the single long page of our monthly publication, "but it's only the beginning."

Jessica Dainty

Then, one day, after May's issue, our fourth, Dr. Isaac's umpteenth refusal to allow our words to reach beyond our walls, she placed a dagger of chance between us:

"Do you know anybody useful on the outside?"

May's issue was dedicated to our lives before Willow Estate. From students, to typists, to housewives, from happiness to the moment of betrayal—luncheons that wound up being black cars and men you didn't know tearing you away, arranged expulsions from school so that you had nowhere else to go but where your family demanded, or a cool October morning, essentially your birthday, and your father's black bag that you wished you'd realized sooner still smelled of his aftershave but now smelled only of the present.

My first submission to my own publication, and I left it anonymous. When Pope visited, and he asked if I'd ever submitted anything, I lied and said no. I didn't want to spend my time trying to remember if my father smelled more of lavender or musk, because I couldn't remember, and I didn't want him to watch me cry, not when I needed him to know I was happy to see him. Plus, I had more important business to discuss.

The secret to keeping a secret at Willow Estate was to do it in the open. If we had gone out to the willow tree, we would have been chaperoned directly, someone within earshot, pretending not to listen but really with nothing else to do but exactly that. Instead, we stayed in the bustle of the commons room, the other conversations mixing together like ingredients so that all one could hear was a completeness of chaos.

Pope had brought me a small painting, colorful and blurred, like he had smeared his hand across it before it was quite dry. It suggested a farm, a barn, red and glowering, white and black splotches of cow, a reflection of water. I squinted at it, wanting to like it, but it was my least favorite of any he'd done. I smiled at it, avoiding him, but he seemed satisfied. I leaned forward to kiss his cheek but instead whispered in his ear.

"I am going to give you an issue. Put it in your pocket and do not take it out until you are home. I've written on the back of it. Let me know next week if you can help."

The Shape of the Atmosphere

I avoided his eyes for a minute. I'd told him of the paper briefly on his first visit after we started it, but Nurse Peters banned any sharing of the paper with visitors. In fact, I was sent to a day of solitary, something I didn't even know existed on Ward 2 after exploding the news of it to Pope on that first Sunday.

"*Four Walls* is a gift for those inside here. Not for those out there. You'll remember that now." And the lights went out for a day.

This day, Pope slipped a copy of the first issue calmly into his pocket as though it were as innocuous as a pack of gum, the contraband I imagined would burn a hole through his pocket before he could get home. My note simply said I'd slip him the others each week until he had them all. We wanted them shared, published, broadcast. And though Pope didn't seem to hate this place as many of the voices on the page did, his relief to be out emanated from every part of him. He was a walking exhale. Though be it a stutterless one at that.

When he left, he kissed me without hesitation. People stared. Susan smiled. I kept my eyes open, but everything else fell into his lips. I had the sudden urge to write a poem.

* * *

Toward the end of May, Explorer 1 ceased transmission. The man on the news had shaved his mustache, and I did not like his lips, the way they flapped excessively with each word. No burnups, no disintegration.

"Apparently the batteries died," the news anchor bantered, his co-anchor laughing. "But not before discovering what professionals are calling the Van Allen Belt," he continued once the laughter subsided.

Apparently we were surrounded by a belt of radiation, held in place by our own magnetic field. Tiny particles, trapped. I imagined them bouncing around, pressing against the invisible nets holding them in place, watching all these objects shoot past them, out of the atmosphere, while they hung, suspended. Left behind.

Jessica Dainty

* * *

My weeks had not changed much, except now during my free time, I did not sit alone or with Elizabeth off to the side. Now I was bombarded by scribbles on sheets of paper, questions, timid suggestions. I no longer could say I had only spoken to a handful of people on my ward. There was no one I had not talked to, no one whose name I could not pull forward from somewhere in my brain, given enough time, even after shock.

I had missed the budding of the willow tree and when I finally made my way there, its leaves waved at me in excitement and I fretted to think of how I could not have noticed.

The garden boasted its brightest colors since I'd come and I imagined Elizabeth, when no one looked, appeared and stroked the leaves, whispered to the blossoming yellows and reds. I could almost see her there, dwarfed by her giant hat, smiling and wiping her sweatless forehead.

But other people had taken up her fallen trowel, her brown-handled spade, and after a while I could no longer watch them dig into the earth with what so obviously should belong to her, dig down toward her into the broken, soft summer soil.

Given the amount of redness on Nurse Peters' and Dr. Isaac's faces, I decided the June issue should be an ode to Willow Estate. People who had thank yous, stories of progress, happy moments to share were to submit by the last day of May by bedtime. On the nineteenth, I had only three submissions in hand, one from Becca Donelson about her free week of grounds privileges and her special walks, which I had to pen myself as she spoke since I could not make out her handwriting. She hugged me afterward, excited because she'd never been famous before.

Two other women submitted stories on behalf of friends who had come and gone, left with a clean bill of health years ago.

With half a page of empty space, I approached Samantha, Ward 3 recover-ee.

"Sorry if it's none of my business, but I heard somewhere that you used to be…um…" I hesitated.

The Shape of the Atmosphere

"Well spit it out, Gertrude. I don't have all day." She said this as she filed her nails behind the nurses' station door, her feet up on the sill.

"One of us. I heard you used to be one of us." In her eyes, a storm brewed. "I was hoping maybe you'd be willing to submit something to the paper about your experience, seeing as you must be grateful, for your recovery and all."

She planted her feet on the ground and put the file on the table.

"I have nothing good to say about this place. I'm here because with their name on my record, I have nowhere else to go. And if you quote me on that, I'll make your life even more of a hell than it already is." She pushed past me and was gone.

I had no choice but to take up the cause myself. I wrote of Elizabeth and Pope, even of Susan toward the end. I mentioned briefly, my family life, my mother's pantry visits, and my sister and my odd estrangement considering we lived half a hallway apart. I wrote that, here, I found a family. The words stared back at me smugly, not untrue, but somehow depressing in their honesty, and I only hoped it was enough for Nurse Peters to take a breath and regain some paleness to her complexion.

I went to bed wondering what my life would be like now, had it not happened this way. Had Dad and Allison not left that afternoon, late, his sought-after watch not sitting in the pantry with my mother and her liquid secrets. Would we reach across the table now that as a human race we'd reached into space? Could we orbit a conversation now that we had orbited earth? Or would we all simply disintegrate as we tried to re-enter the atmosphere? Or be trapped like those new particles, unable to be anything but what we were?

I had no answers and I fell asleep, St. Christopher and my sister, wrapped in a crooked heart, limp on the floor beside me. My mother watched my dreams from inside a closed drawer.

* * *

Jessica Dainty

When the June issue came out, the font commanded the page. I had to handwrite the masthead to make the letters bigger, no one's story of praise enough to fill the space.

Still Nurse Peters downgraded to peach and even taped the month's issue up on the commons area bulletin board.

I was out of ideas, and I announced that July was an open submission issue. All entries were to be anonymous, no more than a handwritten page tops. I'd accept poems, confessions, whatever they wanted to give.

Pope was now caught up. He owned a contraband copy of each publication. On his next visit, I gave him the June issue, to complete his set. I wanted him to take a year's worth at once, a cycle of life as I saw it. In the meantime, he researched, memorizing names, looking up addresses. He agreed that starting locally was best.

"You've done a lot. Can I ask you to do one more thing?"

He answered, without stutter or hesitation. "Anything."

"I haven't received a letter in a long time."

The address was 376 Sparrow Street. Her name was Alice. He would go. I told him to pretend he was selling Bibles. My mother always loved the Word of God.

XVI

July meant mostly rain so far, while April had been surprisingly dry. The world of Willow Estate hung waterlogged. Everyone hummed with pent up energy. Women sat at windows, waiting for the sky to break open, for gold to fall down in rays. When it finally did, daily activities were canceled, and we set up the badminton net in the sloshy ground.

We re-entered, a study in brown, and were given a second shower visit before bedtime. One towel each took less to wash than a set of sheets each. They weren't really doing us any favors. We were never the sole beneficiaries, but we took it gladly, laughing and scrubbing, as though in a sprinkler, for fun.

Susan still shared showers with me, and the awkwardness of the bathroom, I have to say, had faded away after close to two years in this place. In fact, the days I entered the stall alone, I felt too exposed. I'd gotten used to the protection of other bodies near mine. There was comfort in shared discomfort.

Later that month, when the ground was a bit drier, the estate social was held outside for the first time since I'd been here. The male aides set up a grill well away from us and off limits. Still we could hear the sizzle of burgers and hot dogs, could smell the melting slices of cheese. We had potato chips and lemonade, cold strawberry gelatin for dessert with little marshmallows floating inside.

In an odd way, I found myself enjoying the socials more now that Pope was gone. Since I saw him each week, not so much rode on each visit. Before, I worked myself up for the brief time we would have together. Now, I played badminton and volleyball, talked with Susan. A group of us sat at a picnic table and braided each other's hair. Laughter once again became a regular part of my day, even the days with hydro and shock. I'd lost one friend in Elizabeth and gained a family of friends in the others around me. I

The Shape of the Atmosphere

still missed her, but with her frail frame gone, all these other potential relationships surfaced. Besides, unlike the unfairness of coincidence my family suffered, Elizabeth had wanted to go. Who am I to wish her back to somewhere she did not want to be?

Jonathan waved to me from across the way, and I smiled and waved back, nodding my acknowledgment. His hand left the air and I followed it to the small of Becca's back. There was a slight shudder of a reaction, an almost invisible recoil before her face fell back into her sloppy smile. A sudden, fierce knowledge attacked me and I bolted up off the picnic table.

"It was you!?" I screamed it. I did not care what they would do to me. I thought back sickeningly to the rush I'd felt when his hand had first touched me. How grateful I was now for that man and his refusal to give up the punch ladle. For Pope interrupting us. I shuddered to think how close I had come to taking a walk with him alone.

Jonathan stared at me, afraid. Not of me, I knew, not of my flailing arms and intent to hurt him, but of what my words could do to him.

"How could you do that to her! Look at her." I grabbed his face and pulled it toward Becca, who stood oblivious to my accusations. Before I could say anything else though, two sets of hands were on me, pulling me away. I did not fight. I did not want to lose more than I already had of myself, of the little bit of predictability I'd grown accustomed to. I latched my eyes onto Susan's as they dragged me away. I could see her face, the darkening curtain of understanding, and I was glad they did not get me over the hill before she punched him square in the groin.

* * *

To my amazement, I did not lose much. Extra shock. A few days of solitary. The worst of it was missing Sunday. Missing Pope.

The next visitation, when they allowed me to return to my "normal" schedule, I had nothing to give Pope. He had all of our issues. I instead sat, wringing my hands, wondering what news of my mother he might let fall from his stutterless, beautiful lips.

Jessica Dainty

Susan and I sat playing Rummikub. Susan never had any visitors. Once, before I came, her mother had tried to visit and Susan had tried to attack her with a brillo pad she'd stolen from the kitchen, she'd told me. Her family had not returned since.

"Good riddance," she'd said, but I could see her eye the room as it filled with familiar faces, people who came week after week. I wondered if she pretended, as I sometimes did, that they were my own family, coming to see me, to hug me, to take me home. I never asked. She wouldn't admit it even if she did.

But her disposition grew generally cheerier and she had begun letting me braid her hair, her wild curls winding mesmerizingly into twists and braids I imagined Elizabeth Taylor would turn green at. She sometimes even let Frances brush her cheeks rose, her lids blue or brown. I had already decided she was beautiful, but I could tell she was deciding it as well, and this made my stomach bubble over in a way it hadn't since my sister had told me I was bound for the type of beauty my mother had.

Pope came in late, only about fifteen minutes left until he would be ushered out, asked to leave as though he had a choice.

"I was starting to think you weren't coming."

He smiled. "You really thought I wouldn't come?"

"I don't know. Maybe you had bad news for me and thought it'd be easier to not come than to tell me." I said this jokingly but his face faltered, a silent stutter although his words stayed steady.

"I went to your house."

"And?"

"And your mother wasn't there."

"Did you leave a note, a message? Try again?"

"No, I mean she wasn't there. No one was."

"I don't understand."

"I looked in the windows and everything. The furniture was covered with white sheets. I don't think anyone's been there for a while."

I sat on the couch and he sat next to me. I didn't understand. The news hit me hard and missed me all at the same time. I felt like I was suspended, as though gravity had not yet decided if it would crash me to the ground.

The Shape of the Atmosphere

"Can you find her? That nurse, her name was, her name was… Ugh! I hate my stupid memory. Why do I remember the awful things best?" I put my face in my hands, but I was nowhere near crying and my breath made my face feel too hot. I sat up and leaned back into the couch.

"Way ahead of you, Gertie." Pope leaned back too and took my hand. "There was a pile of newspapers on the front step, at least three weeks' worth, so I waited around for the paper boy. He knew nothing, but your neighbor, oh what did he say his name was, Mr. Perkins, he said that she left about a month ago. That she looked well, walked down the stairs with help from two men in white coats, but then had been wheeled to a car in a wheel chair."

"Mr. Perkins grew tomatoes in his garden. Always gave them to us when they were still too green. My mother mushed them up and mixed them in the dirt of our own garden. She thought it might work like fertilizer. We ended up with maggots in our turnips."

"Are you even listening to me? Your mother was taken somewhere, to a sort of home or hospital I think. None of your neighbors know where, but they did give me the number of her old nurse. I guess Mr. Perkins checked on your mom during her days off and he had her number for emergency purposes. I haven't called yet. Should I or do you want to?"

"Do you think she'll tell me anything?"

"I don't know. I guess it probably depends on what's wrong with your mother."

"Maybe you should call then. We can think of a reason why it's crucial for you to know. Maybe…maybe…" I closed my eyes. "Maybe tell them I'm all better and being released. That her daughter needs to see her."

Earlier in the year, right after I returned from the darkness, our country had become a union of forty-nine rather than forty-eight. Some Russian territory that wasn't even directly connected to any other part of the United States. Pope had told me it was a land of ice, that a people called Inuits lived there and killed whales with their bare hands.

I'd marveled at the chasms between everything. Between the knowledge and power to send a metal object into space and the lack of resources so that an entire people lived in houses of ice. Between Ward 1 and Ward 4, between my mother and me. Between the sane and the not.

Jessica Dainty

Now I thought of Elizabeth and Susan, and all the stories I had heard since my personal four walls had exploded open to include all the walls of those around me, and I realized they weren't so much as chasms but wide open roads with no obstacles that we simply decided were not worth our time.

When Pope left, I said my first prayers of the new year, technically closer to the end than the beginning. I prayed for forgiveness for my lies, and that my mother was well enough that I didn't have to see her. Perhaps some things weren't meant to be crossed.

* * *

The August issue of *Four Walls* spoke its words from regular sized font and a full page. There were poems, confessions, everything I had suggested was welcome. The paper was a safe place where our voices were both released but held. Women wrote of tragedy and happiness, but mostly of things that were not proud or boastful, things that had sat in corners of souls and collected the heavy dust of guilt and shame.

> *When I was twelve I killed a man*
> *Not in life but in mind*
> *When I was fourteen, I did it again*
> *A father of five that was kind*
> *I wondered what part of me wanted to hate*
> *And for years, I had no confession*
> *And then at eighteen, it was too late*
> *My mind made real my transgression*
> *I bloodied my hands and bloodied my fate*
> *My mother cried when they took me away*
> *I like to pretend I'm sorry for what I've done*
> *But I'm happier here, if I may*

One wrote a letter to her daughter, admitting her father was not her father. That instead of divorcing her, he had sent her away when he'd found out. Another confided that she'd tried to end her life seventeen times.

The Shape of the Atmosphere

Not all of the entries were about misery though. Francis suggested we start a news section at the bottom corner of the paper. Here we highlighted only the nice things we heard on the news, like the Alaska statehood, the launching of new satellites, sports events, and celebrity weddings.

Juniper, on her last stay, pushed for a gossip column, but since we figured our stories were gossip enough we started a horoscope instead. We only covered predictions for the current sign because we lacked the space to cover everyone at once, and we only predicted niceties. Wealth, health, fortune, forgiveness, recovery. Women loved using their voices and being told by another's that everything was going to be alright.

Still, when the August paper found Nurse Peters' hands, her face remained red. She called a ward meeting during free time.

We sat and stood, filling the commons area with anticipation and awkwardness.

"I want to know who submitted this entry." She pointed to a block of text. "Who wrote this?"

Her fingers choked a story at the bottom left of the page, her nail turning white from pressure. It was an entry about rape within our own walls. About abused power and corruption, about an innocence taken away. Becca had not come to me. I had written it on my own, on her behalf, whether she wanted it or not, whether she even knew that what had happened to her had been what it was.

We all looked at each other. Or I should say, I looked around at everyone looking at me.

"Gertrude, who submitted this to you?"

"The submissions are anonymous to those who want anonymity, Nurse Peters. I don't know who submitted it."

"*Four Walls* is suspended until I find out who wrote this."

Objections rang out in a wave of muffled gasps.

"But you can't do that. You said we had free press. How are we supposed to feel safe expressing ourselves if you can do this?"

"Gertrude MacLarsen, you open your mouth again and it's extra shock for a week."

Jessica Dainty

My mother would have slapped me. She would have slapped me and sent me to my room for a month. I stared right at the beet redness that had become Nurse Peters. I cocked my head to the side, and without a sound, I opened my mouth as wide as I could. And glared.

* * *

I had been drugged and taken from a room at Willow but never dragged from a room, by a hand on my ear, like I was seven again in Catholic School and Mother Mary had caught me sticking gum under my desk.

I spent what I can only imagine was more than two days in isolation. The room was white with a mat in one corner and a toilet in the other. The lights were off during the day and turned on glaringly at night, at least that's what it seemed like before I lost track of the time, of the day, of whether I was really there or somewhere else, floating above the world like Explorer or Sputnik or whichever one was still out there circling somewhere.

Water appeared somewhere between head nods and eye blinks. I never saw food. I pinched the skin on my arms and wondered how long it would take before I was a bird like Elizabeth, my bones thin and hollow. I wondered if I could fly.

"Are you ready to tell me who gave you that submission, Gertrude?"

A voice floated through the door. I reached out to touch it.

"I don't know who sent it. I swear."

"Very well then." And the voice was gone again, along with the smell of something that hinted of pot roast and gravy, maybe even a tab of butter.

* * *

I remembered light so bright I knew I had made it to the sun, surprised at its incredible whiteness.

"I always thought the sun would be orange. Or at least yellow. Why is it white?"

The Shape of the Atmosphere

And then the coolness of refreshing water on my head, a wet towel on my temples. And then a squeezing that seemed distantly familiar, the taste of leather between my teeth.

"We're too close to the sun. It's too hot," I tried to say through the slab of hide in my mouth, but the fire had already begun to burn and I blacked out watching my body twist and float above me, toward the flames.

* * *

"Why is this so important to you?" I asked. The light was still bright, and I didn't remember eating, but I had a moment of lucidity where I knew what was being done to me.

But Nurse Peters was not there. Instead there were three aides I did not recognize, plus Sarah.

"Just relax, Gertie," she said, her voice bordering eerily on kind. She wiped my forehead with a cloth.

"Why is she doing this? I don't know who sent the story. Why does it matter anyway?"

The towel washed over me in a chill of coolness but it felt good.

"That's enough, thank you." Sarah's voice reached me from too far away, but I could sense that we were alone now. She was next to me, her voice closer. I reached out as though I could hold onto it. "I don't know. But things are different here. Less staff, more patients. The state doesn't give us any funds because we're privately owned. We rely on patients and reputation. Nurse Peters cares what people think. That's my only guess."

"But no one reads this but us." I pushed her hand away. The water was too much.

"No one did read it but us."

"What do you mean?" My tongue crumbled like a pile of sawdust in my mouth. I choked on it. Sarah sat me up.

"One of the papers got out."

Why would Pope do that? I'd asked him to wait. I'd wanted him to wait.

"The one praising Willow Estate got published."

Jessica Dainty

"But why? Who?" Pope wouldn't do that. If he was going to publish one before we agreed, he'd have made it worthwhile. "Wait, why are you all of a sudden being nice to me?" Sarah smiled, or at least appeared to. Her face looked like runny eggs, a yellow melting mess. "I'm hungry," I said.

"I'll get you something."

She stood with her back to me. "Nurse Peters," she said.

"What?"

"You asked a question. Nurse Peters. Think about it after you eat. You're smart, I bet you can figure it out."

She handed me a glass of something orange. The sourness overwhelmed me and I immediately thought I would vomit.

"I know it's rough, but try to finish it. It'll help. And please don't mention me. I don't want to be mean, but I know about Jessica and the key. If someone knows about me, they'll know about that too."

The room melted around me, and I spewed orange onto the cold, concrete floor, no eye-like drain to drink it down.

*　*　*

I ate something akin to oatmeal the next time aides came in the room. The room no longer melted. Instead it vibrated, the edges blurred and humming. Sarah didn't return, and I didn't recognize any other faces that came in and out over what had to be a day's time, though I wouldn't have known the difference between a year and an hour.

I sat up on my own, my body feeling pulled down as though the ground were a magnet and I metal.

I remembered Sarah but didn't trust myself enough to determine whether her words were real or imaginings. What would Nurse Peters have to do with any of this? She hated the paper. What did she say about the publication getting out?

I looked around. I was somewhere in the basement, no doubt, but I didn't know where. My body was gummy, moist in a bad way and sour. I pinched my skin again and it stayed peaked before melting back into itself, like dry dough. I thought for a second that I was in an oven, being baked, but

The Shape of the Atmosphere

I was more lucid now, and I knew I wasn't. That something far more unjust was going on.

"When can I go back to my room?"

The aide I directed my words at stood like stone, her eyes wide like I had shot her through.

"Um, I'll find out for you."

She hurried away, and when she came back, Nurse Peters came with her.

"Hello, Gertrude. How are we doing? I'm real sorry about all of this. Do you remember what happened?"

"You asked who submitted the story and I wouldn't tell you." Her face dropped low. "Because I don't know."

"Oh dear, I did ask you that, and I would like to know, but that's not what happened. You became enraged when I asked. You were a danger to the rest of the girls. You don't remember."

"I do remember." I sat up, a sudden surge of strength. Anger. Whatever. "And that's not what happened."

Nurse Peters smiled, her lips pressed together like dry, cracked snakes. "Very well. Feel better, Gertrude." She turned to leave, whispering something to an aide that looked no older than I.

"Wait," I said. "Why do you need to know so badly? Why does it matter? You tell me that, and I'll see if I can find out who submitted it."

"There has been a leak, Gertrude. Luckily it was an issue favorable to the reputation of Willow Estate. However, now there is interest in the rest of our publications. If there are questions about the content, we need to be prepared. Some can be passed off as creative experiments, with these women expressing a voice. But blatant accusations will not be taken lying down. Willow Estate will not fare well in the light your little experiment shines on us." She got very close to me. Her breath smelled of vinegar. "If we are going to continue helping people here, we need to know. Now are you feeling better? Shall we get back to the ward and get to know your fellow Debutantes a little better?"

I was feeling better. But my fellow Debutantes were not the ones I was interested in.

Jessica Dainty

* * *

Sarah did not work for a few days, and Jessica, I heard, was doing a rotation on Ward 1 since the student nurse's numbers were lower than anticipated. She had come in excited last week, telling me she had passed her final tests.

"You look disgusting," Susan said to me when she saw me.

"Gee, thanks."

"I mean, it's good to see you, but yuck. What did they do to you?"

I had showered and changed, but it was obvious I had lost weight. The mirror taunted me with a sallow face and harsher cheekbones than normal.

"I don't really know what they did. Most of it's a blur."

"Well, shit, Gertie." She heaved back in her chair.

I shifted in my seat. "How long?" I asked.

Susan leaned forward, her head down. "Four days. Why? Did it seem longer or shorter?"

I sighed and shrugged, a forced smile. She put her arm around me and pulled me toward her. I rested with my head on her shoulder. Her body was warm and I could feel my cheeks filling, my body gaining something back from what it had lost.

"I'm glad you're back." She didn't have to say it, but I was glad she did.

* * *

I had no intention of actually seeking out the source of the story, obviously since I had written it, but I had to pretend like I was. I'd woken up in a panic, glad to find myself in my own room. I had been floating in space, a pale Elvis next to me, a bullet hole through his forehead. I'd kissed his cheek and sang "Blue Moon" to his cold ear. In his hands he held an issue of our ward paper, the headline in giant letters: SOURCE INDICTS OWN FACILITY. I looked at him, shocked. He opened his eyes and winked.

However, it made perfect sense. I felt ridiculous admitting that a dream had actually foretold, or simply told me what I had not yet been able to figure out,

The Shape of the Atmosphere

what Sarah had told me in ambiguous terms. What Nurse Peters herself had sort of admitted to through blatant abuse and misplaced accusations.

Nurse Peters had sent out the newspaper. The issue she was proud enough to hang on the wall. The only issue that boasted success and hope, directly attributable to Willow Estate, to the staff, to Nurse Peters herself.

But now, she had put herself in a bind. She had piqued interest. People wanted more and she had nothing else to give them that would keep patients coming in, student nurses rotating through, money circling around. She was looking to either save herself or damn somebody else. And the former looked like an increasingly slimmer option.

I gathered as many as I could together during free time.

"Alright, I'm going to say some stuff that you can just ignore after I've said it, okay?" I said this under my breath, barely loud enough to earn the silent nods I received in response. I cleared my throat, and announced, "September's issue is again an open book. However, Nurse Peters has requested, more like demanded, to know the source of the story from August's issue. If September's issue is to be printed, it needs to include the name of that person, in print. If anyone has any information, please come see me. Thank you."

I was happy to be left alone the rest of the afternoon.

*　*　*

By my count, I had about three weeks to plan whatever it was I was going to plan. That really meant I had three two-hour visitation periods to plan whatever it was I was going to plan.

When Pope and I walked out to the willow tree, I was happy for the nurse and aide shortage. A handful of aides were scattered across the grounds but no one was personally accompanied if they had a visitor, a healthy person trustworthy by virtue of not being insane.

"I'm leaving," I said.

"They're letting you out?"

I shook my head. He put his hands in his pocket and leaned against the tree.

Jessica Dainty

"What do you need me to do?" he asked.

Two hours later, he knew what had happened. What I was going to do about it would have to wait.

*　*　*

Hydro remained my least favorite, though shock caused me the most anxiety. I was left again in the water too long, but this time I caught only a cold, not pneumonia.

Sarah returned to work, and she offered to walk me out to the willow tree during free time. I was finished being surprised in this place.

The summer sun was hot this day, the sky a low film of clouds and colors, like a glowing gray, not quite silver, but hazy and glistening still.

The willow hung full, its branches brushing the ground, heavy with green.

"So did you figure it out?"

"I did."

Sarah picked at the bark. I still could not say I liked her.

"What are you going to do about it?"

"I can't tell you."

She looked at me, something almost like hurt in her eyes.

"Did you take my towel that day?" I stood tall, my frame gaining pinches of skin each day, though I knew I was less than formidable.

"Why does it matter?"

"Because this seems big, this new stuff. And I do think I can trust you, but I still don't know if I want to."

"Fair enough." Sarah slid down to sit on the ground. I sat next to her. "I didn't take your towel. But I could have given you a new one. And I should have. I'm sorry."

"Who did take it?"

"I don't know. It doesn't matter though. The aides had just had a meeting and we were told that close to a third of us were going to be let go. This is from the whole hospital, not just our ward. Everyone was upset. Honestly, it could have just fallen and been picked up by someone trying to go above and beyond to save her job. Who knows."

The Shape of the Atmosphere

"Why do you all of a sudden want to help me?"

"I need my job. I want to keep it. But I also don't want to hate myself on my days off. I heard what Jessica did for you. And in a way, it bit both of you in the ass. How you'll ever get over"—she eyed me—"seeing what you did, I don't know. But I asked her why she did it, if she regretted it."

"And?"

"She doesn't. She's glad she did it. She wasn't off that weekend. She had been suspended. They all know what she did. But they couldn't fire her. They didn't have anyone with enough experience to replace her. Even if they'd fired her, she'd still be glad she did it. I guess I'm just ready to be glad of what I do."

"I'm writing an exposé. Next issue. If I find out you're lying to me, I can put you in it."

She looked down. "She'll destroy you, you know. She's not a bad lady. She has good intentions. But she's been here forever. She'll do anything to keep this place open. She believes so much that Willow Estate can cure that she doesn't realize how much damage she causes."

"I've got it taken care of."

I'd have asked for her help, her solidarity, but I still didn't know if those small hands, those lips that had once called me cunt, could be entrusted with the whole of what I had to give.

* * *

Nurse Peters wasn't rude, kind, or aggressive during the course of the next week. My activities were normal. There was no more isolation, no more glowing white sun of a room. But eyes and whispers followed me everywhere. If I didn't know I wasn't crazy, I'd have related to the woman from Ward 3 who thought the War of the Worlds was still being waged against only her.

Susan had told me in the time that I'd been back that there had been something on the news about a new government program or department dedicated purely to space. NASA. Apparently it had been started a while ago, before Elizabeth, before my own revolution through the darkness after her death, but the news broadcaster was talking about it more. The organization had opened its doors almost exactly a year after the atmosphere had opened its doors to foreign objects wanting to fly.

I am sure my father would have marveled at that, even had he known it was coming the night we sat up to watch the evidence of such possibilities travel over us in trails of gold. Still, I do not think he understood or cared much for things beyond his comfortable office, our tiled foyer, our robin's egg blue front door. He reached for the stars because he knew I thought he could make it there. That's what parents did. He reached and fell. My mother knew she would never make it, so instead of trying, she sent me away so I could not be disappointed.

Such things I was coming to terms with.

Susan drank tea in the afternoons, as Elizabeth used to, probably because Elizabeth used to. I sat with her and brushed Helen's hair. She would close her eyes and hum softly, so low that had I not been right behind her I may have thought it was a breeze from an open window, a melodious exhale from the corner radiator. I would close my eyes too and think of what words she would put to her song should she choose one other than *apples*.

I would also think that I was going to miss this place, that I was going to something much less of what I knew to be home. That the best thing to do would be to stay.

"You look like you've got gas or something."

Susan watched me from above the lip of her mug, a smirk on her face.

"How ladylike of you."

She lifted her chin and burped, shrugging her shoulders. We both laughed.

I went and lit a candle in the chapel, asking my sister to forgive me for forgetting the color of her eyes.

* * *

The next week when Pope came, Susan came with us on our walk. An aide hung a little too close for comfort, so after a while Susan said she wanted to head inside so that the aide would have to walk her back to the main building.

The Shape of the Atmosphere

"So what's your plan?" Pope asked me once we were alone.

"Any more word of my mother?"

He said he had called the nurse and that my mother had fired her in a rage one day when she couldn't find her rosary beads. That the nurse insisted she had not touched them, that she never touched anything she wasn't supposed to, but that my mother had been becoming increasingly irascible as she forgot more mundane things such as where she put her prayer beads.

"'I didn't have the heart to tell her they were around her neck, and the old woman threw me out,'" he said she'd said.

"The last she had heard, she was at a new place in Bridgetown, a home that specializes in the care of elderly and infirm people. I got an address, but I haven't been there yet. So what is your plan?"

I hadn't figured everything out yet, but two weeks from now I would no longer be a physical patient at Willow Estate.

"Jessica has already done too much for me, but I don't know if Sarah is on my side or not. There's only so much Susan can do. She'd rip her hair out again if she had to, I have no doubt. I just need a bit more time. Next week, I'll be ready. I have to be. The issue comes out mid-week the week after. If I don't have a plan, I have a feeling I won't be given the chance to make any choices for myself. I need an excuse to have to go see her. Do you think you can make that happen?"

We sat on the roots. They wormed into the ground with more purpose than I'd ever noticed before.

"Look. They're trying to get away." The bark nibbled at my fingers. I wondered how far the roots reached down.

"Are you okay, Gertie?" I looked at him. His eyes were so blue, and so concerned I thought they would run out and lay in pools at my feet. "I mean, are you going to be okay?"

"I love you." I said it too loud and my voice scratched the air between us. "Do you love me?"

Pope squinted through the branches. The days were still long, but the night gained stealth and the sun was dropping behind the trees even though I wasn't ready for it to. He did not look at me or speak. He took my hand, and pressed it into the ground under his. My hand felt squished and when he finally

Jessica Dainty

released it later, the grooved surface of the tree roots lined my skin like veins. The phantom pressure of his hand pulsed through them like blood.

*　*　*

I think Jessica was hurt that I was not asking her for help. She knew the situation. She had to know that Sarah had spoken to me. I couldn't use her after what had happened last time, but I had to know if I could use Sarah. I trusted Jessica's advice.

"Were you really suspended over giving me the key?"

"What?" Jessica laughed. She carried a stack of pressed linens and put them in a closet, locking it before moving on. "Sounds like you're not getting enough sleep."

I stood, baffled at her ambivalence toward me, until sometime after lights out, I felt not a check-in tap, but heard a breathy, "Gertie, are you awake?"

I sat up and flipped my bedside lamp on. Jessica was in regular clothes, her white cap still pinned to her brown hair.

"I was suspended. Sarah was telling you the truth, but I would be careful with her. She cares more about her job than anything."

"She told me that, but that she was tired of not being happy with herself the rest of her time when she left."

"She says that. But I guarantee she knows she'd be a lot less happy with herself if she couldn't pay her bills."

We sat in silence. I wished I had a clock that audibly ticked, to mark the passing time in a measurable way.

"The people here really do care, Gertie. But everyone has their priorities. They want the best for you, but not at the expense of what's best for them. There are things they do here that you can't even imagine. Things that don't just happen on Ward 3 and 4. I started my nursing rotations."

"I saw a Negro aide bite her own tongue off when I was in Ward 3. Did you hear about her?"

Jessica shook her head.

"Can you find out for me if she's still there? What happened to her? Her nametag said Rose or something. It started with an R."

The Shape of the Atmosphere

"I'll see what I can do." She flipped my light off and I knew our conversation was over. That our conversations were over. That this would be the last one we had, like this, on a level that meant we might have been friends, somewhere in the midst of it all.

"Goodnight, Gertie." She stumbled over her second syllable, as though her initial instinct was to say something far more permanent than *night*.

* * *

On Sunday, before visitation hours started, I was called into the nursing station and taken over to Dr. Rosslins' office.

"Gertie, have a seat please." Dr. Rosslins and Nurse Peters sat across from me, solemn with their folded hands. I actually wished they had their pens poised instead. The whole body stillness unnerved me.

"Yes?"

"We've received a call. Your mother has been moved to a facility in Bridgetown and is not doing well. They've requested you visit. And as it stands, your finances seem to be in a bit of a debacle. Your mother has fallen behind. We're sorry about her health, but hope that when you visit you can try to clear this up. We have a very strict policy. If the payments aren't made, we have to either clear you or you'll be transferred to a state facility."

"How will I get there? To my mother, I mean."

"Well, normally we could take you, but the short staff limits this ability." I tried to hide my sigh of relief.

* * *

"I have someone who can take me," I said, placing the words gently in front of them, so that they may be more tempted to take them.

Pope and I did not go to the willow tree. We instead went and sat in the garden, nestling in behind the overwhelming growth of colors, reds, and yellows, but mostly a rainbow of greens.

"The issue comes out on Wednesday. I don't know what they'll do to me, but Sarah will either help me in my way or hers. Nurse Peters told me this morning that the facility called. Was that you?" He nodded. "They also said my mother hasn't been paying, that if I can't figure it out, they're going to send me to the state facility."

I had heard passing conversations when patients discussed their theories about Sarah's father working for the state hospitals. I also deduced abstractions of horror from Elizabeth's piecemealed file. Nurse Peters and I weren't exactly best friends. I wasn't hopeful of being let out, between the two options, with her having a say in the decision. And while much of what happened here at Willow was awful, I knew the unbroken parts of me might not survive those other places.

Pope and I sat quiet. There had been no actual news of my mother. He had faked the phone call, sent a letter on false stationary. But the money issue was real. He said we could check together, when the time came.

"You know, next week. When we're out there together." He said it without a stutter, but I could still hear the falter in his words, that behind the steadiness, he couldn't quite believe it would be true.

* * *

Nurse Peters Sells the Very Paper She Aims to Ban, Caught in Own Web!

Nurse Peters, of Willow Estate submitted a copy of Four Walls *to an outside news source in order to boost the reputation of the facility. However, she did not foresee the overwhelming success and resultant continued interest in Ward 2's publication. We are certain, however, that what she views as non-complimentary toward Willow Estate, the world will simply view as fascinating and thought-provoking. The voices of those deemed crazy do not indict the places in which they reside. It indicts those who listen to us and who fear the realization that we are not so different from themselves. Those that would continue to send their mothers, wives, and children to become singularities behind foreign walls.*

Some of us here are sick, but even those who may be ill are not so different from those out there reading our paper. And perhaps that is what Nurse

The Shape of the Atmosphere

Peters fears so much. That those who sent us here may realize it does not matter what four walls we are put behind.

We will not fade away. We are not disappearing. We matter. And we should be heard.

XVII

Tuesday night, before the Wednesday handout, Susan and I snuck into the small kitchen and baked a cake. We worked by the light of my bedside lamp which was brighter than I thought it would be, and I hoped no one noticed the glow from beneath the closed door, the wafting smell of fluffed eggs and powdered sugar.

We sat in the dark while the cake baked, the warmth sticking to my skin, licking at my nostrils and making my mouth water, though I was not hungry. We did not talk and sometime between the soft smell of sugar and the slight tinge of something burning at the edges, Susan leaned into me through the dim space. Her lips were softer than Pope's but not by much, and I did not lean either away or into her. I knew this moment meant something different to her than it did to me, and that was okay with me. I did not know if she was glad it was me or if she wished I were Elizabeth, if she loved me or just trusted me. All I knew was that when she pulled back she did not look away, and her eyes were almost black in the darkness of the room. I held her hand while she cried.

Earlier that day the women had been allowed to lie on the grass in their bathing suits, if they owned one. I did not. I instead read by the window, watching Susan in her full pants and blouse sit on the bench outside near where the other women lay. I wondered what it would be like to look at a woman and love her, to follow the curve of her hip or breast as I followed the curve of Pope's jawbone, the bony tips of his elbows. I thought of my father's rolled up blankets on his office floor, of my mother's increasingly longer stints behind the pantry door. I thought of my sister's refusal of boys on our front stoop but her insistent smiles and waves to them from behind the bus window, the line in the hallway at school. I thought of the pressure of Pope's hand on mine, his visits each week with no guarantee as to a

The Shape of the Atmosphere

different future. I watched Susan and thought that it must be an awfully lonely, singular thing, this loving of a woman.

The cake was browned but okay. We sat around it at the counter, the freshness too hot and soft to cut. Susan lit and sucked on a cigarette until the tip glowed red. I stuck it into the yellow sponge like a candle. I had no wishes to make. I turned off my lamp. We sat there and watched it burn.

* * *

"I'll do it."

The crowd of women from Ward 2 looked around at who had responded to my question of who would be willing to distribute the paper that night, since I would not be available.

"I have a feeling I won't be around here after today. I've enjoyed hearing all of your voices," I had said.

And then one voice rang out that none of us had heard but one way, a two syllable word that rang with inherent sweetness.

Helen looked surprised at our surprise, but I never heard another word from her, and I doubt anyone else who was to stay at Willow Estate would hear anything but *apples* again.

She hugged me as the crowd dispersed, squeezing my shoulders once and pulling away. It's amazing how much one could say without the words to do it.

* * *

Later that evening, after dinner, when I would normally be playing cards with Susan or reading with her feet in my lap, I was instead packing two days' worth of clothes in my father's black suitcase.

"All set?" Sarah had come in behind me.

"Pretty much."

She peered into my bag. "Is that all you're taking?" I smiled at her question and was grateful she knew I would not be back. In a way it made things easier.

Jessica Dainty

"Is he here yet?" I asked, zipping up the black bag, and a smell I almost remembered reached me but faded too quickly to place.

"He called a while ago. He'll be here in a couple hours. I think it's about a three-hour drive for him."

I nodded but did not have words left for who stood in front of me.

"Well, thanks, you know, for the past few weeks. I know we haven't always gotten along," I finally said.

"Sure." She blocked the doorway but shifted her body to the side, to let me know I was welcome to leave whenever I felt ready.

"Well, I better go. Good luck tomorrow, when…well you know."

"When the shit hits the fan? Already have my umbrella set."

I pushed past her and the air of the hallway felt lighter and easier to breathe.

"I did take your towel." She said it suddenly as I was about to walk toward the commons area. I stopped, turned back, and let her speak. "But only because someone paid me to. I honestly don't even remember who. Someone who wanted ice cream more than you." She laughed, a single exhale, and I did too, for how little ice cream seemed to matter in the midst of any of this. "But I shouldn't have taken it and I'm sorry."

"Thanks," I said. "For telling me. When you didn't have to." She nodded and I turned again.

"Oh, and Jessica wanted me to tell you." She pulled a scrap of paper from the pocket of her white uniform and squinted at it. "Her name was Rosalyn. But she's not here anymore. She doesn't know where she is. Who's Rosalyn?"

"Just a girl I think about sometimes." I stood outside facing in, taking one last look at my room. I couldn't say I wasn't sad to say goodbye. I'd have liked to capture the memory without Sarah there, but like so many of my goodbyes, I would have to accept an intrusion. "Tell Jessica I said goodbye. And good luck, with the nursing and stuff."

"I will. But you'll be back in two days. So you can tell her yourself."

Samantha, the recover-ee, walked behind me, and I stiffened at her avoidance of us, but knew if she'd heard she would go running.

The Shape of the Atmosphere

"Thank you," I said. For everything, I thought, but could not bring myself to give it to her in words, in a way that she could interpret as me really owing her anything.

I turned to go, but then faced her again. "What's an oophorectomy?"

"Gertie, I—" She took a step toward me. I stepped back, on instinct. She almost looked hurt, but we both knew we weren't friends. Never had been.

"Tell me, Sarah. If you want to do something for me. Telling me about the towel was nice, but that doesn't matter anymore. This might."

She sighed and looked at her hands. Her nails were bit so low that lines of red shone. I looked at them and was reminded of my father's office, of my own arms. Of the marks on Elizabeth's cell. Sarah cleared her throat. She looked me straight in the eye. "They took your ovaries, Gertie. That's what they did."

I felt sick, immediately ill, like I might vomit. Not at the loss, but that someone had had the ability to do such a thing to another human being, without telling her.

Me. Without telling *me*.

I didn't know how to absorb this information. I knew they had taken something. But this. I'd noticed my lack of period over the past few months but assumed it was just stress. Susan said that could happen sometimes. I'd never shown her my scars directly, and people were kind enough to look away in the showers. She couldn't have known. Or I'm sure she would have told me.

"Do you hate me?" I asked.

"A little."

I had expected a pause, a brush-off. Her words shocked me only because they existed in the room between us, not because of what they were.

"Can I ask why?"

"You know when I told you I wanted to like myself at the end of the day. I wasn't lying, you know. I meant it. I want to do good. I do. But people like you, you make it really hard to go home and feel good about what I do." She brushed her cheek so fast, even if there had been a tear there, I couldn't have proved it for anything. "Helen, Elizabeth, even Susan with her…condition, they all have something wrong with them. I can feel like what I do can help them. But then there's you." She paused and huffed, as though she needed a breath deeper than she had time for. "There's nothing wrong with you, Gertie."

I had waited two years—no, my whole life—to hear someone tell me that, and here it was, coming from the one person in my life I might have hated. I nodded at her and smiled, and she made a move like she had something else to say, but I was done. I didn't even take a last glance back. I just walked away.

* * *

Outside in the commons area, Susan sat in the green chair, the gilded Bible of Elizabeth in her lap.

"Almost time for me to go." I poked my head in front of her but she did not move, and for a second I felt as though I were looking at Elizabeth, before she slumped back to life.

"Don't say goodbye to me. Just go."

"Susan." I reached out to her, but she shrugged me away.

"I'm not mad at you. Or trying to be cruel. I just don't want to say goodbye. So I won't."

"Okay," I said, putting my bag down and extending my hand. "See you."

She looked up and I could see her mouth tugging at the corners, her eyes brimming but holding solid like a dam. She took my hand and held it, turning the back of it to the ceiling, and I could see her tracing the lines of my scraggly veins with her eyes. I turned to go, but came back, not caring what she had said to me. I grabbed her and pulled her close. One hand rose to meet me and squeezed me closer.

"I love you, you know. And I'm sure Elizabeth would have loved you too, had she gotten the chance to know you."

She said nothing, and I walked away, my shirt wet, the dam shattered and broken behind me.

The Shape of the Atmosphere

* * *

I had not brought anything with me except what I would need for the two days of freedom I was supposed to have, not even the still mostly unread letters from my mother. Not even the photograph of my sister. Pope's first drawing to me remained under my pillow. St. Christopher protected them, and here I was on my own. The only object I brought other than what was expected of me was a single copy of the last issue of *Four Walls* tucked into my bra where they were unlikely to look.

Pope and I stopped halfway to his home and slept in the truck, parked in a gravel lot in front of what at one point may have been a gas station or a small store. He thought it would be better to show up tomorrow, in the day, instead of at night, with the pressure of meeting his family. We barely talked, and I felt like the sky I saw through the windshield was pressing down on my chest until I couldn't breathe. I woke up to paved gray whirring by and Pope next to me, already driving.

"We'll go to my house first to get you some clothes. I have a sister about your size."

"You have a sister?"

Pope smiled, but I knew we were both thinking about how this may have been easier if I was back in the commons room waiting for him each Sunday.

No one was home at Pope's house. And he was right, it was easier this way.

He lived in a large colonial with columns that screamed pretentiousness, but once inside, the handmade pottery, the framed scribbled drawings, obviously years old, warmed the whole of the house, and I began to relax for the first time since I'd left last night.

He disappeared upstairs, and I traced the edges of shelves and spines of books, noticing little piles of dust stuck in random corners. Did his mother not see them or not care? What type of woman sent her child away to be cleaned and left her shelves dusty?

On one shelf was a brick of parchment solidified into form with a knotting of twine. The threads were loose, and I pulled one corner off and slid the papers out. They were all letters from Pope to his family, a combination of wordless drawings and drawingless words. Each was dated, some reaching as far back as 1954. Pope had been in Willow since he was sixteen or seventeen. He'd never told me that before. I thought of what he'd shared with me, about being in special classes at school. I knew what he was talking about. I'd seen those students herded down the hall in single file, if they ever came out at all. They were like a sideshow attraction at a carnival when they emerged from behind that classroom door, which was hidden in a corner of the building.

How much of his life he must have spent locked away somewhere. We were so much alike that I felt my heart ache for a second, but I knew perhaps he had had it worse than I, even though his family was still alive and had taken him back. His entire family had allowed him to be shut away. I was confident that if my father had lived, I'd still be watching the sky every night, with his quiet, lonely person next to mine.

"Here, try these." Pope's presence startled me, and I dropped the letters. They scattered like tiny living things, trying to get away.

He handed me a garbage bag of clothes and bent to pick the letters up. A curt clearing of his throat was the only conversation he allowed on the topic before closing the twine around the stack and putting it back on the shelf.

I tolerated, even welcomed, the avoidance. I opened the bag and glanced inside. "Won't she miss these?"

"Nah. She just got new clothes for the school year. She would have given these away anyway. It's just a start anyhow. We'll get you some more once we are a bit more settled."

I liked how he said *we*.

I took the bag into a closet-sized bathroom on the first floor. I liked the dungarees but I knew my mother would prefer to see me in a dress. Pope's sister only had ones too short for my mother's taste, so I put on a pair of black pants and a blouse and cardigan instead. The clothes fit fine, too loose if anything, and I yearned to see this person related to Pope, to know if she was brunette or blonde, funny or serious. If she had fought to keep him home when his parents sent him away.

The Shape of the Atmosphere

"Are you ready?" His voice reached me from some interminable distance.

"Coming." I looked at myself once more in the bathroom mirror. I did not see the face of my mother anymore as I had sometimes over the past two years, as my sister had promised me when I was younger. I was almost eighteen now and I resembled no one. I belonged to no one.

"Do you and your sister look anything alike?" I asked Pope when we were back in the truck.

"A little, maybe. I don't know. My mom thinks we have the same nose. Why?"

"I don't think I look like anyone."

"What did your sister look like?"

Outside, the town blurred past in streaks. I was unfamiliar with this area. We were at least an hour from my own house, and my mother was apparently at least forty miles outside of where we were now. It's strange to think Pope and I had grown up within one hundred miles of each other and never known it. I breathed onto the glass and counted the seconds until it cleared again.

"Did your sister look like you?"

"I don't remember," I said. It must have been colder outside than I thought. The breath clung to the window stubbornly for over ten seconds. "I barely remember any of them anymore. I'm afraid I won't recognize my mother when I see her. Even more than I'm afraid of her not recognizing me."

"You might not think you remember but you do. You'll know her when you see her. Don't worry. I felt the same way when I was at Willow. JoAnn, my sister, never visited, but I recognized her scrawny excuse for a body the moment I saw her." He smirked at me from across the car. He had always been a cute boy, but I saw him now for the first time as a man. His hands looked bigger, his jaw stronger, his eyes more capable. I had been nervous to even think of being alone with him in a way not possible at Willow Estate, but now something low in my stomach ached at the thought of it. I crossed my legs, uncomfortable being so close to him while I had these thoughts.

"What's wrong?"

"Nothing. I have to pee," I lied.

"We'll stop in Porter. Can you wait fifteen minutes?" He squinted at the road like it was a map he could read.

"I can wait until we get to my mom. I don't have to go that bad."

"Are you sure?"

I nodded and leaned against the window. I pretended the hard glass was Susan's shoulder, the breeze from the cracked top of the window her breath, soft and even, smelling of tea and loneliness. I breathed back, the window fogging again. I drew a heart in the middle, to let her know I was there.

XVIII

The sign read "Bridgetown Home for the Elderly and Infirm," but the building looked like a house. A small house. We entered through the front and stood at a low desk until someone came out to greet us.

"Can I help you?"

I was about to speak when Pope did it for me. I held his hand, grateful.

"Yes, I spoke to someone on the phone. We are here to see Alice MacLarsen. Her daughter is here."

"Yes, sir. Let me check, sir."

We sat in two chairs in a row of four. They were brown and hard and did nothing to make me less nervous. My sides pulled, as they sometimes did, even though my stitches were healed, cut and removed, only a glistening line of skin on either side marking their places.

"Do you know what an oophorectomy is?" I asked.

"A what?"

"An oophorectomy."

"No, I've never heard of it. Is it bad?"

I shook my head, more shaking off his question than intending to answer it. What would he think when I could not offer him anything but myself?

He was about to speak when the woman came back and said we could follow her.

She led us down a narrow hallway and out a door. We walked under a breezeway. From here, I could see a much larger building, though just as low. We entered through a side door and stood around while she spoke to a nurse. After a few moments of soft words, the nurse approached us with the type of smile Nurse Peters used before hydro.

The Shape of the Atmosphere

"Hi. I'm Claire. Nice to meet you." She extended her hand. I took it. So did Pope. "I understand you're here to see Miss MacLarsen? You say you're her daughter?"

I nodded. I had no words.

"Miss MacLarsen informed us her daughter had died. I'm sorry we didn't contact you when she came here. How awful for you."

"She did die. I mean, my sister. Is dead. But I'm"—I took a deep breath to gain my composure—"not." I nodded once at the end, as though no one could know I was done speaking otherwise.

"I see. I'm very sorry for your loss. I'll tell her you're here."

"Could you not?" She looked surprised. "I mean, could I just go in and see her? It's been a long time. I need to know if she remembers me."

Claire smiled and nodded and took my hand. "Very well, dear. But she doesn't remember much of anything anymore."

My mother was sitting in a large high-backed upholstered chair, rocking slightly. Pope was right. I recognized her immediately. When I saw her I thought of a time when I was six and my mother was sitting in her chair in the living room. I ran to jump on her lap, and she did not notice me. She put her hand on my head like I was a dog. My father had come and carried me away.

"Let's give your mother some time," he'd said, and before I knew it I was distracted by checkers and licorice laces, my father's overwhelming laugh and my sister's obvious ability to worm her way in.

I see her now and wonder if whatever it was that was inside her, clouding her sight of me, her memory of any of us, had been there then, brewing behind those vacant eyes.

"Miss MacLarsen. You have a visitor."

Miss. She was as unclaimed as I was. A singularity in this world.

I sat next to my mother in a chair Pope pulled over for me. Her hands rested in her lap, bundled up like marshmallow drumsticks.

"She was scratching at her face. We had to cover her nails," Claire said before walking away.

"I'm going to go walk around outside," Pope whispered to me, his hands on my back. "Unless, of course, you want me to stay." I shook my head that he could go. I did not want to be alone with my mother, but saw no other way. This was how it should be.

I was convinced I could still walk the halls of my childhood home, navigate its rooms, scale its L-shaped stairs with the foyer landing, all with my eyes closed. The natural wood railings, floorboards that when the sunlight hit from the giant second-story window of our foyer looked like honey, amber-colored and glistening like the bottles in my mother's darkened hideout. The awkward blue carpet of the living room, the brown plainness of the family room, the black and white checkered floor of the kitchen that, when linked together, seemed ridiculous and mismatched, but that each provided a space comforting and of use. The blue a setting for an ocean adventure or outer space exploration, the black and white a giant checkerboard, a trap set by some mastermind. The dark sandiness of the family room a threat of quicksand, or, on some days, just a place to sink away.

I remember the bedspread of the downstairs guest room, its pattern fitting for the older guests who usually stayed there, floral and paisley, in muted tones, that though new, made it look years older, faded and aged.

The second story deck off the kitchen, that in the winter, when the snow was deep and soft enough, had a three-foot railing we would brave, gripping with gloved hands the outer side, and fall or jump to the whiteness below. My parents must have known, had seen us once or twice take the leap, but I look back amazed at our freedom to choose, especially after the past two years. To make decisions for ourselves about our safety and well-being.

Our house was hugged by rolling green lawn, a pond that croaked in the spring and froze solidly under our skating feet in the winter, and woods that stretched back enough for my imagination to truly believe I was somewhere far, far away from it all.

I looked at my mother now and knew she did not remember any of this. That were I to scream Allison's or Dad's name, that she might blink at me and smile but she would not pluck their familiarity out of the air in front of her and taste her memories of them.

"Miss MacLarsen?" My voice faltered. "I'm Gertrude."

The Shape of the Atmosphere

"Hello, Gertrude." She reached out to shake my hand. I took the soft mass of cotton in mine and did not let go. I sat beside her, her hand melting inside mine, feeling small even bundled up.

"I knew your daughter," I said. I do not know why I made it singular. Perhaps because she did and I did not want to tarnish any little memory she had left.

"How nice. Did you say Gertrude? My daughter's name was Gertrude." I searched her eyes, but she had not yet looked at me. "She died though. Years ago. In an accident."

"I'm very sorry to hear that. Would you tell me about her?"

I sat with my mother for over an hour. She told me things about myself, some of which were true, like her pulling me out of Catholic school and how I sat with her on the kitchen floor when she cried after burning a cake. I barely remembered this but I knew it was true. I could see the white lace of her apron, sense the mix of burnt lemon and my mother's exaggerated sobs. I wished I had done the same the day of the pie.

She also told me some things that were true only of Allison. That I was a great soccer player. That I had beautiful blonde hair.

Even my father was wrapped up in her memory of me.

"She had such beautiful hazel eyes. And she gave me a silver pocket watch for my birthday one year." It had been gold and on her anniversary, from my father.

I did not know what to make of my mother weaving all she had left into me.

"Do you miss her?"

"What kind of a question is that, child? Of course I miss her. She never once comes to visit me."

"I thought you said she had died." I tread lightly.

Her eyes absorbed this. "Yes, oh, right. You're right."

Claire came in then, to announce that it was time for everyone to have their afternoon rest. I had wanted to take my mom outside, to walk with her. Claire said I could come back, but today was done.

"Goodbye, Miss MacLarsen. It was nice to see you."

Jessica Dainty

I pulled her hand to my cheek. I wanted to rip the gauze off so she would have to touch me, to feel me. Her eyes found mine and she stared. I fought every day to remember my family. To remember the color of my sister's eyes, the exact sound of my father's laugh. In this woman's eyes I sensed no such fight. I believed my mother could not remember, but I also believed that she had willingly let it all go. That she had sat in her empty house and decided what pieces she would keep and she threw them in a pile together and some broke and some remained intact but all were misplaced and tragic. I looked at her and saw the irony of us. That she had sent me away when she in fact was the one who was sick. I did not know if I wanted to burden her with memory or rob her of the little she had left.

"What did you say your name was again, dear?"

"Gertrude, mom. My name is Gertrude."

"Ah yes. I had a daughter named Gertrude. I sent you away, didn't I?"

"What did you just say?"

"I sent her away, I think. Or she died. I think I need to rest. Will you be back to see me again?"

I nodded. Claire came and helped her into a wheelchair. She moved away from me.

"Wait!" Before I thought it through, I was face-to-face with my mother, my eyes no more than a few inches from hers.

"Dad. Allison. Gertrude. Do you remember them, Mom?"

Her eyes flickered and she started to reach up to me but then let her excuse for hands fall back to her lap.

"I have a daughter named Gertrude." She smiled at me then and I could not say for sure, but I felt that she knew me. Not that she knew it was me, that I was Gertrude, that I was her daughter, but that I was someone somewhere in her pile of memories. A shape she may have known, even from so far away.

"Come back tomorrow if you want to visit again. It takes a lot out of her though. When your friend came the first time, she was in bed for a week."

"My friend?"

"Your friend that you came with. When he visited her. All they did was play checkers and talk. She smiled a lot that day. But it exhausted her."

The Shape of the Atmosphere

"Okay, thanks." I watched my mother roll away, the light of her fading with distance, the memory of her face already blurring around the edges.

I found Pope down by the water.

"How was it?" he asked, as I was still walking toward him.

I did not stop when I got to him. Instead I put my hands out and shoved. He stumbled backward and fell to the ground but stood up quickly.

"What's wrong with you?" He wiped off the back of his pants.

"You came to see her. You came to see her without telling me."

"Gertie—" He tried to cut me off but I wouldn't let him.

"You told me you hadn't found her. That we would do this together. Why did you come here!?" I yelled this last part and didn't realize it until my throat scratched back. I fell against a tree and slid down. I did not want to cry in front of Pope, but there were a lot of things I'd done by now that I had never wanted to do.

Pope shoved his hands in his pockets. He did not sit with me. He stood and faced the water.

"I just wanted to meet her." He kicked at the dirt. "I wanted to be able to prepare you, but I also just wanted to meet her. To know what she was like." He came and leaned against the tree. I flicked dirt from his shoe. "You're going to meet my family. You'll learn things I'd never tell you on my own. I'll never get that from you. For the rest of my life, I'll only know what you choose to give me. And that's fine. But, I still wanted my chance to know you through someone else."

I wanted to stay angry, but I thought of peeking through Pope's letters. How he had replaced them without questioning me, allowing me to absorb whatever knowledge I had from them, outside of his giving.

I sighed. "She doesn't remember me. I mean she does, but she remembers me as everyone. My father, my sister. I think she even put me to a memory about Bobby, a policeman she was in love with."

"She still remembers you then. In fact, she remembers you the most. Above all others."

"Because she feels guilty."

"Because you're worth it."

"I'm still mad at you."

Jessica Dainty

"I'm still glad I came. I'd do it again."

"You plan on knowing me for the rest of your life?" I stood now, facing him. He leaned against the tree.

"Depends on if you're going to be mad at me for the rest of my life."

"Susan kissed me." I did not know why I said it. "And I let her. I just thought you should know."

He angled forward, toward me. "Will you just let me kiss you or will you kiss me back?"

I smiled and shrugged. I was not cool enough to play it cool. I fell into him like I had nowhere else to hold. I had not felt free enough to let myself go at Willow. Here, I let my womanhood fall to pieces around him and I smiled to hear him sighing, frantic to catch every one before it hit the ground.

XIX

I felt more guilty breaking into my own home than I did breaking out of Willow Estate. Dust floated around me like tiny stars, illuminated by the filtered light through the windows. The furniture in their white sheets haunted me, and I felt a chill. I wish I had come earlier, before the sun began to fade. The house felt dead, even more than it had when death surrounded us here.

My father's office remained untouched. I ran my fingers along the dark desk, the defined edges of his empty cross. His desk was clean, uncluttered, but I noticed as I sat in his chair that someone had been here. My mother's handwriting called out to me from a piece of stationery. This is where she wrote her letters to me. I'd always pictured her hunched over below the pantry's low ceiling, scribbling in the dim light her short notes to me. But no. She had sat here, in my father's space, avoiding his name while surrounded by all that was left of him.

She never did write either of their names to me, save for Allison's in that first letter. Under the top piece of paper, though, was a stack of pages with nothing but my father and sister on them. Henry and Allison whispered to me from tiny script, screamed at me from large, blackened marks, cried to me from shaking, vibrating letters. My mother had not been able to escape them after all. Or perhaps this was her fighting to remember them, to hold onto them as they slipped away, out of her consciousness.

The letter on top was addressed to me. Here is all it said.

Dear Gertrude,

    I hope you are well. I am not. I remember the wrong things and forget what I should remember. I hope to visit you. I am

The Shape of the Atmosphere

And there it ended. She was what? Sorry? Miserable? Happy I was gone? I thought of all the possibilities of what she could have written to complete the sentence and I decided I was glad she didn't. I did not want to know what she was. What I had left was enough.

I remembered my nights in here before I'd been sent away, purposefully surrounding myself with my father, spending my nights where I knew she would never go. I blamed her too heavily and forgave my father too easily. His things in drawers, my mother locking herself behind a door. He had locked himself away too, and I forgave him without thought. I looked around now, at her scrambled search for them on the stacks of paper, and I knew that it was not just my mother who had left us alone, not just this woman who perhaps had lost interest in us as a family. That I had lost them all, my sister too, long before I'd realized. That my father focused me on the sky, so I did not look too closely at what was right in front of me.

I found Pope fingering the shelves of books in the living room. I'd forgotten we had so many. I'd grown used to the few shelves in the commons area at Willow, grateful and surprised at what we had been given there. Here the books announced themselves and could not be ignored. I'd had so much. And now I had an empty house, a mother who did not know me. And then, this man in front of me, who had found his voice and decided to spend it on me.

"Are you done? Did you need to see anything else?"

"Just a few more minutes. Come with me."

We walked through the foyer my mother had fallen on, that I had vomited on how long ago? Two, three years? I was an adult now but I did not feel it standing on the black and white squares. My mother's memory was giant and took up the entire space. There was no room for me to be bigger than a child.

Upstairs, my room's normalcy shocked me. I had not remembered it being so plain. I grabbed some clothes, but they were older and I could tell they would no longer fit. It didn't matter where I had been. Growing up, it turned out, was not a choice.

Jessica Dainty

My telescope sat directed toward a window where it was met by a closed shade. A layer of dust covered the exterior, the lens filmy with neglect. I wondered what the stars would look like through the haze, but I didn't touch it. I left it where it was, staring at nothingness, and walked away.

My sister's room seemed the most quiet. I stood in the middle, afraid to move, to disturb the stillness, as though she was there somehow and could only remain if nothing changed, if the air did not stir.

I took a photograph from her mirror. I was nowhere in this tiny world of hers. It was a picture of only her, but she smiled out as though to say, *yes take me with you, I am for you. You may have what is left of me.* I put her in my back pocket and hoped I remembered to take her out before I sat down, so I did not bend or crinkle her.

"One more stop," I said, and Pope followed me to the kitchen. The pantry was smaller than I remembered and not just because I may have grown taller. I'd had to wear dresses more often during my last months at Willow, the pants entirely too small now so that I could not button them.

Small bottles lined one of the shelves, next to the beans and condensed milk. I held them to the light, the amber liquid, glowing warmth. Some had clear liquid, some no liquid at all. I opened one closer to brown and took a sip. The color burned my throat. I coughed, and sipped again. It took a few minutes, but I replaced the bottle, empty. Pope simply leaned back and let me do what I needed.

"I don't know what she was able to find in here that she couldn't find out there. I guess she sort of sent herself away like she did me. What does it mean for a majority of a life to fit in a handful of glass bottles?" I said this quietly but, beginning with one, threw the glass against the wall. It broke but did not shatter, the larger pieces clinking on the floor. The next bottle I threw directly down and that one shattered and spread, like a cluster of stars exploding outward.

After three, Pope stopped me. He did not speak. He simply grabbed my arm and pulled me in. He took the bottle from my hand and placed it back on the shelf. It was better there, where she had left it. He took the broom leaning against the wall and swept the glass into a corner. I sat in my

The Shape of the Atmosphere

mother's chair, a sudden warmth flooding my cheeks and burning through my chest.

When he was done, he came to me, stood me up, and pushed the chair back. He knelt and I followed. We faced each other, the ground hard on my knees and I swayed slightly, partly from the drink and partly to keep the weight moving from side to side so I did not need to stand.

He looked nowhere but my face as he unbuttoned his shirt and pulled it off, exposing a white undershirt. I noticed the moist stains of yellow beneath his arms as he pulled that over his head. We did not speak. When he started unhooking his belt, I began my own journey toward nakedness. I unbuttoned my blouse, embarrassed at wearing his sister's bra, at my inability to fill it. I cowered forward. He took my shoulders and straightened me out but then took his hands away and did not touch me.

Soon he knelt, just in his underwear. I tried to remove my pants without standing but could not. My face red, I stood and stepped out of them. I shivered. The room was not cold.

This time when he reached out it was not for my shoulders. He crawled toward me until we were only inches apart and put his hands on my waist. They found their way behind me and around my back. He pulled my straps down and exposed my breasts. I looked down, nervous. He put his finger under my chin like the first time we'd danced.

Soon, I was lost in him, and I wondered what my mother would think of such a thing happening in here. Her crucifix stared from the wall, her remaining bottles, unblinking, held their posts. The ground around me still glittered slightly from the glass the broom could not catch. I closed my eyes and tried to feel everything, the air around me, the pressure of fingertips, of lips, of torso and legs. Of the undeniable presence of my past, the weight of the room around me, and the lightness, the promise of hope, in my future.

XX

We slept on the floor of the pantry and the next morning, we drove from town to town, stopping at the local papers. Pope had used his own money to get photocopies made so that we'd have enough.

I grieved as I handed over each page, each story that had in some odd way become my own. My situation wasn't liked Pope's. I couldn't go back. I couldn't visit. These black and white pages may be the last I'd ever see of them, of those who had become my friends.

My family.

One paper wanted only the scandal, one had no interest at all, and one agreed to publish a mishmash of both the positive and the negative. I highlighted the ones I required to be published—Susan's story and Becca's—but also my own, along with Elizabeth's tribute. I marked some others and handed them over, feeling no lighter for the weight I had given away. Some things just stay with you.

* * *

We had just sat down to dinner with Pope's family. His sister did look like him, but it was not the nose as his mother said but the eyes, and the shape of the face, how it came together in a point at the chin without seeming harsh. Pope's father was a large man, round and always laughing so that he jiggled constantly. I couldn't imagine him going through shock, his body vibrating for weeks at a time without reprieve.

The phone rang, and Pope left to answer it.

"And what will you do now, Gertie?" His mother asked me, as I lifted a bite of chicken to my mouth. What could they think of me coming from where I'd come? What did they think of their son? Of themselves?

The Shape of the Atmosphere

Their child had come back whole. Their decision had been verified, stamped with approval. I had emerged, emptied of parts of myself I'd never used but that labeled me broken for their lacking. I was not a success story.

"I'm not sure. I—" And Pope came in, his hands shoved in pockets, his voice low.

We drove back toward Bridgetown. They had to call in the middle of dinner. Of getting to know these people who may, given time, be called my own.

I had planned to take her outside, toward the water, to the tree Pope had pressed me against the day before with an urgency I thought could not be topped until I came to know the final breathless moments in my mother's pantry. I had dressed feeling amazing, to be alive, to know that I had come from such a moment. That my parents had in fact loved each other at some point.

She had died in her sleep they'd said, during her afternoon rest. They had hired a home to deal with the remains. What would I like done?

I did not have money to bury her and I did not want money from Pope to do so. I'd told them to cremate her, though I imagined my mother's screams from inside the flames at her body's desecration.

I had not wanted to see her before it was done. I couldn't help but think she had used whatever will she had left, whatever strength remained in her to ensure she did not wake up. Did not wake up and have to face these things she only recognized vaguely. I did not know that I blamed her.

We were going to pick up the ashes in a couple days, but first there was a box of her things at the facility.

There were a few strings of rosary beads, a Bible, a hairbrush and mirror that had always been my favorite part of her room, but that I had not noticed was missing from her dresser on my walk past. I had not gone in. And my letters, neatly pressed in the front cover of her daily reading. I browsed back through my words to her. Even the best, most kind ones were avoidances. I was glad she could not remember me anymore, to know that I had forgotten her as well. Had tried, anyway.

I sat in Pope's truck, what was left of my mother on my lap. We did not speak. I wondered if my father had ever showed my mother the stars. I wondered if it would have made a difference. I stretched the seatbelt around the both of us, as though I could make up for anything as we drove away.

Jessica Dainty

* * *

We didn't buy an urn. The funeral home provided boxes but even these were outside my price range. I carried my mother out in a giant plastic bag. She was heavy and I held her in both arms, to my chest. I gave her my heartbeat, faster and faster, as we made our way to the cemetery, but she remained still.

I had not bought a plot, but Pope had brought a small shovel, and I, a trowel. I left my mother in the car and we found a spot under a tree on the edge, far enough away from any headstone that we were sure we would disturb nothing.

The hole was shallow and took all of twenty minutes. Pope got my mother from the car.

We each took a minute to say good-bye, the two of us who at this point probably knew her equally well. We'd each seen her once since she had become this new person, this empty page I had no words for. I was about to drop the bag in when I changed my mind. I ripped it open. I took a handful of ash and went to the hole, dropping my mother inside. Pope did the same and we alternated this way, until the bag was half empty. The hole looked dusty but my mother blended with the earth and I thought if she could see it, she may have liked this choice after all.

"Hey, Gertie."

Pope turned and blew his hand clean, ash floating into my hair.

"Uh! Pope! Gross!" But I smiled at his boldness, his equal claim to this woman whom we held in our hands.

He reached back into the bag for another handful and threw it at me, gray dust flaking off my eyelashes and cheeks.

Soon my mother was flying through the air. We dodged her, ducking behind gravestones and statues. She was in our hair, down our shirts, in my ears and nose. Pope was fiercer, picking up fallen piles from the ground to throw again. I watched him and had no doubt it was he in the yard that day, flinging snowballs at his fellow patients.

The Shape of the Atmosphere

I stumbled, my eyes clouded with ash, back to the bag, but it was empty. I sneezed and ash billowed from my forehead. I watched it fall and had to understand that this was what we were, what we all were in the end. A slight panic tugged at my stomach, but I realized I was not afraid.

We did not talk as we drove away. We were peppered gray over our clothes.

When we finally reached a main road, on the way to drive past my house one last time, Pope finally spoke. "I looked up that word. Oophorectomy."

My mouth went dry.

"It's the removal of a woman's ovaries. Some kind of surgery." I nodded, which he must have noticed. "Did you already know what it was?" He turned to me, watching me longer than he should while driving.

I fumbled into my words. "Um, it was in Elizabeth's file. She'd had it done to her. Isn't it awful though? That they'd do that." His silence settled over me, and I relaxed that he would not press me any further. The pantry had been dark, but not everywhere would be. At some point he would notice my scars, like evidence that did not have to be dug for. I would have to tell him eventually but, right now, my mother still clinging to me, I did not want to talk about it.

"Stop the car," I said, after a while.

The familiar fence of my childhood swimming pool loomed at the top of the hill. The sun sank down, as though telling me, *yes, shhh, I won't tell.* I climbed over the fence and Pope followed. He did not follow when I jumped into the water. He did not follow when I lodged myself beneath the ladder, looking back up through the water to the sky that was not yet dark enough to show any stars. The water grayed in front of me, my mother swirling up toward the surface.

I saw my sister at about age twelve. I smiled to think of passing her in the hallway, whether at school or at home, eager even for her avoidance of my pleading eyes; I was important enough to ignore. I realized that it was not just me my mother was unable to love, to reconcile into her fraying mind beside all those saintly beings.

We didn't stand a chance.

Jessica Dainty

I saw Allison standing there, her knobby knees like wrinkled Easter hams nuzzled between her striped socks and the hem of her lime-green shorts. She would be standing next to Pope, who I somehow knew would replace her gently and become my family.

I didn't know what would happen to Willow Estate, if Nurse Peters had nothing to fear. At first I hoped that the hospital would be shut down, the women released. But then I thought of all those ladies, exiting out into a world that had already said it didn't want them. I knew in this moment that the only worthwhile result to hope for was compassion. And maybe hope. I thought of my father and smiled. "I hope for hope, Daddy," my last bubble of breath trickling up in front of me.

My chest burned. I could hear the muffled voice of Pope trying to reach me. I pushed toward the surface.

On one of my last nights at Willow, the newsman on television told us NASA said there were five layers to the atmosphere. On my way to the surface I pushed past my father, then my sister in her green shorts, her soccer uniform, her bobbing ponytail. I pushed past the dilution of my mother, through all that had tried to break me behind the four walls of Willow Estate. I did not know whether I was leaving or entering, but I made one final push, past the girl below me, clinging to the ladder, holding her breath for I could not remember what. "Breathe," I wanted to tell her. "Breathe."

I pushed past all of these, taking some things with me. I grabbed at them, tiny pieces of the sky that got caught in my hands. They whispered to me as I floated past, *yes yes, take us, we are yours.*

I grabbed my final moments with my mother, my kiss with Susan. I held tightly to the frame of Elizabeth, to the drawings of Pope, to Jessica and a smooth, golden key. I pushed into my pockets the branches of a giant willow tree, a cigarette shooting out of a cake like a rocket. I even found myself clinging to my sister's avoidance, to the sound of her nightshirt outside my bedroom door, to a promise of beauty that did not quite come true. I left most of my father floating but took his empty cross, his dim green lamp, a string of red licorice, the warmth of his lips on my forehead. I left the foyer and my mother but not without kissing her goodbye first, not without wiping away the vomit on the floor, not without helping her to her feet. I floated past hydro

The Shape of the Atmosphere

and shock but took Rosalyn with me, dropping her off on a comet shooting by. She smiled, her teeth perfect and unbroken. I did not keep much but my arms were full by the time the trees came into view from beneath the water. I clung to them, but they were only the shapes of things now, nuzzled in my grasp, already partly misshapen from the journey and melting.

    The surface hit me and I gasped, the air filling my lungs like a stream of stars. I held them in my mouth and floated, breathing them out. I stared at the sky and watched, waiting for them to shine.

Acknowledgements

First, I would like to thank my parents, Helen and Jim Dainty, my brother, Ryan Dainty, and my sister-in-law, Nicole Dainty, for all their support and belief in me. For your love, forgiveness, acceptance, and constant faith, thank you.

Thank you to my teachers, both writing and non, but especially to Rosalie Andrews, Carole Ivey, Michael Knight, Arthur Smith, Rachel Kadish, and AJ Verdelle.

To Hester Kaplan, thank you for being not just a mentor, but a blinding light of talent and support to me both during my time under your guidance at Lesley University and beyond.

To my forever and early readers, thank you for stomaching my words before they were passable for actual writing and for telling me there was something there. There are so many of you, and I hope you know who you are, but specific thanks go out to Jenna Shemwell, Erin E. Moulton, Christine Junge, Laurie "Auntie" Roberts, Helen Dainty, and other family and friends who helped shape early drafts of *The Shape of the Atmosphere* into what it is now.

To my real and virtual writing community, especially Sarah L. Blair, Sarah Fox, Erin (again), Amber Moulton, and Katrina Otuonye, thank you for always being there and loving words as much as I do.

To Jenna Shemwell, who gave me my first "published" copy of my writing and to whom I entrust all my words. You're irreplaceable.

To Jessica Thomas for being my biblio-BFF and my oldest friend. I love you.

To my book club girls—Jillianne, Rachel, Devin, Jill, Allison, Karen, and others—thank you for keeping my reading shelf full and being so supportive.

To my free local therapy, Rachel, Hannah, and Jillianne. You're just the best.

Thank you to Gregory Johns for his early support of my writing career.

Thank you to Faith Kasparian, Erik Weisman, and Frank and Ethan Kasparian Weisman for their amazing support over the years. I wrote chunks of this book on your couch and in the bookstore around the corner from your house. Thank you for always being so excited for me.

To those who helped with information for this novel, including Mary Moulton and Helen Dainty, I thank you.

To Jay McPherson for the author photo that made it and the bazillion others you patiently took that I tyrannically vetoed. You're wonderful.

To Nicole Tone, thank you thank you thank you for favoriting my Tweet. I wouldn't be here without you.

Thank you to my agent, Linda Camacho, whose feedback on another manuscript made me a much better reviser of this one. I look forward to the next step with you.

To my editor, Saren Richardson, thank you for loving my book and for helping me make it better. Your guidance was invaluable. To Rachel Schoenbauer, thank you for your keen eye.

And finally, to Pandamoon Publishing, especially Zara, Allan, and Don, I thank you with all I have for believing in me and this story. Thank you for the business and family you have created at Pandamoon. To all members of the Panda family, especially the Gamma class of Dana, Sarah, Brian, Penni, Francis, Meg, and Elgon (because he belongs in every class), I am so excited to be on this journey with you.

To anyone I did not mention by name, but who played a role in me being here, please forgive me. I think I'm still dreaming.

About the Author

Jessica Dainty is a native New Englander, who has bounced back and forth from the Northeast to Tennessee over the past 20 years. Jessica works as an English/Special Education teacher and Reading Interventionist in her county school system. When she is not writing her own words, she loves helping her students fall in love with reading, especially those who may have given up on it long ago. In addition, she coaches her high school swim team, does contract editing, tutors, and is an avid knitter.

She received her undergraduate from the University of Tennessee-Knoxville, where she started in poetry. She took her first fiction workshop for the simple reason that it terrified her, and after that, she never looked back. She continued on to earn her MFA in Creative Writing from Lesley University, in Cambridge, Massachusetts, where she studied with Hester Kaplan and AJ Verdelle, among others.

Jessica is drawn to darker literature with a slight silver lining of hope, and her writing reflects this. Jessica's short stories have been published in various places, including *SNReview*, *Fiction Weekly*, *Scholars & Rogues,* and *Composition Cooperative*. She is represented by Linda Camacho of Prospect Agency.

Connect with Jessica on social media! She's on Facebook at www.facebook.com/jessicadaintyauthor and Twitter at the handle @daintywriterj3.

Thank you for purchasing this copy of ***The Shape of the Atmosphere*** by Jessica Dainty. If you enjoyed this book, please let Jessica know by posting a review.

Read More Books from Pandamoon Publishing.

Visit www.pandamoonpublishing.com to learn more about our other works by our talented authors and use the author links to their sales page.

122 Rules by Deek Rhew
A Tree Born Crooked by Steph Post
Beautiful Secret by Dana Faletti
Crimson Forest by Christine Gabriel
Everly by Meg Bonney
Fate's Past by Jason Huebinger
Fried Windows in a Light White Sauce by Elgon Williams
Juggling Kittens by Matt Coleman
Knights of the Shield by Jeff Messick
Looking into the Sun by Todd Tavolazzi
Love's Misadventure by Cheri Champagne
Rogue Alliance by Michelle Bellon
Sitnalta by Alisse Lee Goldenberg
Southbound by Jason Beem
The Coven by Chrissy Lessey
The Hunted by Chrissy Lessey
The Juliet by Laura Ellen Scott
The Kingdom Thief by Alisse Lee Goldenberg
The Long Way Home by Regina West
The Secret Keepers by Chrissy Lessey
The Shape of the Atmosphere by Jessica Dainty
The Trouble with Love by Cheri Champagne

Made in the USA
Middletown, DE
10 December 2016